CONFESSIONS: THE PRINCESS, THE PRICK & THE PRIEST

ELLA FRANK

Ella Frank, LLC

COPYRIGHT

ALSO BY ELLA FRANK

DEDICATION

To the three men who broke all the rules.
You made me believe.
You have made others believe.
Now be happy, and love freely.
I will miss you.

Xx Ella

CHAPTER ONE

I'm not sure why everyone dreads their thirties.
As far as I'm concerned, it's going to be
the best decade ever - Robbie

Six months later...

"LOVERS, I'M HOME," Robbie Bianchi called out to his boyfriends, as he juggled several shopping bags in one hand and kicked the front door shut behind him. He stuffed his car keys into the pocket of his shorts, and as he evened out what he was carrying, he took the stairs that led him up to the first floor of their new home.

With the same smile on his face that he'd left with that morning, Robbie headed across the hardwood floors past the dining room, and into the kitchen, where he spotted a note waiting for him: *We're upstairs, princesse. Come find us when you get home.*

Robbie grinned at the messy crown drawn above the *i* in *princesse*, but then quickly did as he was told. With one hand on the steel rail, he took the stairs two at a time, and as he reached the second floor where the bedroom was located, he walked inside to find it empty except for the fish swimming around the tank that lined the wall facing their bed.

Dropping his shopping bags on the end of the mattress, Robbie headed up to the final floor, where he knew his men were waiting for him. He opened up the glass door that led to the penthouse deck, and when he stepped outside and the warm rays washed over him, Robbie took in a breath of fresh air.

Ah, he'd always loved summer. Everything about it. The sun, the smell of the freshly cut grass, and the clothes—*or lack thereof*—Robbie thought, as he reached for the edge of his white tank top and drew it over his head.

As he tucked it into the back of his shorts, Robbie scanned the wide deck, his eyes roaming over the wooden slat floor, the hot tub over in the corner, and the glistening water of the lap pool surrounded by the potted greenery bordering their rooftop oasis.

This space had been the final selling point with all three of them when they'd made the decision to leave the condo after what had happened there with Jimmy. It was the perfect place for Julien to relax and do his yoga, for Priest, who loved a good soak to clear his mind, and for Robbie, for whom it was all about the calm he got from finally seeing his men happy and at peace. And *that* was exactly how he found one of them right now. There, stretched out on one of the sun loungers, was the brand-*new* reason that Robbie loved summer—an almost-naked Julien Thornton.

Dressed in tight, black, barely there swim shorts that left little —*okay, nothing*—to the imagination, the only other thing Julien was wearing was a pair of Aviator sunglasses. His rich, olive-colored skin was glistening with water droplets as he lay sprawled out with his hands behind his head, and *oh my God* was he a feast for the eyes.

As Robbie walked to the end of the lounger, his eyes roamed

up Julien's toned legs to his muscular thighs, and ended at the bulge that tight material was cupping like a glove.

Oh yes, this was hands down the best part about summer now, and luckily for Robbie and Priest, tanning was a favorite pastime of their seriously sexy Frenchman.

"*Bonjour, princesse.*" Julien's honey-toned voice wrapped around Robbie, informing him that he'd been caught staring. But he didn't care—not one little bit.

"One second, please. I'm concentrating here," Robbie said, his gaze trailing up all he could see to finally land on Julien's face. "Now, sorry, what were you saying?"

Julien chuckled as Robbie walked alongside him. "*Bonjour, princesse.*"

"Oh, yes," Robbie said, and bent down to brush a kiss across Julien's lips. "*Bonjour, Jules.*"

Robbie went to straighten, but before he got too far away, Julien took hold of the back of his neck and craned up for a deeper kiss. Robbie's lips parted, and Julien slipped his tongue inside, making Robbie's cock jerk to attention, as he braced his hand on the back of the lounger and sank into the deliciousness that was all Julien.

"Hmm," Julien said against Robbie's mouth. "We missed you, birthday boy."

"Good." Robbie nipped at Julien's lower lip. "That's just the way I like it. You two here at home, *pining* after me."

"Cheeky boy," Julien said, and shifted on his lounger so Robbie could sit beside him. "You taste like strawberries."

"Strawberries and *cream*," Robbie said with a wink. "Don't forget the best part. El gave it to me with my birthday present. It's my favorite."

"Mine too, now," Julien said, and slicked his tongue over his full bottom lip. "Did you have a nice lunch with Elliot?"

"I did. I got myself a new pair of swim shorts," Robbie said, and Julien's lips curved.

"Did you now?"

"Mhmm."

"Then why aren't you in them?" Julien said as his eyes shifted to Robbie's purple shorts with white flamingos.

Robbie grinned. "I just got *home*, Mr. Thornton. At least let me come and say hello before I get naked. Sheesh. Anyone would think you only want me for my body."

Julien sat forward and tapped Robbie's nose. "Then they would be stupid. I want you for many reasons, *princesse*. One of which, I can't deny, is your lovely body."

Robbie bit down on his lip as Julien ran a finger down the center of Robbie's naked chest. Then he reached for Robbie's arm and raised it, looking at the new leather strap that was wound around his right wrist. "Do you like?"

Julien stroked his fingers over the braided leather and nodded. "I do. It's beautiful."

"Right?" Robbie said, and looked down at the present Elliot had given him. "I'd been looking at it forever. I can't believe he remembered."

"I'm not surprised. He's a good friend."

"Yes, well, I *suppose* he is," Robbie said. "Despite how much crap he gave me for finally turning the big three-oh."

"But can you blame him, *princesse*? You barely look a day older than twenty-five."

"Well, okay. I'll take that," Robbie said, preening from the compliment, even though he wasn't *really* bothered at turning thirty. In fact, as far as he was concerned, this was the start of a brand-new Robert Bianchi.

That's right, bitches. Best decade ever, coming right up.

"Where's Priest?" Robbie said. "He promised me he wasn't going to work this weekend."

"And I'm not."

Robbie looked over his shoulder to see Joel Priestley—the missing person from this conversation—walking across the deck toward them in a pair of hunter-green board shorts and a black

tank that showed off the musculature of his arms. He h
on, a pair of sunglasses in place, and, as the sunlight
hair, he rendered the two men staring at him mute.

Priest came to a stop by Robbie, leaned down, pressed a kiss to Robbie's lips, and said, "I was in the bathroom changing my clothes so I could go for a swim."

"Well, you didn't have to put on shorts for my benefit," Robbie said. "You could've just stripped. Or better yet, you could've waited and let me unwrap you. I mean, it is my job *and* my birthday."

"You weren't here, and it's not your birthday yet," Priest reminded him. "You told us August eleventh at ten in the evening."

"Of course you remember that."

"Of course I do," Priest said. "There's nothing forgettable about you."

Robbie's stomach flipped at the offhand comment. Would he ever get used to people loving him the way that these two did? As though it was as natural to them as breathing? Robbie wasn't sure. It still felt so...unreal to him.

"Oh, and Julien," Priest said, as he removed his top. "You do know that tormenting the two of us by lying around in those swim shorts every day is eventually going to catch up with you, yes?"

Robbie's cock went from alert to rock hard in an instant at that threat. Not to mention the look in Priest's eyes as they trailed down over his husband. Robbie turned to look at the man stretched out behind him, and when Julien pushed his sunglasses onto his head, the heated look in that jade stare had Robbie palming himself.

"I sure hope so, *mon amour*. I'm certainly not wearing them for *my* benefit."

"Uh huh," Priest said, and Robbie let out a soft moan and got to his feet.

After hours away from these two, Robbie wanted to strip right there and demand that someone do something to him, or vice versa. But with the afternoon sun blazing, he didn't think any of

them relished the idea of getting a sunburn where they'd rather...
mmm *not*. So the best course of action was to go and get changed
so he could get in the damn pool.

"I'll be back up in a minute," Robbie said as he walked by Priest
and trailed his fingers across his chest. "*I'm* going to go and change
into my new swim shorts."

"Mm, you do that," Priest said, and then looked down at Julien.
"And now that the birthday boy is home, why don't we kick off the
afternoon right? Let me go get us a drink before I get in the pool."

"Oh, I can do that," Julien said, but Priest bent down and
kissed his mouth. "You stay put. If you come downstairs, none of
us will come back up."

"You're probably right," Julien agreed. "Hurry back, then."

"With you waiting up here dressed like *that*?" Robbie said.
"Count on it."

PRIEST SWATTED ROBBIE on the ass as the door shut behind
them and they headed downstairs. Robbie disappeared into the
bedroom, and Priest continued down until he was in the kitchen
making all three of them a sangria.

As he opened the freezer to get out some ice, he heard Robbie
switch on some music and smiled at the throbbing beat that was
now coming from the bedroom. It was, in a word, horrible. Yet one
of the things he looked forward to hearing every single day.

Priest was forever thankful for the man who was likely dancing
around in the room above him, and the one who was relaxing up
on their deck, and it was moments like this that reminded him
how lucky he was to have them in his life—and just how damn
close he'd come to losing them.

Most days, the three of them were back to a fairly normal
routine. Well, as normal as people could be after one was
kidnapped, the other shot, and the other left waiting to know the
outcome of such a horrible night.

But once the finality of Jimmy's death had sunk in, they'd decided they needed a fresh start, and after finding this place, the three of them had begun to establish a sense of security again. A stable ground on which they could finally nurture and grow this relationship between them. Something Priest and Julien planned to discuss further with Robbie this weekend.

Priest put the drinks on a tray and, after cleaning up, headed upstairs to see if Robbie was ready. As he neared the bedroom, the music became louder, and when he walked inside, the sight that greeted him had Priest stopping in his tracks.

Down on his hands and knees, his delectable ass in the air, Robbie was peering under the bed in search of something. Priest put the tray down on the dresser and walked across the hardwood floor, and once he was directly behind Robbie, he said, "Lose something?"

Robbie's head snapped up as he looked back at Priest over his shoulder, and then frowned. "Yes, my flip-flops. Have you seen them?"

No, no, he had not. But that didn't stop Priest from saying, "I think I saw them on Julien's side of the bed the other day."

Lies. All lies. But with Robbie's tight ass on full display, save the strip of material bisecting it, could anyone blame him? And Priest's words had the desired effect. Robbie moved back to his hands and knees and crawled around the foot of the bed to Julien's side.

"I don't see them," Robbie complained, but Priest had stopped listening. "Priest? Priest? I don't—" As Robbie looked back and caught where Priest was focused, Robbie arched an eyebrow. "Did you *really* see my flip-flops under here?"

"What do you think?" Priest said, as Robbie got to his feet and strutted over to him.

"*I* think," Robbie said, and licked his lower lip, "that you like the swim shorts I bought today."

"Robert?"

"Yes, Priest?"

"*These* are not shorts. There is no back to them."

"There's a back," Robbie said, and then slowly pivoted until his very *naked* one was only inches from Priest. "*My* back."

Priest placed his hands on Robbie's hips, and then tugged him backward to fit his hardening length against the thin strip of material wedged between Robbie's ass cheeks. "Has Julien seen these yet?" Priest growled.

"No," Robbie said, as he squirmed against Priest's cock, and Priest dug his fingers into Robbie's soft flesh and spun him around. "I bought them especially for my birthday. You like?"

Priest walked Robbie backward until his ass hit the wall. "Can't you tell?"

Robbie aimed a mischievous look at Priest from beneath his lashes. "I can, but a boy never grows tired of hearing the words."

Robbie reached for the button of Priest's shorts, but Priest was quicker. He wrapped his fingers around Robbie's wandering hand and drew it up over his head, pinning it to the wall. Then he did the same with the other, until the handsy little minx was secure.

"I don't like," Priest said, and lowered his mouth until it was a whisper above Robbie's. "I *love*. Your swim shorts, your lip gloss, this god-awful music. But most of all..." Robbie's blue eyes darkened as Priest fingered the leather strap at his wrist. "I love that you're mine and Julien's."

Robbie shivered, and Priest leaned in and dragged his tongue along Robbie's bicep to his elbow. "*Ah...* Shit, Priest," Robbie said, as his head fell back against the wall, and Priest nipped at the tender skin at the crook of Robbie's arm.

Robbie rolled his hips forward, rubbing his erection against Priest's thigh, and when a moan escaped him, Priest growled.

"Between you in these, and Julien..." Priest brought his mouth back to Robbie's. "I don't know who is more fucking trouble."

Robbie panted against Priest's lips. "You love us anyway."

"Yes, I do. But you know what else I love?" Priest trailed the backs of his fingers down one of Robbie's arms, then he let go and took a step back. "I love making you wait for it."

Robbie's breath left him in a rush. His jaw about hitting the floor when he realized Priest was stopping. "But...but it's my *birth*day."

Priest chuckled at Robbie's put-out tone and took in his swollen lips, flushed face, and that long, stiff cock he had no hope of hiding in his tiny pink thong.

"Not yet it's not," Priest reminded him. "And Julien and I have decided a little birthday game is in order tonight."

"A game?" Robbie said, his interest clearly piqued. "What kind of game?"

"If you can behave yourself until your *actual* birthday, then you can have anything your heart desires."

That piece of information got Robbie's attention. One of his perfectly shaped eyebrows arched, and he eyed Priest in a way that made him think that Robbie was now imagining about a hundred different things he wanted, and planned, to ask for.

"Anything?"

"Anything. Provided you can keep your hands off this." Priest cupped Robbie's erection and squeezed. "Do you understand?"

Robbie bit his bottom lip as he sized Priest up, clearly weighing the pros and cons of this little game—then he nodded.

Priest crowded in, trapping his hand between them, and then whispered in Robbie's ear, "That means no sneaking off to take care of this. No matter how much you might want to."

"Oh *God*," Robbie said, his eyes opening as he writhed against Priest's hand. "So basically, you're both going to torture me all night."

Priest's lips quirked. "Yes, but in the best way ever. Happy birthday."

Robbie's eyes glittered with arousal and frustration, as Priest dropped his hands and walked back to the dresser where the drinks sat.

"Now why don't we go and make this afternoon just as hard on Julien?" Priest suggested. "You strutting around in this scrap of material is going to be a lesson in restraint for all of us."

"Serves you right," Robbie said, and flashed an unholy grin as he sashayed by Priest, who was seriously questioning his own sanity.

"Since you're so into self-denial and all of that," Robbie said, "*you* can follow *me* up the stairs. Enjoy the view, and just remember, you could've had it right here, right now. Your loss."

Robbie made his way up the stairs, adding an extra swing to his hips, and Priest climbed the stairs, two at a time, after him.

THE SUN WARMED Julien as his mind began to relax along with his body, and he waited for his men to come back upstairs and join him. Now that he was home from his weekly meeting with his therapist, he was ready to enjoy the weekend.

He couldn't believe how fast the last few months had passed, or the fact they were now fully settled into their new house. But here they were, mid-August, about to celebrate Robbie's thirtieth birthday, and the six months since they'd asked their *princesse* to make the huge commitment of buying a new house with them.

Things finally felt like they were back on track. However, there was one last thing that was unfinished. Something that Julien and Priest planned to discuss with Robbie very soon. But before they could, they needed Robbie to do something. They needed him to—

"Don't grumble at me," Robbie said, as he pushed open the door to the deck and appeared in far *less* than what he'd left in minutes earlier. "You're the one who put the rules in place."

Priest was barely a step behind him, and as Julien took in the tiny string of pink fabric that clung to Robbie's hips, Julien's mind blanked and his body reacted with the same hunger he could see swirling in Priest's eyes.

"*Mon Dieu.*" Julien took his sunglasses off. "*Viens ici, princesse.*"

Julien sat up and spread his legs on either side of the lounger, and waited for that delectable body to be within touching range. When Robbie came to a stop beside him, Julien ran a finger up the length of the erection that thong was doing nothing to conceal.

"I don't want to alarm you," Julien said. "But it appears you bought the wrong size."

"Blame Priest. He made them a little…tighter than they should be," Robbie said, and glanced over his shoulder to where Priest had put down the drinks and was walking around to the deep end of the pool.

Ahh. Operation drive-their-*princesse*-crazy was now in full effect. The little birthday game Julien and Priest had come up with. "Did he?"

"Yes," Robbie said with a pout. "Teased me mercilessly, he did, and then left me hot, hard, and all kinds of bothered."

From across the deck, Priest laughed at the accusation, clearly not repentant at all as Julien swung his leg over the lounger and got to his feet.

"That wasn't very nice of him," Julien said, as his eyes found his husband's.

"Nice wasn't exactly my mood when I walked into our bedroom and found him on his hands and knees," Priest replied.

Julien chuckled, knowing he would've had the exact same reaction. "*Non?*" Julien brought his gaze back to Robbie's. "What kind of mood *was* he in?"

"A mean one," Robbie said, as he trailed his finger down the center of Julien's body to his navel. "But…he *did* say if I behaved myself this afternoon, the two of you would give me anything I want, the minute it's my birthday."

A splash in the water behind them indicated that Priest had finally dived in, and Julien wondered if it was to cool off from whatever had happened downstairs or what he was watching right now. An aroused Robbie in next to nothing always tested their control, and Julien knew the goal tonight was to tease, which meant playing, but not coming—at least not yet.

"That's several hours from now," Julien said, and caught hold of Robbie's sneaky hand. "You better stop flirting with trouble."

"Aw. But I love flirting with you, Jules."

"Are you trying to say that I'm trouble, *princesse?*"

Robbie adopted an innocent expression and gave a small shrug. "Priest's words, not mine."

"*Vraiment?*"

"Yes. Really," Priest said from the water, where he had his arms folded along the edge of the pool and his hair slicked back from his face. "You're *both* trouble. Now get in the pool, you two. I think you need the cooldown."

"I don't know what you mean," Robbie said, and batted his lashes. "I'm just standing here thinking about *all* the possibilities I have to look forward to when I win tonight."

"*Oui,*" Julien said. "That devious grin of yours gives you away."

"Hey," Robbie said as he walked to the pool, his spectacular ass flexing with every step he took. "I'm just playing by you and your husband's rules. If you don't like them, then that's on you."

As Robbie dove into the water, Julien made his way to where Priest was standing with a smirk on his handsome face. "You're going to enjoy this, aren't you, *mon amour?*"

Priest ran his eyes over Julien in a way that had him reaching down to adjust himself. There was so much heat in those steel-colored eyes, and it was clear that Priest was in the kind of mood that both Julien and Robbie would greatly benefit from...eventually.

"Yes, I am," Priest said, his voice gruff, his control clearly being tested as much as Julien's and Robbie's. "Now get in the pool, Julien, before our neighbors see even more of you than they're used to."

"Bossy *salopard.*"

"I'll show you how bossy tonight."

"*If* that's what Robbie wants," Julien reminded him. "If not, you're in trouble."

Priest chuckled, letting Julien know he wasn't worried in the slightest. And why would he be? There was no way he or Robbie could resist a bossy Priest.

So no matter which way things went tonight, Julien had a feeling that this would not be the last order he would be following from his sexy-as-sin husband.

CHAPTER TWO

Even after all this time,
he still makes my knees weak - Julien

"ROBERT? ROBERT, YOUR phone is ringing." Priest's voice filtered into the master bathroom, where Robbie stood under one of the three showerheads, washing up from the pool. As the door opened, Robbie looked through the glass to see Priest walking inside with his ringing cell phone in hand.

With shampoo in his hair, Robbie made sure to clear the soap away from his eyes as he moved to the edge of the shower and poked his head out. "Who is it?"

Priest eyed him for a beat, and then said, "Your mother."

"Oh, ah, I'll call her back," Robbie said, his gaze dropping to the phone as though it were a grenade, and when Priest aimed a look of disbelief his way, Robbie added, "I *will.* Just let me finish in here, and then I'll call her."

"*I* could always answer—"

"No, no. That's okay," Robbie said, cutting off Priest's offer, and when he tried for a smile, Priest raised an eyebrow. "She's calling about my birthday, that's all."

"And you, once again, are avoiding her. *That's* all."

"I am not," Robbie said, even though Priest was right. "I'm just—"

"Lying through your teeth?" Priest suggested. "This discussion is not over. But your shampoo is about to get in your eyes."

Robbie swiped his hand across his forehead and huffed. "Fine. Let me wash it out and I'll be right there."

Priest put the *still*-ringing phone on the vanity in front on the three-sink basin—to no doubt emphasize his point—and as he left, Robbie let out a deep sigh and shut his eyes. Moving back under the spray, he tipped his head up, let the water wash over him, and tried to shove aside Priest's words. But it was no use—he could still hear them and knew them to be true.

He *was* avoiding his mother—his whole family, really.

Over the past several months, Robbie had gone out of his way to be busy, working, or otherwise engaged whenever he'd been invited back home or his ma told him she was coming to visit Nonna.

He wasn't proud of the fact, but he had a good reason—or should he say *reasons*—for the whole avoidance routine, and they were currently down in the kitchen waiting for him so they could celebrate his birthday.

Ugh, I just need to bite the bullet and take them home already. Rip the Band-Aid off, Bianchi. The problem was that every time he had that thought, it was quickly followed by a mild panic attack over what would happen if his two worlds didn't mesh.

What if the two groups of people he loved the most hated each other?

He couldn't think of anything worse, and for that reason, every time the opportunity for him to come clean and bring his men home arose, Robbie quickly thought of a reason why they should wait.

Because honestly, no matter how well his family knew him and his tendency to be a little less traditional than most, the thought of sitting down and telling his parents that he was in love, and involved with a married couple, seemed much more difficult than he'd originally anticipated.

Hell, at this stage, he wouldn't blame Julien and Priest if they didn't *want* to go now that he'd postponed it for so long.

Robbie turned off the water and snagged one of the plush towels hanging by the shower to scrub it over his hair. Once it wasn't dripping anymore, he toweled himself off and wrapped it around his waist, and then headed across the tile floor to where the phone sat.

A notification that his mother had left a voicemail was flashing across the screen, and as he opened it up and brought the phone to his ear, Robbie looked at himself in the mirror, checking to see if thirty was indeed being as kind to him as Julien had suggested.

With his hair sticking out all over the place, and his skin flushed and dewy from the shower's humidity, Robbie couldn't see any lines or bags under his eyes, and decided that if this was thirty, then he could totally deal.

"Robert Antonio Bianchi," his mother said. "I don't know where you are or what you're doing that you can't answer your phone on your birthday, but—"

"It's not his birthday yet," his father cut in, making Robbie smile.

"Oh hush, Antonio. He's ignored *two* phone calls from me this week, and I will not put up with that."

And, of course, she was right. Usually, Robbie would have called her back by now, but he had a feeling that she was going to—

"We want you to come home so we can celebrate your big day with you."

—ask him exactly that.

"Do you hear me?" his mother continued. "If you can't come this weekend, then pick one where you can. Your pa will make sure to be home from work, and we can just make it a small family affair."

Uh, yeah, okay. Small and *Bianchi did not go hand in hand...like, ever.*

"Call me back, young man, or I am going to turn up on your new doorstep. Don't think I won't." With that final threat, his mother ended the call, and when Robbie looked at his reflection this time, the fear of her following through on that threat was there in his wide eyes.

Not wanting a surprise visit in his near future, Robbie decided there were no more ways to avoid the inevitable and hit the "call back" button, and after two rings, it was answered.

"*Pronto,*" his mother said, and despite his reluctance to call, just hearing her voice made a smile curve Robbie's lips.

"Hey there, Ma."

"Robert, baby, it's about time you called me back."

Robbie turned away from the mirror to lean against the edge of the vanity. "I know. I'm sorry. I was in the shower when you called just now."

"And the time before that?" she asked. "Were you showering then too?"

There it was. No one could guilt a person quite like an Italian mother. "No, I was just..." While Robbie tried to find an excuse that wasn't a flat-out lie, his mother cut in.

"Avoiding me? You weren't *avoiding* your mother, were you, Robert?"

"No, Ma, I—"

"Robert," she said. "I don't want to hear your excuses. We haven't seen you in months, baby. The last time was at Mr. Thornton's restaurant, which was lovely, but are you really trying to tell me that you've been too busy to come and visit your family? Your sister is pregnant, for heaven's sake. With the rate you're going, the child will be two years old and walking before you get back here."

Robbie's lips twitched at the thorough dressing down he was getting, but couldn't disagree. It *was* time to go home and see his family. He missed them. But the problem was that he wanted to take Julien and Priest with him, and that was going to be a...delicate situation, to say the least.

"I have to work next weekend," Robbie said, not believing he was actually about to commit to this. "But the weekend after, I can totally be there. Maybe Friday through Sunday?"

"Oh, that would be wonderful," his mother said as though she hadn't just threatened an ambush. "A little late, but we can work with that. Plus, it'll give your pa time to arrange being home, and the girls can decide who is going to do what."

"Ma. Small," Robbie said, thinking he'd much prefer introducing Julien and Priest to his *immediate* family first, before subjecting them to, well, everyone else. "You said you'd keep it small."

"Yes, yes, I know. But it's my baby boy's thirtieth birthday. We need to celebrate, and since when have you ever said no to a party?"

"Never. But, um..." Robbie chewed on his lower lip. Shit, how did he bring up this next part in any kind of casual conversation? *Oh, just spit it out. It's not going to get any easier tomorrow.* "I'm going to be bringing my boyfriends home with me to meet you guys. I hope that's okay."

There was a long pause, and Robbie shut his eyes. God, he was nervous about this. More so than he'd expected to be. He'd never brought anyone home to Oshkosh before, and certainly not anyone he was in a serious relationship with. And suddenly, he found himself praying that his mother wasn't about to hang up on him.

"Boy-*friends?*"

Robbie nodded, but when he realized she couldn't see him, he said, "Uh... Yes?"

More silence greeted him, and Robbie wished he could see her face. He wished he could gauge what she might be thinking. His parents had always been so understanding of who he was, and embraced it. But would this be too much?

"Robert?"

Robbie gulped. "Yes, Ma?"

"I hope that's not the reason you've been staying away." The seriousness in her voice made Robbie's guilt magnify. He was about to try and half-ass his way through an apology when she said something that had his jaw just about hitting the floor. "We'll see you in two weeks. And Robert? Say hello to Mr. Thornton and Mr. Priestley. I look forward to getting to know them when you bring them home with you. Talk soon, baby boy. Bye."

Robbie stared at the now-silent phone in his hand.

Well, I'll be damned... She really *had* worked it out from that one meeting at JULIEN, and she didn't seem *too* upset. More annoyed that he hadn't been home to visit. *Huh.* Well, it seemed the three of them would soon be heading up to Oshkosh, but not tonight.

No. Tonight, he was going to celebrate his birthday in the best way possible. By winning this little game his men had devised for him, so he could claim his prize.

"JOEL." JULIEN CHUCKLED. "Get your hands off me. I'm trying to make dinner here," he said, as he expertly sidestepped Priest's wandering hands and moved down the counter to where a knife sat on the cutting board.

Priest leaned against the counter behind him and stared Julien down. "Well, you should've thought about that before you decided to invite me to assist."

"If my memory serves me correctly, I *made* you come down here because I found you with your ear pressed up against the bathroom door."

"I was just—"

"Eavesdropping?" Julien suggested, as he began to chop the basil.

"I was just making sure Robert was okay."

Julien shook his head as he scooped up the herbs and then moved to sprinkle them in the pot. "Sure you were. Have you forgotten who you're talking to? *You* are being nosey. Admit it, *mon amour.*"

When Priest pushed off the counter and walked toward him, Julien grabbed the wooden spoon and pointed it. "Stop right there, thank you very much."

Priest smirked, but Julien knew his limits, and ever since Priest had re-entered the kitchen, he'd had his hands, mouth, or body pressed up against Julien. Not that that was surprising. After all, Julien *was* naked, except for the white apron he'd tied around his waist.

A few months back, when they'd been having dinner at Tate and Logan's, Tate had let slip a conversation he'd once had with Robbie about white picket fences and naked men cooking for him. And while they'd all laughed, and of course joked that Robbie already *had* a naked chef whenever he wanted one, Julien hadn't quite gotten around to fulfilling that particular fantasy yet.

Tonight, that was going to change.

"Did you honestly believe for a second that I would sit all the way over there, when you're standing here in next to nothing?" Priest said.

Julien stirred the pasta sauce and then raised the spoon to his mouth to taste. It was the exact recipe that Robbie had taught him —his favorite, the one his nonna used to make—and once Julien was satisfied, he turned his eyes on Priest, who had, *oui,* moved a little closer.

"I want a taste," Priest said, but his voice and eyes implied that he was talking about much more than the sauce that was now dripping down the handle of the spoon and along the side of Julien's hand.

Julien dipped the spoon back into the pot, and when he brought it up between them, he blew on it, cooling it, before he offered it up to his husband. Priest leaned in and sipped it off the edge of the wood, and before Julien could lower his arm, Priest wrapped his fingers around Julien's wrist and dragged his tongue along the edge of his hand.

Julien hummed in the back of his throat, and when Priest's potent stare found his, he marveled that even after all this time, Priest still made his knees weak.

"Delicious," Priest said, licking his lips.

"*Bien*. Do you think our *princesse* will like it?"

"Oh, we're talking about the food?"

Julien's lips curved as he sidled closer to Priest and put a hand on his chest.

"Hmm," Priest said. "Then yes, he will. That's delicious too."

Julien shook his head. "And you think Robbie and I are trouble. Don't try and charm your way out of what we were just discussing."

"I'm not doing that."

"*Si*, you are," Julien said as he turned back to the stove.

"Fine," Priest said, and finally walked over to sit at the island. "But if you want me to actually stay over here, keep talking, or Robert is going to walk in on much more than cooking."

Julien aimed a pointed look over his shoulder. "Okay, then. How about you admit that you were being nosey upstairs."

"I—"

"Admit *it*, *mon amour*. It's driving you crazy that he hasn't formally introduced us to his family yet."

"I *admit* that I was a little bit curious about what he was saying to his mother, yes," Priest said, and then aimed a look at the stairs. "I just wish he'd talk to us about this. He does about everything else, but at the mention of his family, he clams up."

"I agree. We need to talk to him about it."

Priest nodded. "We do. He's always so open about us with everyone. But whenever we mention telling his parents—"

"I know," Julien said. "He's dodging it."

"His mom wants him to come home for his birthday."

Julien snorted. "See. Nosey."

"I just want to help make this easier for him," Priest said, as if that excused the fact that he'd stood outside the bathroom a little longer than necessary. "His mother already knows about us. She knew from the first time she saw us all together. I'm positive. And so is he. This is absurd."

"*Oui*," Julien said, finding Priest's frustration slightly amusing as he bent down to open the cabinet and look for a pot for his pasta. "But introducing your married boyfriends to your family has got to be kind of daunting. *Non?*"

Priest conceded that point as Julien wrapped his hand around the handle of the pot and pulled it free, straightening to his full height.

"Why don't we talk to him about it tomorrow?" Julien said, as he filled the pot with water and added it to the stove. "Then we can see if he wants to do something with them for his—"

"Oh. My. *God.*"

Robbie's voice interrupted the two of them, and when Julien turned around, he found their *princesse* frozen by the dining room table. His lips were parted, his eyes wide, and his gaze was locked on Julien like a tractor beam.

Shelving their conversation for now, Julien walked across the kitchen as Priest stood so he could hold his hand out to Robbie.

"I believe I have *you* to thank for this particular treat tonight," Priest said, as Robbie slipped his palm into his. "Why don't you come into the kitchen, birthday boy, and meet your personal chef for the evening."

CHAPTER THREE

Delicate and fragile or fierce and sassy...
I wonder which Robert we'll see tonight.
I bet I know - Priest

I DON'T KNOW what I did to deserve the good karma coming my way right now, but I am not *about to stop and try and work it out.* No siree, Robbie thought, as he slipped his hand into Priest's and took a step forward, his eyes locked on the hottest chef in the world standing naked in their kitchen. *Well, naked except for the tiniest apron I've ever seen in my life.*

"A pretty good start to celebrating your thirtieth year on the planet, wouldn't you agree?" Priest said by Robbie's ear.

Uh, yeah, he would. Robbie swallowed, trying to find his tongue, as Priest guided him into the kitchen, closer to Julien, closer to heaven.

"We were trying to think of something...special to give you tonight," Priest said, making gooseflesh break out over Robbie's skin. "Something you would never forget. I've always found a private meal prepared by my very *own* chef is something I never forget. What do you think?"

As Priest drew them to a stop in front of Julien, he let go of Robbie's hand, and Robbie blinked a couple of times to make sure he wasn't dreaming. When he tried to speak again, nothing came out, and a sensual smile slowly curved Julien's full lips.

Priest chuckled. "I believe you've rendered him speechless, *mon cœur.*"

Julien held his hand out, and as Robbie slipped his palm over the top of it, Julien drew him forward and bowed down to press his lips to the back of Robbie's knuckles.

Sweet. Jesus. As if all of that wasn't enough to make Robbie's heart thump wildly, Julien looked at him from beneath his lashes and said, *"Bonsoir, princesse,"* and Robbie close to swooned under the power of that smile and dimple.

"Um..." Robbie licked his lips. "You're naked."

Julien laughed, and when he straightened, he tugged on Robbie's hand and drew him in close. *"Oui,* I am."

"Wow." Robbie put a palm on Julien's chest to steady himself. "This is, like, one of my top fantasies ever coming to life right now."

"Mhmm. I remember," Julien said, as Robbie gripped the back of his neck. "It's fast becoming one of mine too."

Now that he'd managed to regain some of his brain function, Robbie leaned back a little and touched the tip of his tongue to his top lip. "I want to see more."

"Greedy," Julien said, but let go of Robbie's waist so he could take a step back.

Once there were a couple of feet between them, Robbie trailed his eyes down Julien's naked torso, to the apron that covered from his waist to the middle of his muscled thighs. "Could you maybe, um...turn around?"

"I could. If you say please," Julien said, his voice as effective as a firm stroke to Robbie's stiffening cock.

"S'il te plaît."

"*Très bien, princesse.*" Julien pivoted, slowly, and it was all Robbie could do to stand where he was and keep his hands to—*and off* – himself. The stark white material was a stunning contrast with Julien's taut, tanned skin, and when his smooth back came into view, Robbie close to whimpered.

Holy shit.

The tattoos on Julien's shoulder, that tapered waist, and the dimples of his firm ass as he came to a stop facing the far wall, had Robbie taking a step forward. Add in the neatly tied bow that sat above Julien's tailbone, and the ends that swished against his round cheeks, and Robbie couldn't contain the moan that left his throat.

"Remember." Priest's voice came from behind, making Robbie's cock even harder. "If you behave yourself, you can do anything you like to that body...later."

"Shit," Robbie said, unable to tear his eyes away. "Have you ever had Jules cook like this for you before?"

"No, surprisingly." Priest wrapped his arms around Robbie's waist and tugged him back into his body. "But I'm starting to think this is the only way we should *ever* let him cook for us."

Julien looked over his shoulder at the two of them, and his smirk had Robbie squirming in Priest's arms. *God, he's fucking hot.*

"If you two are done ogling me, I have a birthday dinner to finish preparing."

Priest massaged the heel of his palm over Robbie's erection. "You done looking, sweetheart?"

"Not nearly— Ah, *fuck*, Priest." Robbie thrust into Priest's hand as Julien walked back to the stove, and when he picked up a wooden spoon, Robbie's mind pictured him doing a whole lot more with that spoon than stirring that pot.

How in the hell do they expect me to wait through a meal to touch him?

"Why don't you go and sit over there at the island," Priest said, "and watch while he finishes up in here?"

Robbie nodded as he walked around to the barstools and got up on one. "Julien Thornton is cooking for me *naked*. This is officially the best birthday ever."

"It's not your birthday yet," Priest said, and handed Robbie a cosmo. "Now why don't you sit there and enjoy your drink while I go and finish setting the table. Remember, you can look, but no touching. Not yet."

AROUND FIFTEEN COCK-TEASING minutes later, Priest ushered Robbie into the dining room, and when he headed toward his usual spot on the right of the table, opposite Julien's seat, Priest shook his head and pulled out the chair at the head.

"I believe this is your seat tonight," Priest said, and crooked a finger. "Come over here."

"So bossy," Robbie said, his eyes full of mischief as he walked over, trailing his fingers along the back of the chair. "But you should probably get it out of your system now, since I'm the one who's going to be calling the shots later."

"*If* you win," Priest said, when Robbie came to a standstill.

He had dressed in Priest's favorite short shorts pajama set tonight, and with his hair swept back and still damp, Robbie's pouty lips and high cheekbones were on prominent display, making it extremely difficult for Priest to keep his hands to himself.

Their princess was such a contradiction at times, and it always fascinated Priest to see which version of him they would get depending on Robbie's mood. In some instances, he looked delicate and fragile, and made Priest want to gently trace every exquisite line of his face. At other times, when Robbie was throwing around that sassy attitude of his, it made Priest want to take him over his knee and teach him a lesson. Fierce Robbie was a force to be reckoned with—like now.

"Since tonight is your show," Priest said, as he gestured to the seat, "it's only right that you sit at the head of the table."

"My *show*, huh?" Robbie arched an eyebrow, and then ran his eyes down Priest's shirt to his shorts. "If that's true," he said, and reached out to finger the hem of Priest's shirt, "how about you undo this and take it off so I can look at you? Seems only fair, since Julien isn't wearing much more than a handkerchief."

"You think so, do you?"

Robbie nodded and stepped in closer to undo the first two buttons. "Unless, of course, you don't think you can control yourself. I mean, I assume the rules of this game go both ways. If *I* can't control myself, I don't get my prize, and if *you* can't control yourself, I do. Right?"

Troublemaker. "Right."

"In that case," Robbie said, as he got to the top button and popped it free, "I want to see the other half of my prize in advance. You know, to make me work extra *hard* to get it."

Priest eyed Robbie's devious grin and wondered when he'd managed to turn the tables, because Priest was suddenly finding it very difficult not to grab Robbie and bend him over *said* table.

Robbie ran a finger down the center of Priest's body to the button of his shorts, and when he saw the erection straining against Priest's zipper, he raised those blue eyes and bit his lip, an impish expression crossing his gorgeous face. "Uh oh. This little game of yours seems to be going down in flames, fast."

Priest wrapped an arm around Robbie's waist, grabbed hold of his ass, and hauled him in against his body until their lips were within an inch of each other. "The only thing that's going to be going down anytime soon is *you*, sweetheart."

"We'll see."

Priest kissed his way up Robbie's jaw to his ear. "Yes, we will. Now sit your delectable ass down while you're still able to."

Robbie sucked in a breath and, when Priest released him, said, "Well, since you asked so nicely," and took a seat as Julien walked in carrying two plates.

Julien looked between the two of them, and after he put one plate in front of Robbie and the other where Priest was now sitting, he said, "I'll be right back. I'm just going to go and put on—"

"Uh *ah*," Robbie said. "If you think for one second you are going to put clothes *on*, forget it."

Julien raised an eyebrow at Robbie, and Priest said, "I think he's practicing giving orders on the off chance he wins tonight."

"For *when* I win, you mean," Robbie said, and picked up his drink to take another sip. "And just so you know, I've never been more motivated in my life."

Julien inclined his head, but his lips twitched as he eyed Priest. "Very well. I'll just go and get my dinner and we can eat."

"The first course, anyway," Robbie said, as Julien walked back into the kitchen.

As Julien disappeared, Priest was about to turn to the rascal beside him, when Robbie said, "He has, like, the *best* ass ever."

"Oh, I don't know," Priest said. "I'd say you're about even."

"No way," Robbie said, shaking his head. "When it comes to *that* particular part of the anatomy, Julien wins, hands down. It's all that yoga. It makes you want to...mm...bite it."

Priest shifted on his seat as Robbie plucked the sugarcoated lime off the side of his drink and sucked on it. "If you win, you'll get to do just that."

"Maybe," Robbie said, as his eyes drifted back to Priest's. "*If* that's what I decide I want. Which, by the way...?"

"Yes?" Priest said, as Julien came back to the table and took his seat.

"Is this like a one-act kind of thing?" Robbie asked. "Or am I allowed to pick a whole scenario?" Julien shook his head, but Robbie continued, not to be deterred. "I mean, that's kind of important for me to know before I narrow things down. Don't you think?"

"That's a good point," Priest conceded, and looked to Julien. "What do you think, chef?"

"I think you two are as bad as each other," Julien said. "Always trying to one-up the other."

"Aww." Robbie put an elbow on the table and leaned toward

Julien. "I want to get all up on you too, Jules. I'm just working out the dirty details first."

Julien ran his eyes over Robbie, and as his gaze lingered on the flirt's lips, Julien's eyes darkened. Priest knew by the end of the night that all three of them were going to be up on each other in one way or another—and he couldn't wait.

"Then I think you can have *any*thing you want," Julien said. "That was the deal, and if you want a whole scenario, then you should get it."

Robbie grinned like a fiend as he sat back in his chair and looked at Priest. "Best birthday game *ever*."

No one disagreed. In fact, with the way the night was going, Priest had a feeling that this little game of theirs just might become a household tradition.

WHEN THE MEAL came to an end, Julien watched as Priest got to his feet and picked up Robbie's plate before heading around to collect his. As he reached Julien's side, Priest leaned down to kiss his cheek and said, "Superb, as always."

"*Merci*," Julien said, and smiled when Priest pressed a harder kiss to his mouth. Julien reached up to hold Priest to him, and when Priest's tongue rubbed up along his, Julien groaned.

Priest growled against his lips before he raised his head, and when they looked over to Robbie, he said, "Why'd you two stop?"

Priest chuckled at Robbie's frustrated tone. "Because you haven't won yet."

Robbie frowned as he looked at the clock. "Close enough."

"Yet still so far away," Priest said.

"Fine." Robbie pouted. "Weren't you taking the plates to the kitchen?"

"I was. But I was taking a moment to kiss the chef. Since I'm allowed to, and you're not."

"Yet," Robbie said.

"Yet."

As Priest left with the plates in hand, Robbie sat back in his seat and said, "Well...since we can't talk about kissing, he's not lying about the food. It was so good. Don't tell my nonna, but this sauce just might rival hers."

"My lips are sealed," Julien said, and Priest called out from the kitchen, "I certainly hope not."

Robbie rolled his eyes, but the cheeky smile that lit his face had Julien's erection threatening the limited coverage his apron provided. It had been nothing short of a miracle that he'd gotten through dinner without having to excuse himself, and therefore break the rules.

But with both Robbie and Priest looking at him as though *he* was what they were eating, Julien had had a hard time—to say the least—making it to the finish line.

As it was, they were around fifteen minutes away from this game reaching a conclusion, and he had to admit, it looked as though the odds were in Robbie's favor. Their *princesse* had been motivated tonight for sure, and he'd somehow managed to keep his hands to himself. Julien had a feeling that wouldn't last too much longer, though. At least, he hoped not.

"Are you enjoying yourself?" Julien asked, as Robbie's bright eyes found him, and *oui*, the arousal and triumph staring back at him was a definite indicator that Robbie was more than aware he was closing in on his deadline *and* prize.

"I *am*."

"*Bien*. That makes us happy."

"Hmm, well, I have a feeling I'm going to enjoy myself a whole lot *more,* very soon."

"That you might, if you don't slip up in the next few minutes."

"Oh, I'm not going to slip up. I've managed to sit here for nearly an hour while you have been *naked* next to me. I have got *this* in the bag."

Julien didn't doubt Robbie for one second. Himself, however? He was walking a fine line, because Robbie was close enough that

Julien could reach out and grab him, and maybe lay him out on this table, where he could eat him for a few good hours.

He needed to distract himself, and the beautiful one beside him, quick smart.

"What do you usually do for your birthdays, *princesse?*"

"You mean instead of eating dinner with a naked chef and his half-dressed husband?"

"*Oui,*" Julien said, as Priest came back to the table and stopped behind him, resting his hands on Julien's shoulders. "What did you do last year?"

"I, uh..." As Robbie's words tapered off, he looked at Priest and frowned. "I spent it with my ex."

Ah, okay, Julien thought, as Priest's fingers tightened a little at the mention of the other man. Clearly *this* wasn't the direction they wanted the conversation to go in.

"And let me tell you," Robbie said.

Or maybe Robbie did.

"I *wish* he could see me right now, because he'd be so damn jealous."

"Of course he would be," Julien said. "He let you go. He's clearly a *crétin.*"

"Uh, not jealous because he doesn't have *me.* Jealous because I have the both of you," Robbie said. "His biggest fantasy was being with two men. Problem was, he couldn't even handle one."

"No offense," Priest said. "But I don't want to think about him handling anyfuckingthing that's now mine. If that's okay with you?"

Robbie's lips twitched as he sat back in his seat. "Jealous?"

"That's the nicest word for what I'm feeling right now, yes."

"Well, there's no need to be. He broke up with me and fired me a week later. What an asshole. But you two have successfully replaced one of my worst memories with a fantastic one. So thank you for that. Speaking of..." Robbie said, and let his eyes drift back to the clock on the wall, which now read nine fifty-five. "Are you ready to concede that I've won?"

"No. It's not time yet," Priest said, as he slid one of his hands over Julien's shoulder, and then bent down to nip at his ear, making Julien's control come precariously close to its boiling point.

"Are you serious?" Robbie said, and turned his attention back to them in time to see Priest's hand disappear beneath the table. "I have five minutes until—"

"*Putain*," Julien said, and shut his eyes, as Priest wrapped the apron around his cock and stroked.

"You have five minutes until...?" Priest said, and when Julien opened his eyes, he found Robbie's locked on Priest's hand—his lips parted, and his cheeks flushed.

"Until I, uh, tell you what I want."

"And have you decided what that's going to be?" Priest asked by Julien's ear, and the rough timbre of his voice tantalized every single one of Julien's nerve endings.

Robbie's gaze found Julien's, and Priest tightened his fist, making Julien's fingers dig into the table.

"Yes," Robbie said on a breathy rush of air, as he reached down and finally pressed the heel of his hand to his dick. "Yes, I've decided."

"Then it's time to tell us, *princesse*." Julien groaned as Priest stroked him again. "Because you just won."

CHAPTER FOUR

A princess, a priest, and a very hard *prick*
walk into a bedroom together...
How would you want this story to end?
My thoughts exactly - Robbie

DAMN RIGHT I won, Robbie thought, as he got to his feet and boldly looked over his winnings. With Julien and Priest as his prize, nothing on the damn planet had been going to make him lose, and now? Now it was time to collect.

Ever since Priest had teased him with this game, Robbie had been trying to decide what exactly it was he wanted from them tonight. But it wasn't until Priest had come back in from the kitchen that it had hit—the perfect idea.

It was something Robbie had never really had the patience for in the past, but since tonight was all about self-restraint, and he'd lasted this long, why not go all the way? *Right? Right.*

"Priest?" Robbie said, and when Priest's grey eyes found his, Robbie felt as though he were about to catch fire.

Shit. That look told him one thing: Priest was done holding back on that indomitable self-control of his. His arousal, his pent-up desire? It was on the surface now for Robbie and Julien to see. Well, if Julien ever opened his eyes again. Right now, they were shut tight as Priest continued to work his cock beneath the table.

"Yes, Robert?" Priest said. He was *daring* Robbie to be the boss tonight, and hell if Robbie wasn't about to take him up on it.

"Take your husband upstairs. I want to watch you take that apron off him."

Priest's eyes flared, and Julien's finally opened.

"Is that right?" Priest said, as he released his hold on Julien and straightened to his full height.

Robbie nodded as Julien finally stood, and it didn't escape Robbie's notice that that apron was doing absolutely nothing to hide Julien's erection. "Yes. It is."

Pretty damn pleased with himself, Robbie walked around the table, and was about to head to the stairs when Priest reached for his arm, halting him.

"Then what?" Priest asked, and Robbie stepped in close and pressed a kiss to the corner of Priest's lips.

"*Then* I'll tell you what comes next." As Robbie moved back, he let his eyes drift between his men and brazenly licked his lips. "But just so you know, it won't be either of you until *I* say so."

Priest scoffed, and the sound was arrogant and so damn sexy that Robbie took a step away, knowing he'd cave in a hot second if Priest ordered him to do something.

But he didn't. Instead, Priest turned to Julien and said, "You heard the birthday boy, Mr. Thornton."

Julien smirked, and when his dimple appeared, Robbie added *licking it* to the top of the list of things he wanted to do tonight.

"Did you put him up to this?" Julien asked, as he looked his husband in the eye.

"I did not," Priest said. "But I have to admit, I'm liking his direction thus far. Get upstairs, *mon cœur*, so I can strip you for our princess."

Robbie's dick throbbed at the wicked promise in Priest's voice, but he didn't linger any longer in the dining room. He took the stairs up to the bedroom two at a time, well aware of the voices still below, and once he was there, he headed around to Priest's workspace and wheeled the desk chair to the far side of the bed, where he took a seat.

Oh yes, Robbie thought, as he propped his feet up on the mattress and crossed his ankles. *The best seat in the house. The director's chair.*

He took in a steadying breath as he heard heavy footsteps heading his way, and when Julien and Priest came to a standstill in the doorway, Robbie gestured that they come in. "Well, don't stop there. I want to see my birthday present up close and...personal."

Priest's raspy chuckle made Robbie's balls tingle, and as Julien's eyes trailed a burning path from Robbie's feet, up his legs, to his stiff dick, Robbie couldn't help but slip a hand between his thighs to palm himself.

"Seems our princess has become quite the demanding queen tonight," Priest said in Julien's ear, and then he urged Julien forward, his fingers on his lower back. "Where would you like us?"

Robbie pursed his lips. "Mm, over there, I think," he said, and pointed to the opposite side of the bed.

As Julien walked to the spot indicated, Robbie's eyes dropped to his thighs. He wasn't sure if it was the peekaboo element the apron was creating that was making the flex of Julien's legs so damn sexy. But with every step he took, the glimpse Robbie caught of his muscles beneath had him close to panting.

Julien's body was unreal, and dressed as he was right now—*or not dressed*—it was difficult for Robbie to think clearly. Add in the way Priest's eyes were zeroed in on Julien's ass, and it all promised that Robbie was about to get the best birthday present he'd ever received.

JULIEN CAME TO a stop where Robbie had instructed, and he could feel Priest's body heat emanating off him, he was so close. But when Julien reached for the tie at the back of his apron, wanting nothing in between them, Robbie shook his head.

"*Non, non, monsieur,*" Robbie said, his eyes sparkling with mischief, and that look promised all kinds of trouble was about to ensue. "That's not what I told you to do. I want *Priest* to take it off, and I get whatever I want tonight."

"*Oui,* you do. My mistake," Julien said, grateful for the freedom the apron afforded when Priest smoothed a hand up his spine and tugged him back, so Julien's bare ass was now cradling his massive erection.

Dieu. That felt good, and clearly Priest agreed.

"Better behave yourself, Julien," Priest said, and his breath on Julien's ear made a shiver of anticipation race down his spine. "It seems Robert is feeling extra feisty tonight."

Robbie gave a flirty shrug. "Fair's fair. You two came up with all of this; I'm just collecting my winnings. And this first part requires *you,* Mr. Priestley, down on your knees."

Priest raised an eyebrow. "I thought I was taking off his apron."

"You are," Robbie said, as his eyes trailed up to Julien's, the glint in them making them practically twinkle. "With your teeth."

Julien cursed, and Priest's fingers dug into his hips.

"And you think I'm the cock tease in this threesome," Priest said. "I think you just stole the title, sweetheart."

Robbie seemed to like that, if the flush that stained his cheeks was any indication. Then Priest let go of Julien and did as he was instructed, shifting down to his knees.

Julien looked over his shoulder, and when Priest raised his head, the melted steel that connected with him promised that whatever was about to follow would be so fucking hot, it would likely melt Julien to the ground.

"You *are* a tease," Robbie said, recapturing Julien's attention as he slipped his hand under the elastic of his pajama shorts. "A big, *mean* one. But now I'm going to finish this the way *I* want. And I want you to take off his apron...with your mouth."

Julien caught his breath as the tip of Priest's tongue flicked over the round curve of his ass, and when one of Priest's hands smoothed up the front of his thigh to circle the base of his dick, Julien swayed on his feet.

"*Putain de merde*," Julien said, and gritted his teeth, not knowing if he wanted to thrust forward into Priest's hand or back toward his teasing mouth.

"Yes," Robbie said, as he uncrossed his ankles and widened his legs. "Take the apron off him, Priest. I want to see what you're doing."

Julien's eyes found Robbie's, and the dark desire swirling there told him that whatever Robbie had in mind for them after this was something he desperately wanted. Lucky for Robbie, they were more than willing to give him whatever his dirty little heart desired tonight.

———

PRIEST HAD KNOWN that laying a little groundwork this afternoon would pay off in the best ways imaginable. But he'd had no idea which direction Robbie would take them in once that clock struck ten.

Still didn't, really. But with Robbie sprawled back in the chair with his bare feet on the bed and his hand in those shorts, he was difficult to ignore—and so was his uppity attitude.

Priest leaned forward and took the end of Julien's apron tie between his teeth and pulled, and as it fell to the ground at Julien's feet, Priest's eyes found Robbie's fevered ones.

Bossy bottom. He's totally getting off on this. But then again, so was Priest.

Unable to resist the lure of Julien's flesh, Priest gently scraped his teeth over one of the rounded curves, and Julien reached back to spear his fingers through Priest's hair.

"Don't tease, *mon amour*," Julien said, his breathing slightly unstable. "Not if you want this to last."

"Yeah, Priest," Robbie said. "Plus, I didn't say you could *bite* him. Now, stand up."

Priest's eyes narrowed on the impertinent man who was trying his hardest to keep his cool. But when Priest inclined his head and slowly got to his feet, he ran his hands up Julien's sides, and Robbie moaned.

"*Shit,*" Robbie said. "Yes, this is... Stroke Jules's cock for me. I want to watch."

So their princess wanted a show tonight for real? Okay. That was more than fine with Priest, as he wrapped an arm around Julien's waist and took his thick erection in hand. The pleasure-filled groan that echoed off the bedroom walls made it crystal clear that it was more than fine with Julien too. The only question that remained was: how far could Robbie take this little show of his before he caved?

With long, sure strokes, Priest began to pull and work Julien's stiff length until Julien leaned back against him, wrapped an arm up around his neck, and began to pump his hips forward.

"Oh my fucking God," Robbie said, and quickly let go of himself to unbutton his shirt. It seemed their princess was getting a little bit hot and bothered.

Robbie threw the material aside, and as he fell back in his chair and stuffed his hand back down in his pants, Priest wished like hell he was the one giving orders, because he really wanted to see the delicious prick Robbie was stroking.

"*Princesse?*" Julien said in a voice that was practically a caress to both the men who were listening, and when Robbie brought his eyes up to Julien's, he nearly whimpered.

Priest couldn't blame him. He could only imagine how breath-taking Julien looked right now with his phenomenal body exposed and his cock sliding in and out of Priest's fist.

"Yes?" Robbie said, his breathing coming a little harder now.

"Can I ask you for something?"

Robbie parted his legs, and his arm flexed, his fingers no doubt tightening around himself, and Priest got the impression that Julicn could've asked for *ten* things right then and Robbie would've agreed.

But as though Robbie sensed he was caving, falling under Julien's sensual spell, he seemed to shake himself out of it. "You *can*...that doesn't mean you'll get it, though."

"*Oui*, I know. But could you take your shorts off so I can see you?"

Thank. You. Julien, Priest thought. He loved it when all three of them were on the same wavelength, and tonight they most certainly were. That didn't mean, however, that Robbie was going to let them off the hook that easy, *oh no*. His blazing blue eyes shifted to Priest's, and whatever he must've seen there made his sweet lips curve into a provocative grin. "Do you want that too?"

"Yes," Priest answered in an instant.

Robbie's gaze shifted back to Julien. "Then I'll think about it. And if you two continue to please me, I just might give it to you."

Priest's lips twitched at Robbie's insolence, and he raised the haughtiest eyebrow Priest had ever seen, and *fuck*, it was so damn sexy.

"Well? Continue, please," Robbie said, and then sat back to watch the show.

BEST DECADE EVER. I called it. And if this was the way it was starting out, then Robbie had high hopes for the rest.

When Priest had moved in behind Julien down in the dining room, Robbie had had a sudden vision of them naked, opposite him, but this time with Priest—

"*C'est bon*, Joel. Harder."

—doing a whole lot more to Julien than rubbing his shoulders, and now that vision was coming to life.

Julien's cock was dripping all over Priest's hand, as Priest brushed his thumb over the swollen head that kept peeking through the end of his grip. But even *that* wasn't enough to satiate this hunger Robbie couldn't seem to satisfy tonight. He wanted more.

He blamed the two of them, of course, for his suddenly insatiable appetite. But come on—Priest and Julien had thrown down this sex gauntlet. Robbie had just picked it up and run.

"Priest?" Robbie said, and when Priest looked over, Robbie reveled in the power he held. He felt lightheaded, drunk on the intoxicating feeling of being in control of these two men—and right now, he *totally* was. They'd handed him the reins, and he had no trouble playing the boss. Really, no trouble at all.

"Yes, Robert?"

"Get naked."

Priest's eyes glittered like diamonds, as he slowly released Julien and removed his shorts and boxer briefs.

Priest was commanding *in* clothes, but without them, he owned any person fortunate enough to be in his bedroom. Luckily for Robbie, that now only included him and Julien, and they were always left in awe whenever Priest stood before them like he was now.

His hair was pushed back from his ruggedly handsome face, except for the one piece that always fell forward on his forehead, and that small thing reminded Robbie of all the times Priest had thrust that powerful body inside either him or Julien, and that hair had fallen down from the force of it. And one look at Julien told Robbie that he was thinking the exact same thing.

With his head turned, and his eyes locked on Priest, Julien was greedily devouring the body moving closer to his, and when the corner of Priest's mouth quirked up in an immoral smile, Julien groaned deep in his throat.

Fuck. While Julien was all sleek and sensual when naked, Priest was full-on power—and this was going to be so damn hot that Robbie thought the room might catch on fire.

"Now, kiss," Robbie said, and when Julien pivoted toward

Priest, their cocks grazed one another, and Priest reached for the back of Julien's neck and hauled him in.

Robbie moaned as though it were *his* mouth Priest was now destroying, *him* taking such a long taste of Julien, and he clamped a fist around his dick to stop himself from coming as he watched the scene unfold in front of him.

This kiss wasn't soft. It wasn't gentle. It wasn't a kiss to see if the other was interested and wanted to go further. *No.* This kiss was rough, passionate, and full of pent-up aggression and frustration.

Priest's fingers dug into Julien's neck and shoulder, as he angled his head and speared his tongue into Julien's mouth. Julien threaded his fingers through Priest's hair and twisted, hanging on as he bit down on Priest's lip, making him grunt, pull back, and then go at him again from a different direction.

Robbie's pulse raced, his blood like a wildfire in his veins as he watched the two on the opposite side of the bed. Priest grabbed at Julien's ass, and Julien thrust his hips forward, grinding his cock along the underside of Priest's, and as they continued to go at one another, Robbie *still* wanted more.

"*That*," Robbie said, and as they tore apart and looked at him, their chests heaved against one another. "I want to watch more of *that* for my birthday."

"Be specific, sweetheart," Priest said. "*What* exactly are you asking for?"

The untamed expression in both Julien's and Priest's eyes told Robbie they knew exactly what he was asking for. But if they needed him to spell it out, then he had no problem with that. In fact, he'd never wanted to say the words more.

"I want to watch you two fuck."

CHAPTER FIVE

A dirty-talking princess
is much more fun than a proper one.
Trust us, we should know
- Julien & Priest

DAMN. THOSE WORDS coming from Robbie had Julien clenching his teeth, as did the way Robbie was lounging back in his chair with his wanton eyes roaming all over them. Robbie looked like a man who'd paid top dollar for an explicit show and expected to get it—and boy was he about to.

As Priest kneaded Julien's shoulders, he couldn't help but groan as his husband moved in behind him and put his lips just under his ear. Robbie nodded, but said nothing, making it very clear that what Priest was doing was exactly what he wanted to see.

Julien shut his eyes and leaned back into the strong body behind him. He reveled in the feel of the hard length that would soon be inside his body, as it found a place for now nestled between the cheeks of his ass, and Priest growled out a soft rumble of approval.

"*Damn*," Robbie said, and Julien opened his eyes in time to see him sit up and put his feet on the floor.

The air in the room crackled with sexual energy, and then Priest lit the match.

"Brace your hands on the mattress," he said in Julien's ear, and as Priest urged him down to their bed, Robbie finally got to his feet.

Julien's palms landed atop their duvet at the same time Robbie's shorts hit the floor, and then Robbie opened the bedside drawer, grabbed a bottle of lube, and climbed onto the opposite side of the mattress.

As Priest crowded down behind Julien, he pressed a kiss to the base of his neck, and Robbie tossed the lube down beside them and settled back on his heels to watch.

Julien arched into the solid pressure of Priest's body, and when Priest reached for the bottle and opened it, Julien's eyes found Robbie's.

"You two like this," Robbie said, as Priest began sliding his slick fingers up and down Julien's crack. "I... It's just... Fuck. It's so goddamn hot. And I'm always so caught up in how *I* feel that I never get to just...watch."

Julien's dick throbbed at Robbie's words, not to mention Priest's fingers. But Robbie didn't have to justify his wants to them. They knew perfectly well what a turn-on it was to watch one another, and just as Julien was about to tell him that, Priest chose that moment to push a finger inside.

Julien's hands flexed around the covers, and as Priest dragged it out and did it again, Julien shoved back, taking that finger in as far as it would go.

"Christ, you're fucking tight, Julien," Priest said as he pulled his finger free and rubbed the pad of his thumb over the pucker he was now pouring a liberal amount of lube on. "We're going to have to get you nice and stretched before anything bigger than my fingers get in you. It's been a while since this ass has had my cock in it."

Julien's arms trembled at Priest's words. It *had* been a while. Months in fact. Now that Robbie was a permanent part of their lives, the three of them had shifted into the roles that came most naturally to them. But Julien had to admit, he was eager to give Robbie this and feel Priest once again consume him.

As two of Priest's fingers slowly eased inside, Julien gnashed his teeth together, and his eyes moved up Robbie's body to the hand that was methodically working his length. His creamy skin had a light sheen over it, and the evidence of his arousal was helping him get a nice, sticky slide going.

"*Viens ici,*" Julien said, and he wondered if Robbie would follow the order, considering he was the one who was giving them tonight. But when Robbie shifted closer on the mattress, bringing that luscious cock mere inches from his lips, Julien aimed his eyes up at Robbie and said, "*Laisse-moi te goûter.* Let me taste you."

With a shameless grin, Robbie said, "I would *love* that. But where are your manners, Jules?"

Priest's deep chuckle rumbled around the room, and Julien gripped the covers a little tighter as he stared into Robbie's gorgeous face. The cheeky minx was paying him back for that moment earlier in the kitchen.

"*Laisse-moi te goûter,*" Julien said again, and then ran his tongue across his lower lip. "*S'il te plaît.*"

Robbie practically purred as he painted his sticky fingers along the same path Julien had just traced with his tongue. And when the salty taste of him hit Julien's senses, Priest slid three fingers inside and leaned across Julien's back. "*Please* give me your mouth, sweetheart."

As Robbie moved that final inch closer to kiss Priest, the sound they made as their lips met and their fingers moved in and out of him was one of the most erotic things Julien had ever heard.

His cock ached as he continued to work it, and then Priest said, "So you want to watch me fuck our Frenchman, do you?"

"Ah huh," Robbie said, his voice breathy, his body swaying even closer until his cock brushed the corner of Julien's cheek. "It's my go-to fantasy. The two of you together like this."

"Really..." Priest said, as he removed his fingers from Julien's body and began to drag the head of his erection up and down Julien's channel. *Teasing salopard.*

"Mhmm," Robbie said. "Always. Even before we all— *Ahh.*"

Robbie ceased talking as Julien captured his erection between his lips and sucked, and not a second later, Priest grabbed hold of Julien's hips and entered him with one solid thrust.

JULIEN'S BODY WAS as tight as a vise, and as Priest's cock disappeared inside, he dug his fingers into his husband's hips and didn't stop until his balls were brushing up against Julien's hot skin.

It had been a long time since he'd been inside Julien, and the toe-curling pleasure Priest got from having him spread open like this made him feel high as a fucking kite.

Robbie's eyes were riveted to Julien's stretched hole, and his hands were now fisted in his hair, and if Priest hadn't been gritting his teeth in an effort not to come, he would've told Robbie how much he approved of this birthday present.

As it was, Priest was having a difficult time keeping a leash on his control, and when Julien clenched his muscles and they contracted around his length, Priest cursed. "Do that again, Julien, and I'm going to drill you into this mattress."

Robbie shoved his hips forward at the threat, sliding deeper between Julien's full lips, and then smoothed his hand down Julien's neck to his back. "Shit. I was so right. He has the best ass on the planet."

Priest's lips curved as Robbie's fevered gaze met his. Those blue eyes were navy right now, and the lust riding Robbie was as intoxicating as the hole Priest was getting ready to annihilate.

Right here and now, there was nothing and nobody in the world but the three of them. Each man connected to the other in this untamed, raw moment that had been dreamed up by the sweet-looking man, who then opened his mouth and issued a not-so sweet request.

"God, Priest. *Move*," Robbie said. "I want to watch. I want to see you slide into him."

Julien groaned between them, making it clear he'd heard Robbie, and as Priest slowly dragged his cock free, Julien pulled his mouth from Robbie and said, "Do it, Joel. Fuck me," and Priest complied.

Priest drove back inside, gripping Julien's hips and yanking him back so he could get as deep as he possibly could, before pulling out to do it over and over until Julien called out his name. Robbie's hand was pumping his cock in time to the pace Priest was pounding out, and when Julien took him back into his mouth, Robbie matched pace there too.

Priest's hands spread Julien wide so he could watch his dick penetrate him, and a shout ripped free of Robbie as Julien took him all the way to the back of his throat.

"Oh fuck. *Fuck*," Robbie chanted, and he pulled free of Julien's mouth, trying to fight off his orgasm.

Greedy boy. Still wants more before he comes tonight, Priest thought, as he reached for Julien's shoulder. *Then sit tight, princess. We'll give you more.*

Priest clamped a hand down on Julien's tense muscles and hauled him up until he was standing. The angle and shift of Julien's body had Priest bucking forward, and once he was back inside that tight hole, Priest kissed his way up Julien's neck to his ear and said, "It's been a while, *mon cœur*. You like that?"

"*Oui*," Julien said, and reached down to pump his cock. "*Bordel, c'est trop bon*, Joel. It's so fucking good." As Julien's words morphed into heavy moans, Robbie's eyes latched on to them, and Priest began to move.

He banded an arm across Julien's collarbone and splayed his other hand over his stomach, and as he began to move in and out, the sounds out of Julien's mouth almost made Priest lose it.

Julien was so free with his pleasure, so sexy, and Robbie must've agreed, because not long after that, he was across the bed and standing on the mattress. His dick grazed over the back of Priest's hand, and when Robbie bent down to kiss Julien's lips, Julien's ass tightened, making Priest hiss.

As the two in front of him took a long, deep taste of one another, Priest bit down on Julien's shoulder. But the sensual reconnection didn't last long, not with how hot this fire was now burning, and finally Robbie gasped and pulled away.

"That's it," Robbie said, and licked at his swollen lips. "I'm done watching." And before Priest could ask what he meant, Robbie shifted until he was lying flat on his back with his feet on the edge of the mattress.

Robbie spread his legs wide and wrapped a hand around his cock, and when his pretty little hole appeared, Julien cursed.

"Mmm, you want that?" Priest said as he kissed beneath Julien's ear, and Julien fucked back on the cock still lodged inside him. "You want to come in our dirty-talking princess tonight and teach him a lesson for teasing us?"

"Me?" Robbie said, then bit his lip as he arched up, showing himself off to them with not one ounce of shame.

Priest planted a final kiss on Julien's neck and slid out, and watched as Julien put a knee on the mattress between Robbie's legs and nodded.

"*Oui*," Julien said, his voice deeper, raspier from his arousal, as he crawled over Robbie and reached for the bottle of lube. "You, *princesse*. Let's finish this together, hmm?"

Yes, Priest couldn't agree more. The only *real* question was: could they all wait until the other was in place?

ROBBIE COULDN'T TEAR his eyes off Julien as he reached for the lube. His hard cock was sliding along the inside of Robbie's thigh, and when he had the bottle in hand, Julien said, "You're lucky it's your birthday, you naughty boy. Or I'd be flipping you over on this mattress to spank you right now."

Robbie turned his head until their faces were so close he could kiss Julien's lips. "How about you just fuck me into it instead?"

"You have a filthy mouth tonight."

"Actually, you do," Robbie said. "But that's what you get when you and Priest *torment* me all day."

"Hmm," Julien said, and nipped at Robbie's lower lip. "In that case, we might have to tease you more often."

When he added a wink, Robbie's entire body responded by bowing up off the bed in an effort to get closer, and when Julien shifted his weight to one arm to open the lube, Robbie's gaze moved over his shoulder to Priest.

He was standing behind Julien now, working his erect cock, his attention focused on the two of them. Robbie licked his top lip, and when a wicked-hot smirk crossed Priest's mouth, Robbie worked himself a little faster.

Shit. Julien needed to get in him, like...now.

As if Julien could read Robbie's mind, he tossed the bottle aside and, not a second later, his slippery fingers were moving over Robbie's tight balls to the strip of skin that led to—

"Ah, *yes*, Jules. In me... Get them in me."

Julien rested a forearm by Robbie's head, and as he began to move his fingers in and out, Robbie wrapped a leg around his waist and pushed up with his other to get them in deeper.

"*Oui*, use them, *princesse*. Use me." Julien crushed his mouth down over the top of Robbie's, and Robbie opened to him as he began to writhe on those nimble fingers.

"Jesus." Priest's gruff voice filled the room. "For fuck's sake.

Get your *cock* in him, Julien, or this is going to be all fucking over in the next few seconds."

Robbie shuddered and Julien smiled against his lips. "Better hang on to something. Sounds like it's about to be a rough ride."

Julien melted away from Robbie's body, and he saw Priest's hands on Julien's waist pulling him to his feet. Once he was there, Priest took Julien's mouth in a bruising kiss, and Robbie frantically pumped his length as he watched them ravage one another until Priest put a hand to Julien's shoulder and halted him.

"Stop. *Christ*. You've got to stop."

Priest maneuvered Julien to the edge of the bed where Robbie lay. "Robert? Pull your legs— *Fuck*...yes," Priest said, as Robbie hooked his hands around the backs of his knees and spread himself open. "What a pretty fucking sight that is."

Julien nodded, his attention focused on Robbie's eager entrance. "I can't wait to come inside you tonight, birthday boy."

Robbie shivered. It was still such a thrill to feel either one of these men claim him in such a way, and tonight it was going to be... "The icing on the cake?"

Julien placed his palms on the bed by Robbie's head, and when his cock brushed over Robbie's entrance, he said, "Or the cream," right before he sank into Robbie's body.

As Julien stilled, and his mouth hovered over Robbie's, he grinned. "Didn't you tell me that was the best part?"

"*Yes*," Robbie said as he stared up into Julien's gem-colored eyes, and Julien gripped the duvet and rolled his hips forward.

Robbie gasped, and the feeling of having Julien bare inside his body was enough to get Robbie off all on its own. But tonight, Robbie was waiting. He knew what was about to happen, and when Priest moved into position, Robbie watched with eager anticipation as he lined himself up with Julien's body and then powered inside his husband, making Julien's entire body surge forward from the impact.

Robbie moaned as Priest pulled out to do it again, until Julien was so deep inside that Robbie wasn't sure where Julien started and he ended. Julien took Robbie's mouth and kissed the holy hell out of him then, and Robbie let go of his legs to wrap his arms around Julien's neck.

After that, Robbie lost all sense of time and place as they each moved within one another, and as his climax threatened, Robbie shut his eyes and let the euphoria of it finally take over his body, much like the two men above him had taken over his heart.

CHAPTER SIX

*Okay, so I'm nervous about introducing
my married boyfriends to my parents.
Don't act like you wouldn't be - Robbie*

THE MOONLIGHT SLIPPED through the curtains and illuminated the tangle of legs sprawled out on the mattress, where the three men basked in the aftermath of the sensual storm that had just passed by.

"I said it before, and I'll say it again," Robbie said into the shadows. "Best. Birthday. Ever."

Priest turned his head on the pillow to look at Robbie, who was stretched out on his side with a leg slung over one of Priest's thighs, and curled around behind him was Julien.

"So that means you'll want to do this again next year?" Julien said.

Robbie glanced back and nodded. "And the year after that, and the year after that. How about we just say this is what we'll do every year for my birthday until I'm no longer able to?"

"I think that sounds like a fantastic idea," Priest said, as Robbie snuggled closer to his side and Julien wound an arm around Robbie's waist. "But there's something else we think you need to do for your birthday. This year, and every year after."

Robbie grinned. "Really, Priest, let me recover first. I'm not a twenty-something-year-old anymore."

Priest arched an eyebrow. "I'm being serious."

"I can tell. My favorite scowl is back."

"I don't scowl at you."

"Any*more*," Robbie said, and ran his finger across Priest's lips. "But you frown, and your lips get really tight. Kind of like they are now."

Priest nipped at Robbie's finger, making the other two laugh.

"Lucky for us," Robbie said to Julien, "he seems to have decided to bite more than he barks these days."

"Can I please talk?" Priest said, and when Robbie looked back at him, he pretended to zip his lips shut, but Priest knew better. He had about five seconds to get out what he wanted to say or their mouthy little spitfire would be back at it. "Julien and I would like to speak to you about going home to visit your family."

Robbie said nothing.

"We know it's a big step," Julien started.

Priest continued, "But if you're ready to take it, we think seeing them for your birthday would be the perfect opportunity to—"

"I agree," Robbie said, surprising them both.

As their eyes met over Robbie's shoulder, Priest saw Julien's lips curve in a knowing smile. *Always so perceptive, aren't you, Mr. Thornton?*

"You do?" Priest said, just to make sure he'd heard Robbie correctly.

"Yes. Shocking as it is, I agree."

Priest rolled to his side, and Robbie pursed his lips.

"I know I've kind of been avoiding the whole *meet my parents* thing."

Julien tightened his hold around Robbie's waist and asked, "Why is that?"

"I don't know. I guess I was...scared, maybe?"

Priest cradled Robbie's face and brushed his thumb across his lips. "It's okay, sweetheart. You can talk to us. Nothing you say is going to offend us."

Robbie took in a deep breath and shut his eyes for a second, and when he opened them, Priest could see the worry there, and it tore at his heart.

"My parents have always been really great about, well, everything. They're supportive, proud, and love all of us more than anything in the world." Robbie smiled. "I've always been super close with them. I could tell them anything and they never batted an eyelash, especially my ma..."

"But?" Julien asked, clearly sensing the same *but* that Priest did.

"But..." Robbie said. "I've never brought anyone home with me before."

"And that's what you're scared about?" Priest said. "Bringing us home with you?"

"It's one of the things. That's a huge step. What if...what if you guys don't get along with my big, crazy family? What if they don't get along with *you*?"

Priest leaned in and brushed a kiss across Robbie's lips. "We've already met Felicity and your mother."

"I know. But that was before I knew *she* knew that *we* were all together."

As Priest tried to decipher that little word maze, Julien said, "But now she knows for sure?"

Robbie shifted until he was sitting up between them, his back against the headboard. "Yes. At first I wasn't. Sure, I mean. I know I joked about her figuring it out right away, but when she didn't say anything, I thought that maybe she didn't."

"She did," Priest said, and when Robbie looked at him, Priest chuckled. "At the opening of the restaurant, she saw us talking at the bar after your little run-in with Henri."

Robbie's eyes widened. "She did?"

Priest nodded. "She did. And if you recall, you were flirting outrageously with me."

"Oh *God*. What must she be thinking? She probably thinks I'm some kind of home wrecker coming between you two."

"If that's the case," Priest said, smiling at Robbie's mortification, "she would be half right. You most certainly came between us that night. But not until *after* we got you home."

ROBBIE'S MOUTH FELL open, and he shoved at Priest's shoulder. "You did *not* just say that. I'm trying to have a serious conversation with you. About my *mother*."

"I apologize," Priest deadpanned.

"Okay, focus, you two. You said she knows," Julien said, and Robbie bit at his thumbnail. "Did she tell you that, or—"

"Not exactly. I told her I was bringing my 'boyfriends' home, and after that she said..."

"What?" Julien asked. "What did she say?"

Robbie rolled his eyes and let out a sigh. "That she looked forward to getting to know Mr. Priestley and Mr. Thornton much better." Priest let out a laugh, and Robbie pinned him with a serious look. "You are awfully jovial about all of this."

"Ignore him, *princesse*," Julien said. "He's been impatiently waiting for this moment, and now that it's happening, I think he's slightly delirious."

"*This* moment?" Robbie said.

"*Oui*. When you tell your family. When we finally get to meet them as your partners."

"Really?" Robbie said, and looked at Priest, who was smiling. "You *want* to meet my family?"

"We do. It's the final step," Priest said. "The final elephant in the room."

Julien put a hand on Robbie's thigh. "But there's something else worrying you. What is it?"

"I..." Robbie paused, and then twisted his hands in his lap. *God, since when am I nervous about talking to them?* "What if you don't like them? There are a *lot* of them. And you are both so...private."

Julien sat up beside Robbie and took one of his hands. "I find it impossible to believe that we wouldn't love the family you came from," Julien said. "You're bright, happy, beautiful inside and out, and if for some unimaginable reason we don't get along, Priest and I are adults. We know how to behave and play well with others."

Robbie sighed. "It's not like it really matters now anyway. I already told her we were coming to visit."

"You did?" Julien said, and Robbie grimaced. Maybe he should've checked with them first?

"I did. But if you can't get free, then we can just—"

"We can," Priest said.

"You don't even know when it is. What if you have to work?"

Priest sat up until he could kiss Robbie's lips. "Too bad. This is more important."

"More important than your *job?*" Robbie said, but a grin was tugging at his mouth. "Your clients might disagree. So might your partners."

"Ask me if I care."

Robbie didn't bother. He stood no chance when Priest got like this. What did Julien call him? A *charming salopard?* He was so right.

"Okay, so we're going to visit," Julien said. "When did you tell her we could come?"

"Um, in, uh, two weeks?"

"*Très bien.* Then we have two weeks to practice being on our best behavior."

"Oh please," Robbie said. "You two are always on your best behavior. You're all French and gorgeous, and Priest is all smart and charming. My mother is already halfway in love, and my pa— Oh *God.* Who am I kidding? I have no *idea* how they're going to react to this." Robbie dropped his face into his hands. "What if the two groups of people I love the most can't stand each other?"

"I don't believe that will happen," Julien said, and pulled Robbie's hands away from his face. "But we aren't going to find out by avoiding them, are we?"

"I guess not." Robbie blew out a breath. "Then there's my sisters and the party..."

"The party?" Priest said, and Robbie groaned.

"You sound more worried about that than meeting my parents."

"I am. I didn't know there was going to be a party," Priest said, and Robbie glared at him.

"Well, now you know. Ma wants to have the family over. That includes aunts, uncles, cousins... Basically every Italian in Oshkosh." Julien laughed, and Robbie shook his head. "This has disaster written all over it. I can already see it, and it's not pretty. There'll be drinking, dancing, karaoke—"

"God help us," Priest said, and slid down into the bed.

"I know. Trust me." Robbie shook his head. "I'm already trying to think of an out for you." Priest aimed his eyes at Robbie, and he looked so appalled that Robbie finally lost it and laughed. "Seriously, though. Maybe we should just call and cancel?"

"*Non*," Julien said. "We are not cancelling on your mother now that she's specifically invited us. Let's sleep on it. Maybe we can come up with a way to make this easier somehow. Less stressful."

Robbie scoffed. "Good luck with that."

As Julien moved down under the covers, Priest tugged Robbie down between them. Once he was fully beneath the sheets, Priest rolled the two of them over to face Julien and said in Robbie's ear, "Want me to sing you a lullaby? It might help you fall asleep."

"Or induce nightmares," Robbie said.

"Brat," Priest growled. "Remind me again why we put up with your sassy mouth?"

Robbie let out a dreamy sigh as Julien moved in so the three of them were entwined with one another. "Because you love me?"

"Mmm. That might be it," Priest said, and ran his hand down to rest it over Julien's where it lay on Robbie's hip. "What do you think, *mon cœur?*"

Julien kissed Robbie's lips and whispered, "I think that's definitely it."

"You know," Robbie said into the shadow-filled room, "sometimes I wish we had gone with a queen-sized bed."

"We wouldn't all *fit* in a queen-sized bed," Priest said.

"We would *too*. With some careful leg placement," Robbie said. "But if we had a queen-sized bed, then we could sleep this close, always."

"I don't know much about sleeping, *princesse*. The problem with being this close to you is I never want to leave, and I *always* want to touch."

"That's a problem?" Robbie asked.

"No," Priest said, and kissed the back of Robbie's neck. "But being half-asleep during the day because we spent all night inside you each night might be."

"Hmm, maybe." Robbie squirmed between them, making sure to rub himself up against all the warm, naked skin touching him. "I still think I'd like it."

Priest groaned, and then said to Julien, "Yet he tells us he needs rest now that he's a thirty-year-old—"

"*Ugh*," Robbie said. "That just sounds wrong."

"*Joyeux anniversaire*," Julien said. "Now sleep. We'll talk more about this tomorrow."

CHAPTER SEVEN

Most people don't understand us.
But they don't need to. We understand.
We have from the moment we met ~ Julien

Two weeks later...

I CAN'T BELIEVE I agreed to this, Robbie thought for the millionth time. *What was I thinking saying* yes *to this?*

But as he rolled his suitcase down their driveway, he spotted Priest at the back of the Range Rover packing the trunk, and knew exactly what he'd been thinking—*I want to show these men off.*

Robbie wanted to finally introduce them to his parents and be able to say, *They are with me. I am with them. We are happy and in love. More than happy. We are crazy, stupid, deliriously in love.* And that was all well and good, when he wasn't actually about to go and do it.

As Robbie came around the end of the SUV, Priest flashed a

crooked smile as he looked at the bag Robbie was wheeling, and the one slung over his shoulder.

"Traveling light, I see."

"This *is* light," Robbie said, as Priest reached for the overnight bag. "I spent a long time narrowing down my wardrobe, I'll have you know."

Priest slid the bag in beside the black one he'd just packed, and then turned back for the suitcase. Robbie wheeled it around and collapsed the handle, and when Priest hefted it up into the back of the car, he looked over at Robbie and said, "We *are* only staying until Monday, right?"

Robbie arched an eyebrow. "Yes. But this isn't like a normal visit home."

"No?" Priest said as he shut the trunk.

"*No.* There's the meet-and-greet with my family. The serious talk with my parents. A party and, of course, the trip back here."

Priest crossed his arms and peered at Robbie over the top of his sunglasses. "All of which means you need one hundred outfits to choose from?"

"Oh, whatever," Robbie said, swiping a hand through the air. "You should know by now that I don't wake up looking this fabulous."

Priest wrapped his arms around Robbie's waist, and then connected their lips in a kiss that Robbie felt through his entire body. Robbie clutched at Priest's shirt and moaned, pushing up on to his toes to get even closer until Priest finally let him go and raised his head.

His lips curved into a full-on smile then, and as always, Robbie felt a sense of accomplishment at pulling that expression from Priest.

"On the contrary," Priest said. "You wake up looking even better."

"Mmm, you're right. I do," Robbie said. "But only because I usually wake up with one of you on me."

Priest let him go and fished his keys out of his pocket, and as he did, the morning sunlight caught in his hair, making Robbie want to run his fingers through it. The light and dark strands of copper, and the short scruff on Priest's cheeks was just...*wow*. You couldn't pay to get such gorgeous colors. It was striking, and coupled with those grey eyes and that serious set of his mouth, it always made Robbie think of the sun trying to brighten up a storm cloud—his and Julien's little storm cloud.

As the thought entered his mind, Robbie giggled, and Priest gave him a quizzical look.

"Care to share?"

"Nope," Robbie said, and sealed his lips. Before Priest could say anything else, Robbie heard the front door open and shut, and spun on his toes to see Julien walking down the driveway.

He was in a casual white and navy checkered shirt, and navy pants that fit him like a second skin, and had on a pair of brown loafers and sunglasses perched on his head. He looked casual, European, and drop-dead gorgeous, and with the tan he'd spent hours perfecting this summer, Robbie thought Julien looked more fit for a trip to the French Riviera than Oshkosh.

"Do you two have everything?" Julien asked, and before Robbie could reply, Priest did for him.

"If I don't, Robert has packed enough for all of us."

Robbie rolled his eyes. "And what did you pack? A toothbrush and a fresh pair of boxer briefs?"

Priest stopped by the driver's-side door and said, "There's that smart mouth I love. Keep it up, sweetheart. I'd love to teach it a lesson."

Oh yes. Please teach me a lesson, Mr. Priestley. "That's not going anywhere anytime soon," Robbie called out, as Priest opened the door and climbed in. "But I'm sure a firm hand would be a good incentive for me to—"

"Misbehave some more?" Julien said, as he pulled open the passenger door.

"Maybe."

As Robbie flashed a grin, Julien said, "How about you give me a kiss good morning, and then get in the car."

Robbie kissed Julien, and as he pulled away, he said, "Sure you don't want to sit back here with me? Priest will be okay up there by himself."

Julien pointed to the back seat. "*In*, troublemaker. Or we'll never get on the road."

"Fine, fine. I'm just saying, Simon Says is so much more fun when you're within touching distance of someone."

As they shut their doors and buckled up, Priest found Robbie's eyes in the rearview mirror. "I'm within touching distance of Julien."

"Yeah," Robbie said. "But I'm not within touching distance of *any*one. So that road game is definitely out."

Julien programmed the phone and then looked at Robbie to verify his parents' address. "Is that right?"

"Yes, *ugh*. Don't remind me." As Julien put the phone in the mount, Robbie settled back in his seat. "Now, the way I see it, there's three of us and about three hours to get there. So that means we each get an hour with the music selection."

"Fantastic," Priest said drolly. But when he looked at Julien and they smiled at one another, Robbie realized there was nowhere else he'd rather be than in that SUV, with these two men, heading to Oshkosh.

JULIEN LOOKED OUT the window as Priest wove them out of the city and onto the interstate. Sinatra was serenading them as they merged with traffic and headed off for the weekend, and surprisingly, Julien felt a sense of peace sweep around him at the idea of being surrounded by people who loved and adored the wonderful young man sitting behind them.

Julien looked at Priest concentrating on the road, his fingers tapping on the steering wheel, and thought, not for the first time, how lucky he was to have both of these men in his life.

It was an interesting dynamic, Julien thought as he then glanced over his shoulder at Robbie, who was happily crooning along with Priest's idol. Most wouldn't understand the three of them at all. But from the second they'd all met—Julien with Priest, and now here, years later, with Robbie—there'd been an immediate sense of acknowledgment and understanding, an instant recognition of someone you knew was meant to be in your life, and never had Julien been more grateful that they were all alive to enjoy this moment and one another.

He was also greedy enough to want to make it permanent. Something he knew was weighing heavily on Priest's mind.

"*Princesse?* Why don't you tell us a little bit about your family, since we're going to be meeting them soon."

Robbie scrunched his nose up and then let out a long-suffering sigh. "Well, you already met my ma, even though it was brief and you were super busy. And the rest, well, they're just as crazy. There's so many of them, mostly females, and everyone talks over everyone else."

"Which explains your motor-mouth," Priest said.

"It *does*, actually." Robbie poked his tongue out. "If you didn't speak up, you weren't heard. So if you're expecting a quiet weekend, you are in for a shock."

"We certainly are *not* expecting that," Julien said. "But what about your sisters? We've met Felicity, and she seems very similar in personality to you."

Robbie cocked his head to the side. "Meaning *what*, exactly?"

"Nothing bad. Just that you're both rather..." Julien looked at Priest, and he shook his head.

"Don't look at me. You're on your own with this."

Julien shoved Priest in the arm, but then turned in his seat to smile at Robbie. "I just mean that you both seem close and rather...mischievous, is the word I think I'm looking for."

Robbie narrowed his eyes for a second, but then grinned. "I

suppose you're right. I have three sisters. Penny, Valerie, and Felicity. Felicity and I are the youngest and the—"

"Troublemakers?" Priest suggested.

"The *closest*, is what I was going to say," Robbie said. But then he gave an impish wink. "And the most fun."

"A.k.a. the troublemakers."

"That's a lot of women," Julien said.

"Huh, tell me about it," Robbie said. "Growing up with them was a lot of fun, though. Never a dull moment in the Bianchi household. Only colorful ones."

Priest raised his eyes to Robbie's in the mirror. "And are they protective of their baby brother?"

"Why?" Robbie said. "Scared?"

"Do I seem scared to you?"

Robbie huffed out a breath. "They're protective, yes. Like lionesses. So you better watch yourselves. They wanted to track Nathan down and cut his dick off after what he pulled."

Priest grunted. "Seems we'll have that in common, at least."

"*Um*, if it's all the same to you," Robbie said, "I'd rather you don't go anywhere near his dick."

Priest snorted. "Noted."

Robbie leaned forward so he could kiss Julien quick on the lips. "*You*, I'm going to have to fight them off of. Felicity and I weren't kidding when we told you the Bianchi women were fans. They're going to be all over you and your accent. And Priest, you might want to keep an eye on Val."

"Why?" Priest said.

"Oh...nothing bad," Robbie said, but Julien didn't buy that for a second. Not with the twinkle in Robbie's eyes.

"Why do I feel like there's more to that comment than what you're letting on?" Priest said.

Robbie shrugged. "I don't know."

"Uh huh," Priest said. "If you aren't going to tell the truth about that, then why don't we go back to the topic of Nathan for a minute?"

"Uh, why?" Robbie said. "I'd rather just forget he exists."

"So would I," Priest said. "But there's something about him that we want to discuss with you, and you always avoid it."

Robbie slumped back in his seat, but it didn't escape Julien that some of the shine in Robbie's eyes had faded—and Julien hated Nathan for that alone.

"Okay," Robbie said. "What do you want to know?"

Julien sensed how difficult this was for Robbie to revisit. But they knew this *crétin de Nathan* had caused a few insecurities once upon a time, and they didn't want them to pop up this weekend— or ever, for that matter.

"Did your parents ever meet him?" Julien asked.

"Nathan?" Robbie let out a derisive laugh. "Are you kidding?"

"*Non*. I'm serious."

It was clear Robbie could see that too, because he quickly sobered and said, "No, they never met him. He said we weren't 'serious' enough for that step."

Robbie picked at a piece of imaginary lint on his shorts, then raised his eyes to Julien. "I'm glad for it now, though. He was an ass. And not in a good way. He made me think that being *me* was, I don't know, somehow less."

"*Je suis désolé*," Julien said, a frown forming between his eyebrows. He didn't like seeing Robbie like this. But both he and Priest knew this conversation had to be had.

Robbie had mentioned several times over that he'd never been in a real relationship, one where he felt truly loved for who he was. And they wanted to make sure it was one hundred percent clear that when they arrived in Oshkosh today, they wanted the real Robert Bianchi to arrive with them. Not some polite young man that he might think they want. The Robbie his family loved.

"Don't be," Robbie said. "It was my own fault. I made several stupid decisions all at once because I'm a genius like that. And it caught up to me."

The car fell silent for a moment, except for the music that was softly playing in the background.

"When did you break up with him again?" Priest asked.

"A few weeks before I got in an elevator...with you."

Priest nodded.

"What?" Robbie said. "What are you thinking right now? And don't say 'nothing,' because I can see your mind working."

Priest eyed Robbie. "I suppose I'd always wondered at the change between that first day in the elevator, and when I met you later with Vanessa and your nonna."

"Change?" Robbie said.

"He means your personality, *princesse*," Julien said. "When you two first met, he told me you were a little more—"

"Subdued," Priest said. "You used to dress like you were going to a funeral."

Robbie's mouth fell open, making Julien and Priest laugh. "I did not."

"Yes. You did. Do you need me to remind you?" Priest asked. "I remember exactly what you were wearing. How you smelled. How much I wanted to push you up against the wall and strip you naked, with no names needed."

"Ah, okay...wow," Robbie said. "You totally just redeemed yourself."

Priest winked at him, and Robbie shook his head.

"But as for Nathan," Robbie continued, "his problem was more with himself than me. He didn't accept who he was, and then tried to make me someone *I* wasn't. I let it go on for a little too long, and before I knew it, I didn't even recognize myself when I looked in the mirror."

Julien reached back to take Robbie's hand in his. "Promise us something this weekend." Robbie turned those wide eyes his way, and Julien squeezed his fingers. "Be you. Don't be someone you think we expect or want. Be you, and enjoy your family. No matter how crazy and wild they are. You've been away from them longer than you should have been because of us, and we don't want you to feel you have to censor yourself just because we're here."

Robbie's eyes glistened, and he nodded. *"Je vous aime.* Both of you."

"Nous t'aimons aussi," Julien said, and punctuated that with a kiss to the back of Robbie's hand. "Now, about these road games. Have you got any favorites?"

WHEN PRIEST MADE the final turn into his childhood street, Robbie's heart began to tap-dance and his palms grew sweaty. The trip up there this morning had been... Well, it had been really wonderful. But now that they were closing in on their final destination, Robbie's stomach was tying itself in knots.

He'd never been so damn nervous in his life, and the only reason he could think of as to why he wanted to bolt was because of how much he cared for the two men sitting in the front of the vehicle.

He still couldn't believe it'd been nearly eight months since the three of them had started dating. Only eight months since Julien and Priest had walked into his life and upended it. It seemed impossible, because it felt as though Robbie had known them his entire life.

Priest, with his dominating presence that was larger than life when he turned his full attention on you, and Julien, with his easygoing personality and compassionate nature. They were a potent combination, a force to be reckoned with, and now Robbie had to somehow act normal around his family while both of them stood there looking all sexy and kissable.

Sure, this is a great idea. Nothing could possibly go wrong.

"Eleven seventy-six. Is that right, Robert?"

Priest's voice cut through Robbie's musings, and he nodded and pointed to the white two-story Craftsman off to their right. There were several cars parked in the driveway, and when Priest pulled up to the curb, Robbie shut his eyes and took in a deep breath.

This is crazy. I'm out of my mind. Why did I agree to this again?

"*Princesse?*"

Robbie's eyes flew open, and he knew he must've appeared slightly manic, because Julien undid his seatbelt and reached for his hand.

"Breathe, *mon cher petit*. Everything's going to be okay."

Robbie licked his lips, not sure if he wasn't about to faint as he looked out at his childhood house again. "Umm... Shit, I just... Give me a second. I'm trying to remember how I was going to introduce you two. It's not like I can just walk in and say, 'Hey, everyone, this is Julien and Priest, they're married, but we all live and sleep together and I'm in love with them.'"

"Why not?" Priest asked with such a straight face that Robbie felt close to apoplectic.

"He's joking," Julien said, and shook his head.

Robbie pinned Priest with a murderous stare. "Not the right time, *Joel*."

Priest's lips twitched. "You and Julien, you both tend to use my first name whenever you're—"

"Pissed off at you?" Robbie suggested.

"Yes. I like that," Priest said, and then shoved open the car door and got out.

"He likes— Of course he likes that," Robbie said. "And where does he think he's going? I still haven't worked this out yet. Tell him to get back in the car."

Julien laughed. "Oh, *princesse...*"

Robbie blinked a couple of times before focusing back on Julien.

"Everything is going to be okay. We're going to be right there with you. We'll go inside, you can introduce us to your mother and father, and then see how you feel. If you want to leave, we have the hotel booked down the road and can check in after three. Okay?"

Robbie rubbed a hand over his face and nodded. Julien was right. Everything would be fine. And if it wasn't, well, they had a backup plan. "Okay."

"*Bien*. Then let's go," Julien said, as Priest walked around to their side of the car. "It's been years since we've been around a happy family. This is going to be a real treat for us."

No pressure, Robbie thought, as Priest opened Julien's door and then reached for Robbie's. He just hoped that a happy family was what the Bianchis delivered—not an insane one.

Priest looked inside the car when Robbie didn't move. "Are you coming? I know you think this is going to be awkward, but it might be even more so if two strangers knock on your parents' door and tell them that their son won't get out of their car."

Robbie squashed down his nerves and climbed out of the Range Rover, and when he saw Julien looking over at the house with a smile on his face, Robbie decided that if Julien and Priest were looking forward to a happy family get-together, then that was what they would get.

The Bianchis might be crazy, but that house had always been full of love, and no matter how damn nervous Robbie might be, he had to believe that wasn't about to change now.

CHAPTER EIGHT

Four nosey Italians and a kitchen?
We've got this - Julien & Priest

JULIEN STARED UP at the home with the blue shutters. It was the quintessential family home, one you would see on TV or in a movie, where kids ran around in the front yard with a dog yapping at their heels.

It was cozy and inviting, unlike the palatial mansion where he'd grown up that sat on several acres and was surrounded by a gate to keep those less fortunate away.

Oui, this place was like a warm hug, and he had a feeling that whoever was behind that door would welcome you with one of those, should you need it.

When the three of them reached the front door, Robbie went ahead of them and then paused and looked over his shoulder. Julien smiled, trying to be encouraging.

But when Priest flashed him a grin, Robbie's eyes widened and he whispered, "Don't do *that*. You look like a wolf at Grandma's house. Just...I don't know, be normal."

Julien scoffed, and then looked at Priest, who said, "I'm not sure normal is achievable in this situation, sweetheart."

Robbie was about to say something when the front door opened wide and Sofia Bianchi came into view. With her hair styled into lovely brown and blonde waves, her face lit up with joy when Robbie whirled around to face her.

"My beautiful boy," she said with a warm smile as she held her arms out. "Come give your mother a hug."

As Robbie wrapped his arms around her, Sofia kissed his cheek, and her eyes shifted to the two men her beautiful *boy* had brought home with him. Robbie straightened, and when he did, Sofia slipped her arm around his waist, and he hugged her into his side.

"It's been too long, young man," she said as she angled her head to look at her son. "But it's so good to have you home."

"I know. It's great to be here, Ma. Really," Robbie said, and kissed her head. Then he turned and swallowed, nervous, as though he'd forgotten his lines in a movie. "You remember—"

"Mr. Thornton and his husband, Mr. Priestley? Yes," she said, and Julien wondered exactly how this was going to play out.

Were they about to be told they couldn't come in? Quite possibly. But then Sofia placed a hand on Robbie's arm and patted it as she looked first to Julien and said, "It's a pleasure to be able to cook for you today, Mr. Thornton. Especially after the wonderful meal I had at your place earlier this year. My only hope is that *cacciucco* isn't too common for someone as fancy as yourself."

Julien stepped forward, took her hand in his, and brought it up to his mouth to kiss. "*Bonjour*, and please, don't worry yourself. I've been looking forward to your cooking from the moment Robbie described your *fettuccine con carciofi*. No matter how many cooking classes one might attend, nothing beats a home-cooked meal passed down from one generation to the next."

A blush filled Sofia's cheeks, like Robbie when he was pleased —or embarrassed—and Julien looked at their *princesse*, who had an expression full of relief stamped all over his face—until his mother turned to Priest.

"And Mr. Priestley. It's lovely to see you again too."

Priest offered up a less wolfish grin than the one he'd joked with around Robbie, and the charm and charisma Priest rarely unleashed was set free on Sofia.

"It's lovely to see you too, Mrs. Bianchi. Thank you for having us."

"Please, both of you. My name is Sofia. And it's only right that we look after the young man who helped out Vanessa when she was in such a tough spot. It's the least we can do."

Robbie looked at Priest, and Julien wondered if they were thinking the same thing. Under any circumstance would they *ever* think of Priest as a young man? The answer to that was simple—no.

Sofia let go of Robbie's arm and stepped toward Priest, and Robbie's eyes widened. But before he could say anything, she was wrapping her arms around Priest in a hug that made Robbie's eyes close to fall out of his head.

Priest embraced her, and she said, "I wanted to do this at the restaurant that night, but I got sidetracked with all the glitz and glam. Thank you. Thank you so much for helping our Vanessa."

Priest aimed his eyes at Robbie and mouthed, *See, not awkward at all.*

"It was my pleasure to help," Priest said. "Plus, it's how I got to know Robert, and *that* is thanks enough."

"Yes, my Robert is quite a treat. *But...*"

Robbie narrowed his eyes at Priest, but quickly lost his attitude when Sofia pulled away and spun around on him.

"*You* are in trouble, mister," she said, and pointed a finger at him.

"Me?" Robbie said. "It's my birthday. I can't be in trouble."

"It is *not* your birthday. That was two weeks ago, which is *why* you are in trouble." She swatted Robbie on the arm, and then said, to Priest and Julien, "Please. Come in. Come in. Robert's father has just gone up to the store to buy the drinks for tomorrow's party. Penelope's running a little late, but Felicity and Valerie are in the kitchen, and they are just dying to say hello."

As she walked ahead of them, Robbie said under his breath, "Brace yourselves. She's just the welcoming committee. The whirlwind is about to take place."

"She's wonderful," Julien said, as he watched Sofia disappear down the hallway.

Priest said, "Don't you worry about us, Robert. I'm rather looking forward to this."

Robbie rolled his eyes, and when he turned around to head inside, Priest brushed his hand over Robbie's ass, making him startle.

"Just reminding you how my hand feels right here, should you feel the need to get bratty like that later."

"*Stronzo,*" Robbie muttered.

As he walked off, the other two followed, and Julien looked to Priest and said, "I don't think that was very nice, whatever it was."

"I don't think so either," Priest said, and winked. "Remind me to ask him about it...later."

HIS MOTHER HADN'T been wrong. From the second the three of them walked into the kitchen until now, an hour later, Robbie's sisters hadn't stopped talking over the top of each other to ask Julien and Priest anything and everything about themselves.

What did they do? How did they all meet? How old were they? *Thirties* was all they got there. But just as Robbie had suspected, nothing was off-limits, and surprisingly, Julien and Priest had an easy answer for every question.

It was weird, really. Robbie had been so nervous about asking these simple questions of these two when he'd first met them, that he'd figured it would be as awkward for his family as well. But somehow Julien and Priest seemed to fit right in, and were apparently happy to stand in a kitchen with four nosey Italians as they prepped the seafood for the big stew his mother was making foi dinnei.

Julien had been put to work on filleting the fish, since he was an expert. Robbie was on the other side of the kitchen with Felicity cleaning and cutting the calamari, while Priest...Priest had been commandeered by Valerie to deal with the filling of the cannoli, and that was quickly becoming the entertainment of the afternoon.

"So you're a lawyer?" Valerie said, as she put a tray of empty cannoli shells in front of Priest.

As Priest smiled down at the shortest of the Bianchi clan, Valerie practically batted her lashes at him, and Priest glanced in Robbie's direction. Robbie quickly looked away, trying to hide his smirk because *payback is so delicious...really it is.*

"I am, yes," Priest said, polite as can be as Valerie handed him a plump piping bag full of the sweet ricotta mixture. "Julien might actually be better at whatever it is we're about to do here."

"Oh, I doubt that," Valerie said as she picked up one of the pastry shells and directed Priest's hand so the tip of the nozzle was at the opening. "You just have to *squeeze* with a firm, steady hand. You can do that, right?"

Robbie snorted, trying to hold back his amusement, but Priest's expression was priceless. His eyes had widened at Valerie's boldness, and he appeared speechless as she brushed her blonde hair over her shoulder and moved even closer.

Robbie *probably* should've mentioned something about Valerie's affinity for gingers. He'd been going to in the car on the way up there, but that would've taken away half his fun, and watching her fawn all over Priest, and seeing him squirm, was making Robbie's afternoon.

"So which one's the better kisser?" Felicity asked under her breath, and Robbie's head whipped around so fast that he was surprised it didn't fly right off his neck. As he gave her a look that screamed, *Shut your face,* she just laughed and blew one of her black curls out of her eyes. "Come on. Don't act like some kind of saint now."

Leaving Priest to fend for himself, Robbie reached for his next victim and started chopping a little harder than necessary. "I'm *not*," he said through gritted teeth. "But a lady doesn't tell. Especially in his mother's kitchen."

"Since when have you been a lady? And I'm sure you've done much worse in this kitchen," Felicity said, then took a sip of her Chardonnay.

"Have not. But I'm not about to tell you now. Ma is right over there. I don't want her finding out that—"

"You're a big slut?" She grinned.

Robbie picked up one of the octopuses and dangled it at her. "Want one of these in your bed tonight?"

She scrunched her nose and held her hands up. "Well, yours will be too full, so yes, he can come sleep with me."

"You're lucky we aren't staying here, or you'd be in so much trouble."

Felicity put her wine glass on the counter and frowned. "What do you mean you aren't staying here?"

Robbie glared at her, but Felicity merely raised her eyebrows, expecting a response.

"We just thought it would be easier if we stayed at a hotel down at the waterfront."

"Easier?" Felicity said, and when their mother left the kitchen, she said, "*Pazzo.* The minute Ma hears you aren't staying here, she is going to have a conniption fit."

"Which is *why* I haven't told her yet," Robbie said, as he reached for the next slippery little sucker. "I'm kind of hoping that Penny"—as if on cue, Robbie's oldest sister Penelope pushed open the back door of the house and stepped into the kitchen —"shows *up*."

Penny looked the picture of perfection with her high-waist A-line dress of white and navy, and cute little cropped cardigan. Around her neck sat the gold crucifix she'd been given on her sixteenth birthday, and as Robbie's eyes dropped to her pregnant belly, all he could think was: *Aw, we're such a good little Catholic family. The unwed pregnant daughter, and the gay son who brought his married boyfriends home. Oh well, we can't all be perfect.*

"Well, well, look who's here," Penny said as she walked to Robbie, then kissed him on the cheek. "I didn't believe Felicity when she said you'd actually agreed to come home for the weekend."

"Really?" Robbie said, as he washed his hands and picked up his wine glass. "Because I believed her in a hot second when she said you got knocked up by golden boy Jack Paulson."

Penny aimed daggers at their sister. "God. You have such a big mouth, Felicity."

Oh shit, here we go.

"He was going to find out anyway," Felicity said. "I don't see what the big deal is."

"The big *deal* is Jack's married and it was a one-night, stupid, drunken mistake."

"So no one knows but...us?" Robbie said. "How scandalous. Does Jack know?"

"Yes," Penny said, her voice lowering. "But that's *it*. He refuses to tell Mary Beth yet, and had a fit when I said I wanted to tell Ma and Pa. So for now, it's easier with the families so close to just—"

"Lie?" Robbie offered.

Penny smacked him in the arm. "I'm not lying, I'm just—"

"Omitting the truth?" Felicity suggested.

"You need to keep a lid on it," Penny said to her. "I don't want to be the focus of any more gossip than I already am."

"Umm, newsflash," Felicity said. "Unless you go into labor this weekend, you're not the one who's going to be under scrutiny for the next three days. Robbie and his married couple are."

"*Felicity*," Robbie said, and when everyone in the room stopped and looked at them, Robbie realized how loudly he'd said that. "I... I *don't* know how many times we have to have this argument. *I* won the karaoke challenge last year. Don't even play."

Priest's eyes narrowed as he toweled off his hands, and Julien grinned. There was no way in hell they believed that bullshit story for a second.

But then Robbie's ma—*God bless Ma*—walked back into the kitchen and said, "I think Robert's right, honey. He did that peppy little song about calling someone—what's the name of it again? It was stuck in my head for days."

Valerie put her hand on Priest's bicep. "'Call Me Maybe.' He was obsessed with it."

Robbie arched an eyebrow at his touchy-feely sister. "Well, he's going to be calling you *never*, Val. So hands off."

Valerie hugged Priest's arm, and Robbie rolled his eyes as she began humming the song, and when the rest of his sisters started to sing the chorus, Robbie's heart lodged in his throat.

If Priest and Julien weren't both standing there staring at his blushing cheeks—*and insane family*—Robbie might've gotten a good laugh out of his sisters singing around the kitchen like they used to when they were teenagers. As it was, he wished the ground would open up and swallow him whole.

"You suck," he told Valerie, who winked.

"As do you, I'm sure."

"*Valerie*," their mother said as she opened the fridge. "That's no way for a lady to talk."

Robbie grinned triumphantly, and thought he was off scot-free until their ma grabbed some butter and turned to pin him with that stare of hers. "Or young men, for that matter."

Robbie's eyes shifted to Julien, who was washing his hands at the center island as he mouthed *cheeky*, and Robbie's legs suddenly felt unsteady.

"Ugh," Penny said, recapturing everyone's attention. "That song is like the plague—utterly contagious."

Valerie started laughing, and then turned to gaze up at Priest. "And I don't do it half as good as Robbie."

"I'm sure he's something to see," Priest said, and when he

turned his eyes on Robbie, it was all Robbie could do not to grab hold of the counter to keep himself upright.

Okay, Julien and Priest needed to get back to work and stop looking at him, because they were making him forget his brain and how to do simple things like, you know, stand and...talk.

"He showed us his rendition of a certain Starship song," Priest said. "Maybe we can convince him to show us this one too."

"*Oui*," Julien said, "Starship has never sounded so good."

Robbie was about to mention one *other* time a Starship song sounded pretty amazing, in a horrible way, when his mother hugged him into her side.

"He always was the little performer, weren't you, baby?" she said. "Dressing up in my high heels and your sister's skirts. He really was quite pretty."

"*Was*? Thanks, Ma," Robbie said, shaking his head. "And I don't think they need to know all of this."

"I'm sorry," she said. "You're still pretty. And I always thought you and Felicity would've made a fabulous little pop group."

"Oh my God," Robbie muttered, his cheeks now burning with embarrassment. "Kill me now."

As the loud rumble of a truck sounded, everyone in the kitchen fell silent as Robbie and his sisters looked toward the back door. Ma put the tub of butter on the kitchen counter and squeezed Robbie's arm.

"Right," she said, and aimed a smile at Julien and Priest. They were also staring at the back door, their smiles from a moment ago having been replaced with serious expressions, because the final Bianchi had just arrived home. "I'm going to go out and help your father. I trust you can all look after our guests."

The girls nodded, and Robbie stood beside Julien and Priest.

As his mother pulled open the door, she aimed one final look across the kitchen to where her son stood with his "guests," and then headed outside to greet her husband.

AS THE BACK door slapped shut against the side of the house, Robbie jumped, and Valerie flew across the kitchen to join Penny and Felicity, who were now peering out the side window.

Priest looked at Julien, who grimaced, and then they both turned to Robbie, who seemed frozen to the spot by the tension that had just blasted through the kitchen like an arctic wind.

Up until now, things in the Bianchi family had been fairly relaxed with Priest and Julien. Robbie's mother had invited them into her home, introduced them to her daughters, and then put them to work in her kitchen. But in the back of Priest's mind, this was the moment they had all been waiting for. The moment when they would finally get to meet the *missing* Bianchi, Robbie's father.

They didn't really know a lot about him, Robbie didn't talk as much about his father as he did his mother and sisters. But Priest didn't take that as a slight toward the man, because whenever Robbie *did* talk of him, it was always with affection and a proud edge to his voice that made Priest...curious.

As Julien wiped his hands on the dishtowel, he leaned into Robbie until their sides brushed and said under his breath, *"Est-ce que tu vas bien?"*

One thing Priest had come to admire about Robbie over the course of knowing him was his strength of self, and he had to believe it came from the people in this house. So he was very interested in how this was all about to go down.

"I, uh, yeah," Robbie said, and then nodded a little too fast. "I'm okay."

"Good," Priest said, and placed a hand on Robbie's back. "I think it's important that your parents have this moment without us there at first."

"I agree," Julien said. "I don't want them to feel they have to put on an act just because we're in the room."

"I know," Robbie said, but his voice cracked a little. "Pa's just... I just don't want to disappoint him."

Julien trailed a fingertip under Robbie's chin. *"Mon cher petit.* I don't think you could disappoint anyone."

"Ugh," Robbie said, and turned toward Julien to rest his forehead on his shoulder. "Then why am I so nervous? Maybe I should just go out there and talk to them."

"*Non. Non.* I think it's best you stay here and help me keep a certain little blonde and her piping bag at bay. I think someone has a crush on our Priest."

Priest let out an inelegant sound, and his eyes shifted to the three women chatting amongst themselves over at the window.

Robbie's sisters were so incredibly different from one another, and yet so lively and animated, just as he was. They never stopped smiling or joking around with one another, and that love of life, that enthusiasm to welcome strangers into their house, made it clear why Robbie had turned into such a vibrant man. This environment he'd grown up in had nurtured a kind, joyful soul and was the very thing Julien and Priest loved most about him.

"Sorry we're being so rude," Penny, the oldest—and pregnant—sister said, when she spotted Priest looking their way. Then she crossed over to the three of them.

She was a beautiful woman, the pregnancy not diminishing that in the slightest. She had the same dainty cheekbones and blue eyes as Robbie and their mother, whereas his other two sisters had more cherubic faces with rich brown eyes.

"I didn't even properly introduce myself. I'm Penny, Robbie's oldest sister. And I know who you are," she said as she flashed a smile at Julien. "*Mr.* Thornton."

"Call me Julien. Please."

"I'm so disappointed I wasn't able to come to your restaurant's opening, but..." She gestured to her swollen belly, and Julien chuckled.

"There's no need to be disappointed," Julien said. "You have an open invitation. Whenever you come to Chicago, let us know and I'll make sure there's a table available."

"Are you kidding?" Valerie said, as both her and Felicity joined them on their side of the kitchen.

"*Non*," Julien said, and ran a hand down Robbie's arm. "Any family of Robbie's is always welcome at JULIEN. At any location."

Valerie brought a hand up to cover her chest and sighed, much the same way Robbie did whenever he was caught in Julien's spell.

"Robbie said there's even a table that overlooks the kitchen," Felicity said. "For *private* dining."

Priest didn't miss the mischievous light in Felicity's eyes as she winked at her brother, and if he had to lay bets, he'd guess that Robbie had filled her in on their first date, and just *how* private that room could be.

"That's right," Julien said, as Robbie's cheeks reddened. "The Skybox. It's our personal table. Always reserved. But if you're ever in town, you have my permission to ask for it by name."

"I'm going to take you up on that," Penny said, and then turned her attention to Priest. "And you must be the famous lawyer who helped out Vanessa."

Priest cleared his throat and nodded. "Yes, that would be me."

Valerie ran her eyes over Priest's frame—not for the first time —and shook her head. "Man did Robbie hate you when you first met."

"*Val*," Robbie said, and tried his best to glare her to death.

"Oh, come on," Valerie said. "I'm sure he already knows how you felt. It's not like you're very good at hiding your feelings."

"Neither are you," Felicity pointed out, then took a sip of her wine. "You're looking at him like you're going to pounce on him. Calm down, Val, he's gay."

Robbie groaned. "Could you all *be* any more embarrassing?"

"It's okay," Priest said, and then looked to Felicity and Valerie. "But to answer you, Valerie, yes, I was very aware of Robert's...less-than-glowing opinion of me."

"*Robert*, huh? No one gets away with calling him that but Ma." Valerie laughed, and Priest couldn't be sure, but he could've sworn Robbie groaned again. It was really a head-trip to see elements of Robbie in each of these lovely ladies. But it was right there: the teasing, the attitude, and the mischief.

"Pa used to call him that too. Whenever he got in trouble," Felicity added.

"Which I'm sure was more often than not," Priest said.

Robbie aimed accusatory eyes Priest's way. "Okay. That's it. I don't have to stand here and—"

"Listen to us talk about you?" Penny said. "Since when have you shied away from the spotlight?"

Robbie poked his tongue out at his eldest sister, and Priest decided to step in and break up the brewing Bianchi battle. "We assume whatever is going on out there right now has to do with us."

"I think that's a pretty safe bet," Felicity said, and her lips curved. "It's not every day your son brings home his married boyfriends to meet the family."

"Oh my God," Robbie said. "Way to be subtle, Felicity."

"Please. We've all been thinking it. I was just the one brave enough to mention it."

Julien nodded. "*Oui*. It is a rather unique situation."

"Yeah. But Robbie's never done anything by the book," Valerie chimed in. "Have you, brother?"

Robbie rolled his eyes.

"But this must be serious," Penny said, as she sized Julien and Priest up. "He's never brought anyone home with him, and—"

"*He's* right here," Robbie said, and put his hands on his hips. "Would you three stop grilling them? *Damn*."

"It is serious," Julien said, answering Penny, as he stepped into Robbie's side and took his hand.

"Very serious," Priest added, taking his other hand.

Three pairs of eyes widened at that, and then Penny said, "Serious as in...?"

Priest opened his mouth, about to respond, when some loud Italian words drifted through the kitchen window, and all of them turned in the direction of the back door.

"Don't worry about that," Felicity said. "If there's yelling it just means they're still alive, which is a bonus, considering all of this."

Robbie took in a gulp of air and then let it out on a rush. "I think I should go—"

"Out there?" Felicity laughed. "Nah, just give them a minute. Pa's been looking forward to meeting your guys."

Her slightly maniacal grin didn't bode well for them, and just as Felicity finished talking, the back door opened and Sofia stepped inside carrying four bottles of wine.

"Well, don't just stand there, you three. Felicity. Valerie. Go help your father and bring in the rest of the alcohol."

"We can help," Julien suggested, but Sofia shook her head.

"No. You've already done plenty. Penny, you can help me, and Robert? Why don't you three head into the living room? Your father and I will be in shortly."

As the girls hurried to the back door, Valerie winked at Priest, and Felicity mouthed, *Good luck.*

"Living room's this way," Robbie said, and then led them down the hallway.

Well, here we go, Priest thought. *God only knows how this is going to play out.*

CHAPTER NINE

Damn, how in the hell are they mine?
- Robbie

ROBBIE'S LEG WAS doing a nervous jig as he sat on his parents' couch between Julien and Priest. It'd been around ten minutes since his mother had told them to go in there and wait, and the longer she took, the more nervous he became. He'd gone from sitting, to standing, to pacing, and now he was back to sitting again.

This was crazy. He knew he had nothing to worry about, and yet he felt worried about everything. *Breathe,* he told himself for the umpteenth time. *Isn't that what Julien always says? Deep breath in. Aaaand a deep breath out.* Yeah, okay, that wasn't doing shit for him.

"Relax," Priest said by Robbie's ear. "I don't think I've ever seen you this nervous."

Robbie's head snapped to the side, and he pinned Priest with a stare. "Thank you for pointing that out, *Mr.* Priestley."

When Priest's lips curved, Robbie shook his head and pointed. "Stop that."

"What?"

"Smiling at me. I told you, you look all *wolf*ish."

Priest leaned in until barely an inch separated them, and said in a voice designed to tantalize, "Get through this and I'll eat you later for dessert."

Robbie shook his head. "*Mean.* That was just mean."

Julien smoothed his hand along the thigh that Robbie was bouncing up and down. "Why are you so nervous, *princesse?* You said yourself your family knows who you are. I can't imagine your father is clueless."

"No, he isn't. That's the thing," Robbie said. "He was so amazing when I came out. Never once made me feel that I was any different from anyone else, even though he's a—" Robbie laughed. "A total Italian. And by that, I mean boisterous, loud, and very Catholic. I just..." Robbie sighed. "I don't think he ever expected something like this." Robbie gestured to the three of them.

Priest eyed him. "You're worried this will be too much for him."

"No." Robbie chewed on the corner of his lip and then whispered, "Yes."

Julien brought Robbie's hand up to his lips, and Robbie shut his eyes and tried to calm his hammering heart. "Let's take it one step at a time, *oui?* Priest and I will follow your lead."

Robbie nodded, and as Priest ran a hand up his back, he let his eyes fall shut. *Okay, maybe I can do this.* But when the sound of the back door opening met his ears, Robbie stiffened and shot to his feet. *Or maybe I can just run now and never come back.*

He could feel both Julien's and Priest's eyes on him and wished he could calm the hell down, but yeah, that ship had sailed.

As the familiar, heavy sound of his father's footsteps got closer, Robbie reminded himself of his father's words when he'd come out.

"I don't care if you like girls or boys, wear blue or pink. You are my son,

Robert. My *son.* I *will always be proud of who you are and who you're going to become. I'm especially proud of how brave you are being right now...*"

Robbie wondered if his father would feel the same way when he was face to face with the reality of *who* exactly Robbie had become.

His mother entered the living room first, and as she did, Robbie heard Julien and Priest get to their feet. *Shit. Shit. Shit. Just breathe. Don't forget to breathe.*

"You don't have to do that. Sit, please," she said as she waved both men down to the couch, but neither moved, and Robbie knew that had everything to do with the next person who entered the room—his father.

As tall as he was, but with broader shoulders, Robbie had always thought his father larger than life, and when he walked into the room and his piercing brown eyes swept over the scene, Robbie swallowed a nervous gulp of air.

Oh Jesus. What is he thinking? Say something, Robbie told himself. *Say anything.*

But as the silent seconds passed, and his father took the measure of the two men standing behind him, Robbie lost the ability to speak.

He wasn't sure how long they all stood there, but after what felt like hours, his father's eyes found his, and he walked across the room and said, "Hey there, gorgeous. It's about time you got your ass back home."

As he pulled Robbie into a warm embrace, Robbie wound his arms around him and closed his eyes. Then his father kissed his cheek and said in his ear, "You ever avoid this house or your mother again, I'm going to give away all your clothes to Goodwill."

Robbie pulled back, his mouth dropping open. "You wouldn't dare."

His father shrugged. "You make my lady sad, I make you sad, pal. We came to that agreement years ago, remember?"

Robbie lowered his eyes, shame flooding him. Nothing cut

deeper than knowing he'd hurt his ma, and as he turned in her direction, she said, "It's all water under the bridge. The important thing is that you're here now."

"Just remember what I said," his father said, and as Robbie nodded, he caught Felicity poking her head around the corner from the hallway. He glared at her. "Now, why don't you introduce me to your guests," Pa said.

Robbie brought his attention back to his father and searched for any sign of disapproval. But all he saw was curiosity. Deciding it was now or never to just lay it all out there, Robbie stood beside his father, and when he caught sight of Julien and Priest side by side, his breath caught in his throat.

Damn, how in the hell are they mine? He had no idea. But somehow, some*way*, these two impressive men were his, and it was time to acknowledge that with the people he loved the most.

"Ma? Pa? This is Julien and Priest—or, sorry, Joel. My boyfriends." There. He'd finally said it out loud, face to face. And the world hadn't ended.

Priest was the first to step forward, of course. Always bold, always brave, but most of all, Robbie knew that Priest stepped forward to test the waters before Julien approached.

Always watching out for his men, that was Priest, and in that moment, Robbie loved him more than he thought possible.

"Hello, Mr. Bianchi. I'm Joel Priestley."

As Priest extended his hand and Pa took it, Robbie held his breath as they shared a firm handshake. Priest's grey eyes then found his, and Robbie instantly felt the message he was trying to convey: *Everything's going to be all right.*

"The lawyer, yeah? We've heard a lot about you."

Yeah, I'm never going to run my mouth around this bunch again, Robbie thought.

"That's right," Priest said. "That's me."

"Antonio Bianchi."

"It's a pleasure to meet you," Priest said, and released Pa's hand to turn to Julien. "This is my husband, Julien."

Oh shit, Robbie thought. *Priest just put it all out there, didn't he?*

Julien stood beside Priest, and as Robbie's father looked between them, Robbie thought that this might be the moment. You know, the one where he decided that Robbie had lost his mind and told him to get out of his house?

But instead, his father said, "The chef?"

Julien held his hand out. "*Oui.* I am a chef."

As Pa took Julien's hand and gave it a hearty shake, he shook his head. "No, that's not what I mean. You're that French chef from the television."

Julien chuckled. "That's right. I was on the first season of *Chef Master.*"

"He *won* the first season," Robbie's mother chimed in as his father continued to look between both men, and Robbie wished like hell this was already over.

One thing about his father? If he didn't want you to know what he was thinking, he was like a vault, kind of like Pr— *Oh, hell no. Don't even go there, Bianchi. You do* not *have daddy issues.*

"And you two are married?" Pa asked Julien, as though testing the truth of Priest's words.

"*Oui.* We are."

Robbie winced at that, and as his father let go of Julien's hand, he looked back at Robbie, who wondered what exactly he saw.

"Are you okay with that?" Pa said, and Robbie blinked a couple of times before managing, "Huh?"

"What have I told you about saying that, Robert?" his mother said, as Robbie continued to look at his father. "It's *excuse me* or *pardon.*"

Robbie caught Priest's lips quirk at the reprimand, and reminded himself to make Priest pay for that later. Right now, Robbie was trying to work out whether he'd just imagined what his father had said.

When it became clear he was having a few issues, his father repeated himself. "Are you okay with the fact that your boyfriends are married, Robert?"

Yeah, okay, that's what I thought he said. "I am, yes."

His father nodded, and then turned back to Priest and Julien. "Then I suppose you two have a busy weekend ahead of you, don't you?" When they said nothing, Pa continued, "You have four women to win over before you get my stamp of approval. And trust me, they are the hardest crowd to convince you are worthy of this one. You make them happy, you make me happy. *Capito?*"

When Priest and Julien stared blankly, Robbie translated Priest's favorite word for them: "Understand?"

Julien was the first to react, and his grin as he looked at his husband wasn't lost on Robbie. Julien saw the similarities there too, and nodded. "*Oui*, we understand. Don't we, Joel?"

"We do."

"Good," Robbie's father said, and slung an arm around his son. "Now that that's settled, where are your bags? I know you have to have a few. Your ma thought it best we put you in the guesthouse above the garage, since your room is a little small for, uh, all of you."

Robbie was still trying to catch up with everything that had just happened. But then he realized he had to tell his mother they weren't staying there, and that suddenly seemed worse than if he'd been about to confess to a murder.

"We, uhh..." Robbie started, and then looked at his mother. "We booked a room down at the waterfront."

"*Robert.* You are *not* serious," his mother said, and Julien—*thank God for charming Frenchmen*—quite possibly saved Robbie's life.

"*Veuillez m'excuser, Sofia.* It was my suggestion. We didn't want to inconvenience you any more than we already had, since there are three of us."

"Oh," she said, and offered him a bashful smile. "Nonsense. It's no problem. We want you—*both* of you—to stay here with us."

When Julien glanced at him, Robbie knew he was testing to see how he felt about that. And how *did* he feel? Less panicked, that was for sure, and he wanted his family to get to know Julien and

Priest. So Robbie found himself nodding, and Julien said, "In that case, we'd love to stay. I'll cancel the hotel."

"Perfect," she said. "It's all ready and made up for you. We can show you there if you like."

"Actually, Ma?" Robbie said. "If you don't mind, I'll take them and make sure they know where everything is. It's been a long day, and I think we'd like to all freshen up a little." *And maybe have a shot of alcohol.*

"Of course," she said, as his father gave Robbie's shoulder a final squeeze and then let him go. "Dinner will be ready around six. Let us know if you need anything."

Julien, Priest, and Robbie nodded at his parents, and Robbie didn't miss the quizzical looks on their faces as they looked at the three of them.

His father nodded in their direction, and as his parents disappeared down the hall, Robbie heard his father say, "Felicity, I saw you standing there the entire time. Didn't I teach you to be stealthier than that?"

His sister's ringing laughter echoed up the hall, and Robbie looked at his men and said, "Well, now you've met my family."

JULIEN AND PRIEST followed Robbie up some outside stairs that were connected to the double-car garage of his parents' house.

It hadn't escaped either of their attention that their *princesse* had become extremely tight-lipped after his mother and father had left them to settle in. But Julien had suggested that they give Robbie a minute or two to digest the fact that he'd just told his parents he was dating a married couple.

Considering how unusual that situation actually was, Julien thought Robbie's parents had handled the news extremely well. They had suspected that Robbie's mother would after meeting her back in Chicago, but since neither of them had met his father, they hadn't been sure what to expect—and what they got was better than they could've ever imagined.

A tall, burly man, Antonio Bianchi had a full head of thick salt-and-pepper hair and eyes that were both intelligent and shrewd. He was an intimidating presence until he cracked a smile. But what had blown Julien and Priest away was how he'd come into the room, sized them up man-to-man, but then taken the time to reel in his obvious curiosity, to first put his son's anxiety at ease.

The hug and genuine care he'd shown as he kissed Robbie on the cheek and greeted him had spoken volumes, and it was that moment that told them that, even if it took years, they would eventually win this man over, because all he wanted was for his family to be happy—and one thing Julien and Priest knew they did well was make Robbie happy. Something they planned to work on right now.

"This is nice," Julien said, as Priest shut the door and put their final bags by it.

Robbie had sat on the edge of the mattress, and Julien sat down beside him.

"How you holding up, *princesse?*"

Robbie shrugged but wouldn't look at him, and Julien suspected Robbie was feeling a little bit overwhelmed by everything that had happened today.

Julien glanced across the space to Priest, who was watching the two of them. He was leaning up against the door with his hands in his jeans pockets and had a frown on his face. He was letting Julien take the reins here, and Julien swayed into Robbie's side, bumping their shoulders up against each other.

"Hey?" Julien said, and this time Robbie looked at him. "Thank you for bringing us here this weekend. You have a lovely family."

"You're welcome," Robbie said, and then his lips quirked. "Sometimes I think they're a little nuts."

"They are," Priest said, and when Robbie looked at him, Priest grinned and pushed off the door. "But to us, that's wonderful."

As Priest took a seat on the other side of Robbie, he took his hand and laced their fingers together.

"Yeah?" Robbie said, and he sounded almost shy. "I thought they might be a bit, I don't know, much?"

Wait, Julien thought. *Is he worried about* our *feelings right now? After he just told his parents what he did? Sweet, sweet man.*

"They're *parfait*," Julien said. "I wish my parents had one ounce of the acceptance I felt in that house today. If they did, I might have some kind of relationship with them."

Robbie blinked, and his eyes misted over a little. "They are pretty amazing, aren't they?"

Julien nodded. "*Oui*, they are. But we aren't surprised."

"No?" Robbie said.

"No." Priest shook his head. "You are a very special man, Robert. It's no surprise to anyone in this room that your family is also."

Robbie raised a hand and wiped away the tear that had fallen free, relief clearly overwhelming him as it finally sank in that his world wasn't about to explode because the two halves of it had met.

"Even if one of my sisters wants to get in your pants?"

"Well, we can't hold her good taste against her now, can we?" Priest said with such a serious expression that Julien couldn't help but chuckle, and Robbie started laughing and flopped back on the mattress.

As they all lay side by side, their fingers entwined, Robbie blew out a breath and said, "God, I can't believe that just happened. That you both just met my family."

Julien winked at Robbie. "And survived."

"The first round, anyway," Robbie said. "Pa wasn't lying. My ma and sisters are going to drive you crazy over the next few days."

"Bring it on," Priest said. "Don't you worry about us. We're not going anywhere."

Robbie bit his lip, stared up at the ceiling, and said under his breath, "I've never been happier in my entire life."

Julien rolled onto his side and kissed Robbie's cheek. "*Bien*."

"Mhmm," Robbie said, and turned to kiss Julien. "And you know what I just realized?"

"What's that?" Julien said.

"This bed is a queen-sized."

Their conversation from the night of Robbie's birthday came flooding back, and as they started to laugh, Julien and Priest rolled into Robbie's side and kissed him until he dissolved into a fit of giggles.

CHAPTER TEN

Don't let the hormonal
pregnant woman out of your sight.
This is advice I never thought
I'd have to take - Julien

THE STEADY HUM of music pounded beneath Priest's feet as he walked out of the en suite and into the guest room to get his clothes for the night.

The music and dance floor for the evening had been set up in the empty garage and driveway below, while food and drink were being handled inside. Julien and Robbie had headed downstairs around thirty minutes ago after Priest volunteered to use the shower last, and it was now closing in on eight. Robbie's thirtieth birthday party was due to begin at any moment—and Priest was looking forward to seeing Robbie surrounded by a family who clearly adored him.

Somehow, Priest and Julien had survived the last twenty-four hours without any threats to their well-being. They'd made it through their first night's dinner before passing out from such a long day, and today they'd been helping with the flurry of activity to get the home fit for a party that would celebrate the favorite Bianchi—and yes, it was very clear that Robbie was everyone's favorite.

Priest picked up his jeans and light knit top and was about to head back into the bathroom when the door to the guest room opened and Robbie slipped inside. Priest had already been showering when Robbie had gotten dressed, but as he shut the door behind him now, Priest took a moment to drink in the man in front of him.

Robbie was dressed in a pair of lightweight grey pants, paired with a three-quarter-sleeve cream V-neck that was made of linen. But what really tied the outfit together, and made it uniquely Robbie, were the loose suspenders over his shoulders.

Tied probably wasn't a word Priest should be thinking about while looking at them, though. Not if they were going to get down to the party anytime soon, because with his hair styled back from his face, and his eyes lined and lips glossed, Robbie had Priest's cock hard in an instant.

"Oh, ah, hey," Robbie said, as he took in Priest's half-naked state, and then flashed a smile—a *forced* smile, Priest noted.

"Hey," Priest said as he brought his clothes in front of him, not wanting to distract Robbie from whatever it was he'd come up there for. "Where's Julien?"

"Downstairs with Ma and the girls. I think they've decided to keep him."

"Well too bad," Priest said. "He's already spoken for—two times over."

Robbie nodded, and then glanced over his shoulder to look out the small window in the door. "Everyone's starting to get here."

Priest sized Robbie up, and his eyes wandered to the hands he was wiping on the sides of his pants. He was nervous again, but Priest wasn't sure why. Robbie had already tackled the major obstacle for the weekend—his parents. So what was this all about?

Priest walked over to Robbie. "If everyone's starting to arrive, then why are you up here?"

Robbie worried his shiny lip, and then gave what Priest knew he hoped was a convincing smile. "I came to check you were all right and, you know, help you get dressed."

"Nice try. But we already decided you were off the hook in that department around your family. We already present a less-than-normal front. So I don't think you excused yourself to help me button my pants. Why are you really up here?"

Robbie stepped around Priest and began pacing the length of the guest room. Back and forth. Back and forth. "*Ugh*, it's just... I know everyone's going to be watching me tonight."

"And this is a problem for you?" Priest said as he halted Robbie. "You've never had an issue being the center of attention. Last time I checked, that's where you're the most comfortable. What's really going on here? Your parents have been incredibly welcoming this weekend, as have your sisters."

Robbie scrunched his nose. "I know. But the rest of my family has always looked at me like the loud, out-there gay relative, who was super amusing but never taken seriously. And tonight, I...I don't want to embarrass you or Julien."

Priest's heart softened, but that was the only thing. "Sweetheart, have you met your family? They're not exactly a quiet, retiring bunch."

How Robbie thought he could embarrass them by being himself was beyond Priest. But it was time to make sure he understood and realized how extremely proud Priest and Julien were to be his. It was *time* to give Robbie something else to think about.

Priest ran a finger down one of Robbie's suspenders, and then he slipped it behind the elastic, smoothed it back up to mid-chest, and tugged on it. "Come closer."

"Any closer and I'll be— *Oh*," Robbie said, as Priest wound his other arm around Robbie's waist and pulled him against his close-to-naked body.

Priest ran his eyes all over Robbie's beautiful face. "You'll be exactly where I want you. You look beautiful tonight. Pretty eyes, shiny lips." Priest brought a hand up and ran his thumb along the seam of Robbie's mouth. "Open them for me." Robbie's lips parted, and when Priest slipped his thumb inside, he said, "Suck."

Robbie's cheeks hollowed out as he swirled his tongue around Priest's thumb, and a growl rumbled in Priest's throat.

"Take my towel off," Priest said as he slid a hand down to cup Robbie's ass, and when Robbie's fingers slipped behind the knot and pulled the towel free, Priest hauled his delectable body back in close.

Priest dragged his thumb free of Robbie's mouth until he was holding his chin in a firm grip. He angled Robbie's head to where he could see all the lovely lines of his face, and then Priest put his lips by Robbie's temple and said, "You could never embarrass me *or* Julien."

"I just—"

"No," Priest said firmly. He wouldn't have Robbie cutting himself down. "You listen to me. You are an incredible man. Smart, caring, and unbelievably sexy." Priest looked into Robbie's dark blue eyes. "Do you know how I know that?"

Robbie shook his head. "No."

"Because you're mine, and I love you." Priest thrust his hips forward and, when Robbie whimpered, added, "And I don't like anyone. So that must make you pretty fucking special."

"Oh shit," Robbie said as Priest walked him back to the wall and planted a hand by Robbie's head.

"I don't want to hear you say another bad thing about yourself. Do you understand me?"

Robbie nodded and wound his leg around Priest's thigh, as he jammed his covered erection up against Priest's naked one.

"You're going to go down to your party, be your usual delightful self, and I am going to spend the whole night wishing I didn't have any objections to fucking you in your parents' house."

"Technically we're not *in* their house," Robbie said as he rubbed himself a little harder against Priest.

"No," Priest said.

"What if I ask *really* nicely?" Robbie said, and batted his lashes. *Good*—Robbie had clearly forgotten why he'd come up there in the first place, and that had been Priest's goal.

"Still no," Priest said, but couldn't stop himself from grabbing hold of Robbie's ass and really grinding his dick up against his soft pants. "I'm trying really hard to let you walk out of here without messing you up."

"Mess me up," Robbie said. "I don't care."

"I do," Priest said, and nipped at Robbie's lower lip. "I want your parents to like us. That means respecting them, which means"—Priest reluctantly let Robbie go—"you need to leave. Now."

Robbie lowered his eyes to Priest's very erect cock and said, "Are you su—"

"Yes. Jesus, Robert," Priest said. "Give me a break here."

As Robbie slipped out from between him and the wall, Priest hung his head and started to count back from one hundred, and right about the time he thought he was somewhat under control, he heard, "Priest?"

Priest looked over his shoulder to see Robbie's eyes all but sparkling.

"Hmm?"

"I think you're really special too."

"Fuck." Priest wrapped a hand around the base of his dick and groaned, and knew he was about to head back to the shower he'd just left. "Get out of here, flirt."

Robbie bit on his lip, opened the door, and left. And somehow, Priest had a feeling Robbie was no longer thinking about how he would embarrass Priest or Julien, but more likely how he'd keep his hands to himself.

A problem Priest knew he was going to have a hard time tackling himself.

WHEN ROBBIE HAD said his family was big, Julien hadn't quite envisioned just *how* big. Really, he should've guessed, considering the sheer amount of food and alcohol that had been purchased and prepared for tonight's party. But as more and more people arrived, Julien found himself staring out at a sea of loud, chatty Italians—and loved it.

It had been several hours since the party had begun, and it was now in full swing as they headed toward the midnight hour. With the alcohol flowing, Julien had found Robbie's family to be kind but...inquisitive. More so as the evening went on.

They'd each made him and Priest feel welcome, and been polite in how they approached the topic of them and Robbie. But as the latest relative—Robbie's Uncle Nico—talked his ear off, Julien had to admit, it was rather amusing to watch him tiptoe around what he really wanted to ask. So far, though, whenever someone got a little *too* invasive with their questions, one of Robbie's sisters saved the day.

With a fresh drink in hand, Julien was about to head out to find Robbie and Priest, when he spotted Penny standing with a couple with an uneasy expression on her face, as though she wanted be anywhere but there.

Wanting to make sure she was feeling okay, Julien made his way over, and when he stopped by her side, she gave him a strained smile, then wound her arm around his elbow and said, "Oh, look who's here. I'm not sure if you've met our celebrity guest tonight. But let me introduce you."

Julien quickly deduced that what was making Penny feel slightly nauseated had nothing to do with her health, but perhaps the people she'd gotten stuck talking to.

Julien's eyes shifted between the man and woman staring at him. The woman beamed, her brown eyes smiling right along with her lips, while the man looked like he was sucking on a lemon.

"This is Julien Thornton," Penny said, as she patted Julien's arm. "He was the winner on *Chef Master*."

"Oh yes," the woman said. "I remember now. You're French,

aren't you?"

"*Oui*, that's correct," Julien said, and then held his hand out to her. "And you are?"

"I'm Mary Beth Paulson. And this is Jack, my husband."

Jack Paulson. Jack Paulson... As Julien ran the name over in his head, he tried to place how he knew it. But considering he'd just met Robbie's entire family twenty-four hours ago, the likelihood of him actually knowing the man was slim to none.

But that name, Julien thought. *It's so familiar.*

"*Bonsoir*," Julien said, and held his hand out to Jack. "It's nice to meet you. And how are you related to the Bianchi clan?"

"He's not," Penny said, and her tone, while friendly, had taken on a slightly sharper edge. Julien glanced her way, but Penny's eyes were locked on the handsome man standing by his smiling wife. "He's a longtime family friend."

Jack nodded. "That's right—we used to take summer vacation by their holiday home at the lake. Our families are close."

Mary Beth laughed and ran a hand up and down Jack's arm, completely oblivious to the tension thrumming in the air. "Robbie used to have a crush on him, right, Penny? He always joked that watching Jack in the lake was the reason he knew he was gay. I mean, could you blame him?"

As Julien tried to process that piece of information, Penny's fingers tightened on his arm.

"No," Penny said. "No one could blame him. In fact, I'm pretty sure each of us Bianchis had a crush on Jack at one time. But it always passed, like a bad case of chlamydia."

And that was when it hit, the exact reason Julien knew Jack Paulson's name. Jack Paulson was—as Robbie had so eloquently put it one night—the Bianchi Baby Daddy.

"*What?*" Robbie had said. "*He was bound to impregnate one of us with all the testosterone he threw around. Hell, I'm surprised he didn't knock me up.*"

"That's really mature, Penny," Jack said, bringing Julien back to the tense discussion underway.

"That's me," Penny said, the happy couple in front of her having clearly destroyed any attempt she'd been making to employ good manners. "Maturing, ripening. More and more every day."

"*Dieu*," Julien said under his breath, as he plastered on his best smile and grabbed hold of Penny's arm. He needed to get her away from these two, stat—especially Mary Beth, who was still trying for a polite smile even through her confusion.

"*Veuillez nous excuser*, but do you mind if I steal Penny? I'm hoping she can help me track down Robbie," Julien said, and as he pulled her aside, Penny aimed blurred eyes his way, an apology written all over her face as Julien led her through the crowd.

As they pushed through the back door and walked out onto the porch, the loud music and conversation greeted them. But instead of heading down to where the double garages were lit up under twinkle lights for the dance floor, Penny went in the opposite direction.

Not willing to let a hormonal pregnant woman out of his sight, Julien followed, thinking he might run into Robbie along the way. But as she disappeared around the side of the house where there were no lights, Julien saw her take a seat on a concrete step and moved until he could take the spot beside her.

"Do you want to talk about it?"

Penny put her face in her hands. "Not really."

"Okay," Julien said, and when he remained silent, she looked at him.

"That's it?" she asked. Confused, Julien frowned, and she cracked a half smile. "Usually when someone in our family asks that and you say no, they give you a few seconds then launch a barrage of questions anyway."

Julien grinned and shrugged. "If you don't want to talk, who am I to make you?"

"My brother's married boyfriend?"

Julien let out a bark of laughter, enjoying himself immensely. "*Oui*, I am that. But don't start pointing fingers, or I might."

Penny laughed along with him, and then shook her head. "I'm a mess. I can't believe I just went off like that."

"You're upset," Julien said. "I assume he knows?"

Penny nodded. "He knows. But no one else does. I mean, except Felicity, Val, and Robbie. Ugh, one stupid night is going to ruin a lifetime of our families being close. God. I'm such a coward."

"*Non*," Julien said. "You're not ready. That's all."

Penny turned her face toward him, and her eyes were so like Robbie's that Julien said, "You remind me so much of your brother."

"Because we've both brought scandal to the Bianchi name?"

Julien grinned. "*Non*. You both follow your hearts. No matter the consequences. That's brave."

"Or stupid."

"No one said being brave was smart. That's why it's brave. It takes courage to go after what you want."

Penny narrowed her eyes. "Do you really love two men?"

Julien couldn't help but think this was more her wondering about Jack than himself. But he answered her anyway. "I do. Very much."

Closing her eyes, Penny put a hand on her belly and whispered, "I wish things could be as easy as that for us."

Julien studied her as she sat in the moonlight, and when a tear ran down her cheek, he said, "Maybe it will be, in time."

"Maybe," she said, and then aimed a halfhearted smile at him. "But can you promise me something?" When Julien nodded, Penny locked eyes with him and said, "Make sure Robbie knows that he's just as important to the both of you as the piece of paper you share with Priest."

As Julien sat there on the Bianchis' back step, he saw a flash of Jacquelyn in her direct stare, and found himself nodding. This weekend he felt as though he'd found a part of himself that had been missing, and he knew that was because of the women in this house, that sisterly love that was in such abundance for their brother, and he was positive he would've done anything to make

Robbie's sister happy in that moment. But this, he already had in the bag—it was one of the main reasons he and Priest had wanted this weekend to happen.

"You have my word," he said, and when she startled, Julien jumped, and Penny began to laugh.

"I'm sorry. She kicked," she said, and shifted her hand on her belly to feel it again. "Give me your hand."

Julien's eyes widened, and he shook his head.

"Oh, come on. You're practically family. You're probably going to be one of this kid's uncles. Feel her kick."

Julien let her pull his hand over to her swollen stomach, and a firm little jab whacked out at his palm. Penny started laughing again.

"You look horrified."

"I am," Julien admitted. "Doesn't that hurt?"

"Does what hurt?" Robbie said from behind them, and Julien turned to see him and Felicity walking through the French doors of the living room.

As the noise spilled out into the small courtyard, Penny said, "Hurry up and shut the door."

"What are you two doing out here?" Felicity asked.

"Hiding," Penny replied. "And then the baby started to kick and freaked out the gay man."

Julien's mouth fell open, but before he could defend himself, Robbie dropped down on his knees beside his sister and said, "I want to feel."

Penny took his hand and placed it in the same spot Julien's had just been, and when the baby kicked again, his eyes flew to Julien's.

"Oh my God," Robbie said. "That's so weird."

"Weird?" Penny said. "How about magical? Wondrous?"

The baby kicked again. "Weird." Robbie laughed. "It's weirdly wonderful. How's that?"

Penny rolled her eyes, but it was clear she was pleased. "That'll do."

"So who are you hiding from?" Robbie asked.

"Jack," Penny said, as Felicity guessed, "Valerie?"

"Valerie?" Penny said. "Why would I be hiding from Valerie?"

"Wait," Robbie said. "Jack's here? Are you kidding me? He has some fucking balls. I mean, I assume. You would know better than me."

"Stop talking. And don't worry," Penny said. "Your man here saved me from the awkwardness."

Robbie looked at Julien, and his eyes softened a little. "Did he?"

"He did."

Julien chuckled. "*Non.* I think I actually saved Jack from a swift death, but—"

Penny shoved Julien in the arm, and Robbie's mouth split into a wide grin at the familiar move. It was clear their budding relationship pleased him.

"So, okay," Penny said. "You know who *we're* hiding from. Why did you think I was hiding from Valerie?"

"Because she's drunk," Robbie said.

Felicity snorted. "*So* drunk. And you know how she gets. She wants everyone around her to be just as merry, and Robbie made me promise to only allow this slight buzz he has right now."

Julien grinned at his bright-eyed *princesse. Oh, oui.* He was definitely buzzed, but not quite as inebriated as the last time Felicity had been tasked to look after him.

Robbie winked at Julien. "I'm *trying* to behave myself around the parents."

"Uh huh," Julien said, and got to his feet, and Robbie followed him before they both turned to Penny and held their hands out.

She accepted their help, and once she was standing, Robbie said, "By the way, where's Priest? I haven't seen him in forever."

The four of them fell silent, and it didn't take them long to come to the same conclusion. They all turned in the direction the throbbing music was coming from, and Julien heard, "I'm going to kill her," right before Robbie headed off in the direction of the dancing partygoers in search of the *her* he planned to murder.

CHAPTER ELEVEN

A flirty drunk.
I didn't see that coming - Robbie

ALL NIGHT I behaved myself, Robbie thought, as he walked toward the laughter and loud music. *I behaved myself at* my *birthday, while Valerie is off doing God knows—*

"You've got to be kidding me."

Robbie came to a standstill on the outskirts of the makeshift dance area and tried to process what exactly he was looking at.

He'd been out there on the dance floor a few times himself tonight, dragged into a dance-off here and there with cousins he hadn't seen in years who actually thought they could beat him—*please*—but as he stood there now, his eyes latched on to Valerie, and he was about two seconds away from saying, *To hell with behaving.*

"Well," Felicity drawled, as she came up beside him. "You *did* say you wanted to find her."

Robbie scoffed and turned his head to her. "She's not *exactly* hard to miss." And the reason for that had nothing to do with Valerie.

No. Valerie was several inches shorter than most of the people moving around on the dance floor, but the person she had draped herself all over—*he* was not.

"*Princesse?* Did you find— Oh." As Julien came to a stop, a chuckle escaped him, and Robbie just shook his head.

He should've known better. He should've kept a better eye on Val. But *no,* he'd left her alone with the one thing he knew she couldn't resist—the redhead.

"I can't believe this," Robbie said, as Julien laughed a little harder, then he dragged his eyes away from what they—and *they* was every single person in the near vicinity—were looking at, and said, "*Non?*"

"No," Robbie said. "This isn't funny. This is... I can't even think of a word because I don't even know what this is."

Robbie looked back out to the scene he was trying to comprehend, and Felicity chimed in, helpful as ever. "I can think of a few words: hot as fuck. Who knew Priest could dance?"

Me, Robbie thought. *But not like* that*, that's for damn sure.*

Yes, it was Priest. And *yes,* he was dancing. But not the smooth, charming foxtrot around the kitchen. *No.* Priest was out there looking drop-dead gorgeous under the twinkling lights getting down to some sexed-up song Robbie couldn't even place right now. He had his arms around Valerie's waist as she hung off his neck, and every now and then they both stumbled into one another and started to laugh uproariously.

As Robbie stood there with his mouth hanging open, someone walked by them with a tray of bright pink birthday cake shots, and Valerie grabbed two, handed one to Priest, and, without letting go of each other, they clinked their glasses, like co-conspirators, and downed the alcohol.

Priest then pivoted and turned Valerie so he was now looking across the dance floor, and when he spotted Robbie and Julien, his mouth kicked up in an inebriated smile so unlike Priest that it was difficult to comprehend.

Valerie had officially stolen one of Robbie's men tonight and was letting her ginger freak flag fly. Unfortunately for Robbie, it just happened to be up *his* ginger pole.

Right. That's it.

But just as Robbie was about to shove his way onto the dance floor and pull Valerie's gorgeous blonde hair out of her head, Julien took hold of his arm and said in his ear, "Where are you going?"

"Out there to pry her damn hands off him," Robbie said. "Look at them. He's actually laughing, *smiling*, for God's sake. Who knows how many drinks she had to give him to do that."

"A lot, I'm thinking," Julien said. "I haven't seen him dance like that for a long time."

"I didn't even know he *could* dance like that." Robbie pouted, and then said in his best Priest imitation, "*I have to behave in front of your parents, Robert.* That's what he said. To *me*. I'm going to kill her."

Cue "It's My Party," because I'm one drink away from crying because I want to.

"Aw, don't be too hard on her, *princesse*. When was the last time you ever saw Priest that...relaxed?"

Umm, how about never? If someone had asked him before tonight if Priest ever got drunk, Robbie would've laughed them out of the building. But that was exactly what he was seeing right now. He knew it as well as he knew his *sister* was absolutely going to pay for this.

"So what you're saying is I should just let her dance all over our man?"

"What I'm *saying*"—Julien slipped his hand into Robbie's—"is that you should come and dance like that with me. We'll get our turn with Priest eventually, and more so than Valerie."

Julien winked as he walked out into the crowd and tugged Robbie along with him, and Robbie shifted his attention to that plan and found his irritation left as quickly as it had appeared.

Really, there was no need for crying when Julien was pulling him into his arms. There was no need for anything at all except losing himself in the scent of Julien's cologne, and the delicious way Julien felt as he spent the rest of the party dancing the night away.

After all, he couldn't exactly blame Valerie, but that didn't mean Robbie wasn't going to keep a watchful eye on his handsy sister who just so happened to share his and Julien's affections for a certain Priest.

"YOU'RE SO WASTED," Robbie said as he pushed opened the door to the guesthouse and Priest came to a standstill in front of him.

It was closing in on one thirty, and everyone had left for the night except Robbie's immediate family. His parents had headed off to bed around half an hour ago, and left him—along with his sisters—to lock up.

Priest tapped a finger on Robbie's chest and nodded. "I think you might be right. *Buuuut* I made it up the stairs, didn't I?"

Priest turned to walk into the room, and as he did, he veered to the left. Julien reached out, hooked an arm through his elbow, and chuckled.

"Actually," Julien said, "*I* got you up the stairs. But who needs facts?"

"Me." Priest aimed a megawatt smile in Julien's direction. "I need facts because *I'm* a lawyer. Facts are my life." Priest stopped talking, seemingly distracted by Julien's face, and then ran his fingertips down Julien's cheek. "Nope. That's not right. You. You and Robert." Priest looked at Robbie and pointed at him. "You and *Robert* are my life. My loves..." Priest drawled. "And my life."

Robbie snorted and closed the door, then headed to his open suitcase for his pajamas. When a loud *thump* met his ears, he looked over his shoulder to see that Priest had just run into the end of the bed.

"Whoops," Priest said, and laughed a throaty chuckle, and Robbie had to bite down on his lip to hold back his own laughter.

"Perhaps you should sit down, *mon amour*," Julien suggested. "Before you fall down."

"Mmm, keep talking," Priest said, and ran a finger along Julien's lower lip. "You have the sexiest voice. Have I ever told you that?"

"*Oui,* you have," Julien said, and urged Priest toward the bed, but he wasn't budging.

Priest leaned in and replaced his finger with his lips, and said against Julien's mouth, "Especially when you're turned on. It gets all raspy, and fuck, Julien—it makes me so hard. Doesn't it make you hard, Robert?"

Um, always. But Robbie was too busy trying to process what he was witnessing to answer. Who would've guessed that Priest was such a flirty drunk? The intoxicating control he usually wielded was currently replaced by a smooth seducer's charm.

Julien shook his head and slapped at Priest's hands, as he reached for the buttons at the bottom of Julien's shirt. "How about you let me and Robbie get you undressed, and then you can—"

"Fuck you both?"

"*Non,*" Julien said, and really started laughing as Priest wound his arms around his waist, grabbed Julien's ass, and pressed his lips to his cheek. "*Mon Dieu.* You're like an octopus tonight. All hands. Everywhere."

"Let me take you to bed. Both of you," Priest said, as he looked at Robbie. "Take off your clothes, sweetheart. I want to look at you."

"Do *not* take off your clothes," Julien said. "You do that, it's all over."

Robbie pouted, because really, there was nothing he wanted more than to take off his clothes.

"But look at him, *mon cœur*," Priest said in Julien's ear. "Don't you want to see what's under that shirt? Those pants...? He wants us to undress him."

I really do, Robbie thought. But then he remembered what Priest had said before the party about respecting his parents, and how that meant a lot to him—and also, apparently, to Julien.

"What happened to making a good impression on the Bianchis?" Julien asked as he took hold of Priest's face, a hand on either cheek.

"Nothing," Priest said, and nipped Julien's thumb. "But they're not *here*, and what they don't know won't hurt them. Like how much I want to suck their son's co—"

"*How* many drinks did you have tonight?" Julien interrupted.

"Umm." Priest frowned. "I don't know. Val kept—"

"He's calling her *Val* now?" Robbie said.

But Priest went on undeterred. "She kept bringing them to me and was asking me to guess what she put in them."

"Other than a shit-ton of alcohol?" Robbie said, and rolled his eyes. "Have you ever heard of the word *no?*"

Priest turned his heavy-lidded gaze on Robbie and grinned. "Yes. But I wanted her to like me, for you."

Okay, really? How am I supposed to argue with that? Robbie couldn't, so instead he directed his ire where it was well deserved. "She's so paying for this when I see her."

"Nooo...don't do that," Priest said, and shook his head. "She's so much fun. Just like you."

Robbie's eyes widened, and he shook his finger at Priest. "No, no. Not like me. I don't have to get you drunk to be all over *me.* Wanna know why? Because I have something you like a whole lot more than her pretty blonde hair."

"Mhmm." Priest's lips curved into that lazy smile again. "Prove it. Take off your clothes."

"*Aaand* we're back where we started," Julien said. "That's it— you are getting changed, Joel, and then going to *sleep.* You're going to have a terrible hangover tomorrow."

Julien directed Priest toward his bag, and as he bent down to rifle through it, Robbie turned his attention to Julien, who was staring at his husband as though he'd morphed into a totally different person.

"Jules," Robbie whispered across the room, and when Julien glanced his way, Robbie waved him over. Julien checked on Priest again, but when he haphazardly tossed a pair of jeans over his shoulder, Julien chuckled and made his way to Robbie's side of the bed.

"Have you *ever* seen him like this?" Robbie asked, and when Priest said, "Ah ha. I knew I packed them," and held up his lounge pants in triumph, Julien's shoulders shook with the laughter he was trying to contain.

"*Non.*"

"*Never?*" Robbie said. "Do you think he's had some kind of allergic reaction to the alcohol?"

"*Non,*" Julien said as he turned his eyes to Robbie's. "I think he's one hundred percent relaxed and one hundred and *fifty* percent drunk. It's quite wonderful. Isn't it?"

Priest got to his feet and reached for his shirt, and just as he was about to pull it off, he turned around, zeroed in on the two of them, and aimed a lackadaisical grin their way.

Julien was right: those grey eyes were glassy as they tried to focus. But that loose-lipped smile on Priest's usually stern lips was a killer. *Damn.* Even one hundred and fifty percent drunk, Priest's magnetic pull was as strong as ever.

Robbie leaned into Julien's shoulder and said under his breath, "Make him stop looking at us like that."

"And how do you propose I do that?" Julien asked, as Priest pulled his shirt over his head.

"Uhh…" Robbie had forgotten what he'd said, and when Priest undid the top of his jeans and unzipped, Robbie swallowed and reached down to massage his ever-growing hard-on. "I don't know, but you better work it out fast. Because if he takes his pants off, I'm getting naked. I don't care if my parents are sleeping in the house across from us."

AS PRIEST STARED at the two of them from the opposite side of the queen-sized bed, Julien had to admit he was tempted to see how quiet the three of them could be if they all stripped down and got in that bed.

But he knew Priest would be mortified if for some reason they were caught and jeopardized the relationship they were starting to build with Robbie's parents.

Luckily for Priest, Robbie's parents hadn't borne witness to his rediscovered dance moves tonight. And by the time they'd come outside to say goodbye to their guests, the music had been shut off and all dancing had ceased.

Now, how in the world he was going to get a determined Priest not to seduce them, Julien had no clue. All he knew was that Robbie had way more faith in him than he really probably should.

"Joel?" Julien knew the second his voice found his husband, because Priest took a step closer to the bed and pushed a hand into the open zipper of his jeans.

Putain. He is not going to make this easy on us.

"*Oui,* Julien?"

Julien reached for the buttons of his shirt and undid it, and Priest watched avidly as Julien shrugged out of it and draped it over the small accent chair beside Robbie.

Priest's gaze then travelled to their princess, who also had a hand pressed between his legs, and when Priest licked his lips, everyone in the room knew exactly what he wanted.

"Joel?" Julien said, then crooked a finger. "*Viens ici.*"

Priest didn't even hesitate. He put a knee on the mattress, and when Julien mirrored him, Priest smirked, thinking he'd won.

As Julien moved closer, he noticed Priest sway a little, and he could tell the alcohol was starting to slow him down, the buzz having turned to more of a hum as Priest aimed his sex-drunk eyes up at Robbie and said, "You should come too, pretty princess."

"*Shit,*" Robbie whispered.

Julien was about to tell Priest to quit it and lie down. But before he could, Priest's eyes fluttered shut and he pitched to the side, and before Julien could grab him, he fell on the mattress.

"Oh my God," Robbie said as he scrambled up onto the bed. "Is he okay?"

Julien studied Priest's closed eyes and relaxed face. Somehow, Priest had managed not to face-plant into the mattress, and his cheek was now squished into the pillow. His breathing was even, and he looked so peaceful that Julien couldn't help but run his fingers across the hair now flopping down on Priest's forehead.

"I think he's just fine," Julien said. "But tomorrow might be a whole other story."

"Right?" Robbie said, a grin spreading. "Priest is a total flirt when he drinks. Who knew?"

Julien chuckled. "He is, isn't he?"

"Uh, yeah." Robbie let out a sigh and looked down at his lap. "Falling asleep is *not* going to be the easiest thing right now."

Julien kissed Robbie and said, "No, it's going to be very *hard*. For the both of us."

Robbie's gaze roamed down to the erection Julien didn't even bother trying to hide. "He so owes us for this."

"I think you might be right," Julien said. "How about we get in bed and dream up ways to make him pay."

"I like the way you think," Robbie said, and wound his arms around Julien's neck. "And the way you smell, and taste, and feel."

Julien pulled back and shook his head. "You're as bad as he is. Sleep. Now. *Allez!*"

"Fine," Robbie said, and got out of bed and quickly changed into his pajamas. "But let it be noted that I don't like this no-sexy-time rule when we're around my family. We need to work on that."

"Noted," Julien said as he got beneath the covers in the middle of the bed.

Robbie flicked off the light and scooted in until he was plastered up against Julien with a leg slung over his thigh. "I *do*, however, *love* this queen-sized bed."

Julien prayed for patience as his cock kicked in response to Robbie, who was squirming up against his side. *Dieu*, between these two, he'd be lucky if he got an hour's sleep. *"Bonne nuit, princesse."*

But the only response Julien got was the soft, even breathing of his two men, who were already in a deep, peaceful slumber.

CHAPTER TWELVE

I want it all,
and I want it my way - Priest

JULIEN STOOD AT the vanity in the guest bathroom the following morning waiting for the water to heat up. He'd woken around ten minutes earlier, his body still set on an internal alarm of *early*.

Last night had been wonderful. Robbie's family was amazing. From his sisters to his parents, each and every one of them were boisterous, loving, and just plain good fun. They were exactly as Julien had imagined Robbie's family would be.

As the water turned lukewarm, Julien put the plug in and filled the basin, and when he went to reach for his shaving cream, he saw the door to the en suite open and Priest fill the doorway.

With his auburn hair sticking out all over the place, Priest winced against the bright light of the bathroom and clutched at his head. He looked...terrible, and he staggered into the room, shut the door behind him, and slumped back against it.

Julien couldn't stop his grin as he stared at his husband in the mirror, and when Priest's eyes finally adjusted to the light, they found his.

"*Bonjour*," Julien said. "You're up early."

Priest rubbed at his eyes. "The drumming in my head woke me up."

Julien chuckled as he shook the shaving cream and squirted some into his palm. "Just drumming? With the amount of alcohol you consumed last night, I'm surprised you don't have a full-on marching band playing in there."

"Fuck me," Priest said, and dropped his hand down to his side. "I feel like shit."

As he pushed off the door and came to stand beside Julien, Priest caught a look at himself in the mirror and grimaced. His jeans were undone and barely hanging on to his hips, and they and his briefs were the only things that remained from last night's little impromptu striptease.

"I look like shit too," Priest mumbled. "Jesus, what happened?"

Julien swished his razor in the warm water, and as he brought it up to his cheek, he said, "Hurricane Valerie." He dragged the blade through the white cream and found Priest's eyes in the mirror. They were narrowed as though he were trying to think back.

"Ugh," Priest said, and ran a hand through his messy hair. "I don't remember."

"I'm not surprised." Julien continued shaving the left side of his face. "What's the last thing you *do* remember?"

Priest braced his hands on the vanity and hung his head down. "Uh...Robert blew out his candles and you went to get us a drink, and then, yes, Valerie. She kept bringing me drinks, and I didn't want to—"

"Be rude?" Julien asked, his eyebrow raised.

"Right. So I thought, *I can have one or two, how bad could this get.*"

Julien clamped his lips together but couldn't hold back the laugh that bubbled out of him.

"Oh God. It got bad, didn't it? What did I do?" Priest groaned. "Please tell me I didn't sing."

Julien eyed him and thought about playing with Priest, but the poor guy looked miserable enough already. "You did not sing, *non*."

"But I did something else?" Priest shook his head. "What?"

"You just got a little bit…footloose."

Priest narrowed his eyes.

"You were dancing."

The expression on Priest's face conveyed his confusion. He didn't quite understand what was wrong with that. "That's not too bad. I didn't trip over my feet, did I?"

"*Non*," Julien said. "Your feet weren't what was moving, *mon amour*. You weren't *dancing* dancing. You were more"—Julien put the razor down and turned to rest his hip against the vanity —"bumping and grinding. With Valerie."

Priest's mouth fell open, and for the first time in as long as Julien could remember, his face flamed the same color as his hair.

"You're kidding," Priest said, and covered his face.

"I'm not. *Je suis désolé.*"

Priest shook his head, but then dropped his hands down, his eyes wide. "Were Robert's parents there? Fuck."

Julien moved in until he was close enough to press a kiss to Priest's naked shoulder. "No, they were inside with a few of the other…adults." Julien chuckled. "As far as I know, you're safe."

"Oh God. I'm sorry," Priest said. "Robert must be pissed."

"I think you might be surprised."

"Meaning?"

"Robbie's not mad at *you*. Although I think Valerie might get an earful today. Plus, you made it up to him last night." Priest frowned, and Julien grinned. "You were rather amusing once we got back up here."

"Amusing?"

"Amusing. Amorous. Take your pick. Either way, by the time you passed out, Robbie was quite entertained."

"Jesus," Priest said. "I'm so ashamed of myself."

"Don't be. It was good to see you finally unwind and relax. Robbie feels the same. It was nice to know that you felt you could."

"I don't think feeling *relaxed* had anything to do with taking one hundred shots."

"*Oui*, it did. Even if you were trying to make sure Valerie liked you, you never would've had a drink if you thought there was a reason to stay alert. Last night, you were finally free."

Priest grunted. "A little too free, it seems."

"Mhmm," Julien said, and reached for Priest's hand. "I was about to have a shower, and since you owe me..."

Priest ran his eyes down Julien's naked chest to the towel at his waist. "Owe you?"

"*Oui*. You left me incredibly...*tense* last night. So why don't you join me?"

As Julien walked back toward the small shower stall, he tugged Priest with him.

"It's pretty tight in there," Priest said.

Julien whipped off the towel, dropped it to the floor, and said, "Yes, it is," before he stepped into the shower stall and turned on the spray.

Not two seconds later, he was happy to hear the rustling sounds of clothing hit the tile floor and the door opening, because while he'd been joking around out there, Priest did owe him, and Julien figured the least Priest could do was wash his...back for him.

AFTER A VERY *frustrating* shower, Priest and Julien dressed quietly in the room, where Robbie still slept soundly. One thing they'd learned about their princess was that it took some heavy-duty noise, a warm pair of lips, or a hard cock somewhere near him to rouse the beauty from his sleep.

But with the added aid of alcohol and excitement from last night, he would likely be out for a little while longer, which worked in their favor this morning, because Priest and Julien had something they needed to do.

Once they were ready, they crept outside and were greeted with the beautiful morning sunrise. Priest was about halfway down the stairs when he stopped and glanced over at the back door of the Bianchis' house, and as Julien reached the bottom, he turned and looked back.

"Joel?" Priest refocused on Julien as he took the final stairs down, and then Julien took his hand and said, "What's wrong?"

"Nothing."

Julien smiled, and when his dimple appeared, Priest reached up to touch it.

"What do you always tell Robbie about lying?" Julien said.

"Not to." When Julien raised an eyebrow, Priest cleared his throat and said, "Point made."

"*Bien.* Then I'll ask again. What's wrong?"

Priest was nervous, that was what was wrong, and as he looked into Julien's handsome face, Priest found it difficult to admit. "I think you should do the talking in there this morning."

Julien frowned and took a step closer. "Why?" Priest went to look away, but Julien moved in his direct line of sight. "Why, Joel?"

"Because you're better at it." As soon as he said the words, Priest knew how absurd they sounded, and so did Julien, judging by the way his lips quirked.

"I'm better at it? You're a lawyer, *mon amour*. It's your job to talk to people. Try again."

"You know what I mean," Priest said. "You are more personable, more...likable."

Julien cocked his head to the side. "You're nervous."

"I'm—"

"Nervous," Julien said again, and his grin grew wider until Priest glared at him.

"And if I am? Why does that make you so happy?"

"Because you're never nervous," Julien said. "In fact, you were the one who was the most excited to come up here. I almost feel like I should go and wake Robbie for this."

Priest shook his head, and Julien chuckled.

"*Je suis désolé*," Julien said, but judging by his smiling eyes, Priest highly doubted it.

"You will be if you don't stop taking such joy from my misery. Why is it you're so understanding with Robert, but my nerves amuse you?"

Julien leaned in and brushed his lips over the top of Priest's. "Because it's nice to be reminded that you're like us from time to time."

"As opposed to?"

"A hero," Julien said. "My hero. Two times over now."

Priest wrapped his arms around Julien's waist and said, "I'm just a man, *mon cœur*."

"You're a man in love," Julien said, and aimed his eyes up at the guesthouse.

"You would be right. And that's why I'm nervous. I was the first time around, too."

Julien took Priest's face between his hands and said, "You have no reason to be nervous." Priest put his forehead to Julien's and shut his eyes. "You didn't then, and you don't now. The man up in that bed worships the ground you walk on, Joel. His parents have seen that all weekend."

Priest reached for Julien's hands and nodded.

"You don't believe me, do you?" Julien said.

"I think you're a little bit biased. But it's in my favor, so I'll take it."

They turned to walk across the driveway, where the lights were still strung and bags of garbage had been collected from the night before, and as they headed up the back stairs to the main house, the door opened and Robbie's mother called out, "*Buongiorno.*"

While Priest and Julien might not have understood a lot of the words they'd heard last night, that one was fairly obvious.

"*Bonjour,*" Julien replied, as Priest said, "Good morning."

They climbed the stairs, and when they reached the top, Sofia beamed at both of them but reached out to pat Priest on the arm.

"How are you feeling this morning?"

Mortified, Priest thought. So much for Robbie's parents not seeing. Best to apologize now. "A little bit embarrassed," Priest said, and smiled. "Sorry for my behavior last night. I—"

"Your behavior?" she said, frowning.

"Yes. I had a little too much—"

"Fun, I hope. The girls told us you are quite the dancer. I only wish I'd gotten to see."

Julien snorted.

"I, um…" Priest stumbled around looking for the right words to say to Sofia and ended up going off on a tangent. "I actually really enjoy dancing to the classics. I'm a big fan of Sinatra, so—"

"Ol' Blue Eyes?" Sofia's expression lit up, and she grabbed hold of Priest's hand, and before he could say another word, she led him inside and called out, "Antonio!"

Priest glanced over his shoulder to make sure Julien was coming wherever he was being taken, and as they made their way through the kitchen, they spotted Valerie slumped over at the kitchen table.

"Valerie, where'd your pa go?" Sofia asked.

Valerie winced and barely looked up as she pointed toward the living room.

"Ignore her," Sofia said. "She drank too much last night."

Didn't he know it. But Priest was pleased to note that he looked a little better off than she did.

"Antonio?" Sofia called out again.

"I'm in here," Robbie's father called from down the hall, and before Priest could pass along his condolences—or tell Valerie he was never taking another drink from her again—Sofia was leading them down the hall.

When they reached the brightly lit living room, Priest spotted Antonio sitting in the well-worn recliner. He looked exactly the way Priest imagined a father should look on a Sunday morning, with a newspaper open and a pair of eyeglasses perched on the end of his nose.

He was wearing navy lounge pants, a white t-shirt, and a blue robe, and when he saw Priest and Julien walk in the room, Antonio closed the paper and set it down on his lap.

"I didn't think we'd see you two up this early," he said, and then his eyes landed on Priest, and he smirked, much the same way his son did. "Especially you."

Okay, Priest thought. *I have some work cut out for me there.*

"We tend to be early risers," Julien said, coming to Priest's rescue.

"I bet Robbie loves that."

Julien laughed. "He hates it."

"I believe you. He was a nightmare to wake up for school."

"He really was," Sofia said. "Always wanted to be up early enough to get ready, but complained the entire time. He was worse than the girls. Except for Felicity. I swear, those two have always been thick as thieves. They could've been twins."

At the mention of twins, Priest looked at Julien to make sure he was okay, and the warm smile his husband directed toward Sofia solidified just how far Julien had come over the months.

"I had a twin sister, Jacquelyn," Julien said. "So I understand that closeness for sure."

As the past tense of that comment registered, Sofia said, "I'm sorry if I—"

"*Non, non.* Please don't be sorry. In fact, this weekend with you and your family has been wonderful. And if it wasn't for your son, I wouldn't be able to talk so freely about her today."

Sofia looked to her husband, and Antonio acknowledged Julien's comment with a nod before clearing his throat and saying to his wife, "Did you need me for something?"

"What? Oh, no," she said, and then beamed at Priest. "I came in here to tell you that this young man has a soft spot for your idol."

"My—"

"Ol' Blue Eyes."

"You like Sinatra?" Antonio said, and then got to his feet, tossing the paper down in his chair.

"I do," Priest said. "Very much."

Antonio looked Priest up and down but said nothing, then he made his way over to the large shelf that lined one of the living room walls. "Come with me."

When they'd all been in there the day before, they hadn't really gotten a chance to look around. But as they moved closer to the shelf, Priest noticed it was full of books and photographs, and saw several of Robbie. Some on his own and some with his sisters.

"Cute, wasn't he?"

Priest was once again shocked by Antonio. He was so accepting of his son, and for Priest and Julien, that was such a foreign concept that it was both strange and beautiful to behold.

"Still is," Priest said, and Julien added, "But we probably shouldn't tell him. He'll use it against us."

Antonio let out a booming laugh. "That he will. My boy is shameless."

"Your boy is wonderful," Priest said without even planning to, and Antonio sobered in an instant and pinned him with a look Priest knew well. It was protective and one hundred percent a warning.

Antonio said, "I'm glad you know that."

"We do," Priest said, and Antonio nodded and reached for the two handles on the shelf.

As he pulled them open, an old turntable came into view, and on several shelves above it was a vinyl collection that would rival any record store.

"*Mon Dieu*," Julien said. "That's a lot of records."

"Damn right," Antonio said, pride filling his voice. "I've been collecting for a lot of years. That shelf right there, that's my man Frank."

Priest's eyes widened. "I'm impressed."

"I'd be disappointed if you weren't. What's your favorite song?"

CONFESSIONS: THE PRINCESS, THE PRICK & THE PRIEST

Priest shrugged. "How can you pick?"

Antonio whacked him on the arm. "You can't. But there's always one or two."

Priest nodded as he looked at Julien. "You're right. I'd say 'Young at Heart' and 'I've Got you Under My Skin'—"

"That's for other people," Antonio said. "We all have those songs. What about for *you*. What's your song? We all have one."

It was slightly uncanny how well Antonio read him, and when Priest opened his mouth to say, Antonio held up a finger.

"I've got it," he said as he reached for a 45, pulled it down, and handed it to Priest. "Tell me I'm wrong."

Priest wanted to, but he was too blown away by the fact that Antonio was spot-on.

"My Way" had been Priest's favorite Sinatra song since the first time he'd heard it. It was the song he'd always lived by. The one that had given him the courage and strength to work and become more than where he'd come from. To not live his life like his father, but instead his own way.

"I can't tell you that. You're spot-on," Priest said, and this time when he looked at Robbie's father, he didn't feel nervous. He felt a sense of acceptance and a strange sense of camaraderie. And that was the only reason he could think of as to why he blurted out what he did next: "We want to marry your son."

The entire room fell silent, and Priest looked over Antonio's shoulder to where Julien stood beside Sofia. Her eyes were as round as saucers, and Julien looked slightly caught off guard. But not because they hadn't planned this, more because Priest had gone off script.

The one person in the room that didn't appear all that shocked, though, was the one who was regarding Priest very carefully.

"You want an awful lot, don't you?" Antonio said, and glanced at Julien. "Both of you do."

Julien stepped around to join Priest. It was imperative that Robbie's parents understood that he and Julien were in this together. That what Priest had just said came from both of them.

"Yes," Priest said, and Julien added, "We do."

"Is..." Sofia started, and then placed a hand on her chest. "Is that even possible? How can you do that?"

"By having a ceremony," Priest said, blunt and to the point, and Julien smiled before turning to Robbie's parents to explain. "We want to invite the people he loves to celebrate this with him. We know we can't have a traditional, legal marriage, per se. But Priest's working on the best way to make everything we own legally equal among the three of us, and we have a plan to make him feel just as connected, just as loved, as we are."

As Robbie's parents stared at the two of them, Priest wondered if this was the moment where they told them to leave and never come back. He wouldn't be surprised at all. This was a lot for most. But then again, most people didn't have someone as unique as Robert Bianchi as their son.

"You're going to make sure he's taken care of?" Antonio said.

Priest and Julien nodded.

"Yes."

"*Oui.*"

Antonio looked to his wife and shook his head. "That boy of ours. You always said he marched to the beat of his own drum."

Priest was positive his heart was beating in time to that drum right now, as he looked into Julien's eyes and saw the same yearning for acceptance from these two, because they both knew their lives would be so much better with this family in it.

"Have you asked Robert yet?" Sofia said.

"*Non,*" Julien said. "We've wanted to for a little while now. But not until we met all of you. Which is why we were so excited he finally brought us up here. We'd like your blessing before we ask him."

Sofia's eyes blurred as she looked to her husband and nodded.

"You have our blessing," Antonio said. "Mainly because I need two more men in the family to balance out all the estrogen. But if you hurt him—"

"We won't," they both said.

"—I will hurt you. *Capito?*"

As the same question from the first night was directed at them, they both answered much more quickly this time around: "We do."

"Okay," Antonio said, and held his hand out to Priest, and after he shook it, Antonio turned to Julien and did the same. "Then we wish you luck. It's probably good there's two of you, anyway. That boy is a handful."

Priest wasn't about to agree *or* disagree with that, and luckily for him, Sofia spoke up.

"All this talk about getting engaged—can I show you two something?" she said.

"Of course," Julien said, as she reached for one of the thick photo albums up on the shelf. As she flipped through it, Antonio put on one of Sinatra's records, and when she finally found what she was looking for, Sofia handed the album over to them.

"I've been telling Robbie and the girls about this place for years —any excuse, really. My only regret is I didn't take more photos than this one," she said, as she pointed to the gorgeous black-and-white image. "That's where we got engaged. Nothing but the two of us...and love. Beautiful, isn't it?"

It certainly was, and as Sofia used this as her latest excuse to revisit the past, both Julien and Priest knew one thing right then. However they planned to do this, they wanted it to be something that Robbie was telling years later, with as much love in his eyes as Sofia.

CHAPTER THIRTEEN

We're never going to be able
to say no to him again, are we?
- Julien & Priest

JULIEN STEPPED OUT of the bustling Chicago street Wednesday afternoon and into the elegant marble lobby of the building that housed Mitchell & Madison. He'd called ahead of time to check if Priest was back from his morning in court, and then Julien had suggested he swing by with lunch.

After their weekend up at the Bianchis', the two of them had realized it was going to take some stealthy planning to pull off any kind of surprise engagement for someone as curious as Robbie. So they'd decided their best course of action was to only talk about it away from the house, where inquisitive ears might overhear.

Julien got in the elevator and punched the button for Priest's floor, and as he leaned up against the back wall, several other people got on including...

"Julien. Hello," Logan Mitchell said.

"*Bonjour*. How are you?" Julien asked.

"Good. Good. Just getting back from a lunch meeting. You?"

Julien held up the black bag with his name on it. "Just going to one."

"I'd never usually be jealous of Priest, but I've got to say, having lunch delivered from your restaurant makes me a little green."

Julien grinned. "I find that feeding him keeps him agreeable."

"I'll have to remember that," Logan said, and slipped a hand into his pocket. "He said you guys had a good time up at the Bianchis' this weekend."

"We did. Robbie's family is exactly as you'd imagine them to be."

"So, loud, excitable, and all talking a mile a minute?"

Julien started to laugh, thinking of Robbie's sisters. "Exactly like that. They're wonderful. It was really quite remarkable to see."

"I'm sure." Logan chuckled. "*And* you made it back in one piece. I was a little worried we'd be down a partner after this."

"*Oui*. We survived. We even managed to win over his parents."

As the elevator hit the floor and the doors slid open, Julien stepped out.

"I have no problem seeing that with you," Logan said. "But Priest? I would be lying if I didn't say I was slightly concerned."

Julien walked with Logan toward the receptionist, and when she looked up, Logan said, "Any calls, Tiffany?"

"No," she said with a winning smile. "But Sherry's looking for you."

"Got it. If you see her before I do, can you let her know I'm back?"

"Will do," she said, and then turned her eyes toward Julien. "Mr. Priestley said you can head straight back, as long as you brought food."

Logan glanced over his shoulder at Julien, who held the bag up. "I don't know about this jovial side of Priest. Him making wisecracks just doesn't seem right."

Julien followed Logan down the hall past the clear walls of the conference room. "He's happy."

"Exactly. It's disturbing," Logan said, and when they reached the doors that led into Logan's office, he stopped with his hand on the door handle. "Have a good lunch, and *if* he happens to leave any leftovers..."

"He never does," Julien said, and waved as Logan disappeared inside his office and called out, "It was worth a try."

Julien walked to the door of the middle office, and when he knocked and heard Priest say, "Come in," a smile crossed Julien's face.

Julien pushed open the door, and when Priest looked up from his computer and spotted him, he smiled.

"Bonjour, monsieur. Je crois que vous avez commandé un déjeuner?"

Priest sat back in his seat, his eyes eating up the space between them as Julien walked in. *"Je l'ai fait.* But now I find myself hungry for something other than food."

Julien smirked, and then pointed to the door he'd just shut. "So you won't mind if I take this down to Logan, then? He was just asking."

"Don't you dare," Priest said. "Bring it, and yourself, over here."

Julien looked around Priest's office and smiled at the framed diplomas hanging on the wall, the dramatic silhouetted cityscape of Chicago, and, of course, the enormous bookshelf that housed Priest's law and reference books. There were tasteful knickknacks, along with framed photos of Priest with his two men, and to this day, it still surprised Julien that Priest had agreed to let Robbie have free rein to do as he pleased to his office.

He had done a fantastic job, of course, and considering Robbie's flair for everything bright and happy, he'd managed to temper those tendencies and keep Priest's workspace more Priest. But it was still quite the shock to see the place look so...permanent.

"Where are your manners, *mon amour*? I slaved over a hot oven to make this for you."

"You slave over a hot oven every day for strangers," Priest pointed out. "But if you bring it over here, I promise to show you how grateful I am."

Julien put the bag on top of Priest's desk and then walked around it to greet his husband with a kiss. Julien shut his eyes and let himself savor the taste of Priest, and as he went to pull away, Priest took hold of his face and deepened the connection.

Julien stumbled forward slightly and had to put a hand on the back of Priest's chair, but when Priest angled his head up, Julien took full advantage. He cradled one side of Priest's face and grazed his thumb along his beard, as he teased and tormented Priest with his tongue until a growl left him.

"I think that's sufficiently grateful," Julien said. "Any more and lunch won't be what you are eating."

Priest smiled as Julien moved back to the other side of his desk, but before he sat down, he pulled out two round containers and put one in front of Priest along with a bottle of water and his utensils. "Today you are eating *Blanquette de veau.*"

"Which is?"

"In layman's terms?" Julien said. "A veal and vegetable stew of sorts, cooked in a heavy cream sauce."

Once they were settled and had uncovered their meals, Priest took a deep inhale and said, "Everyone on this floor is about to hate me. This smells fantastic, Julien."

"*Bien.* A happy wife means a happy life."

Priest raised an eyebrow, and when Julien laughed, Priest said, "No wives allowed. But speaking of marriage, let's see if we can come to an agreement on how we want to ask Robbie to join ours."

PRIEST PICKED UP the fork and took his first bite. As the delicious flavors hit his taste buds, he hummed. The dish was incredible. Actually, it reminded him a lot of the chef who had made it. It was warm, rich, creamy, and very French, and when he looked across his desk to see Julien watching his every move, Priest said, "This is divine."

A pleased expression crossed Julien's face, and Priest loved the fact that, even to this day, after all the accolades and training, this talented man still looked to him for approval.

"That makes me happy," Julien said, as if he could somehow read Priest's mind.

"I know. And that, in turn, makes me happy."

"Of course it does," Julien said as he picked up his own fork and began to eat. "Have you given any more thought to what we could do for Robbie?"

Priest nodded as he reached for the bottle of water and twisted off the lid. "A little bit. What about you?"

"The same. I feel like however we do it, it should be—"

"Big?" Priest suggested, remembering just how much Robbie enjoyed a grand gesture.

"Not necessarily big," Julien said, and then took another bite of food. "But certainly something memorable."

"Agreed. And something he won't guess."

Julien nodded as he picked up the baguette he'd brought and ripped off the end. As he dunked it into the sauce and took a bite, Priest said, "I think we can safely cross off singing."

Julien swallowed and brought his hand to his mouth as he laughed. "Especially if we want him to say yes."

Priest glared at his husband. "I *meant* because we'd already done it. But thank you for that, Julien."

"*Je t'en prie,*" Julien said. "We could go on a vacation."

"I thought about that too," Priest said. "But he might think something's up if we plan a getaway out of the blue."

"You're right. Maybe we can save that for the honeymoon. *Paris?*"

Priest's cock jerked at the way that city's name sounded falling off Julien's tongue, and as he shifted in his seat, Julien's mouth curved into a sensual smile.

Just thinking about the three of them spending a week or two in that city had Priest wanting to pick up his phone to book the tickets. "That is a marvelous idea, Mr. Thornton."

"I think so. I'd like to show our *princesse* my home country, and enjoy the both of you as only the French can."

"Jesus, Julien. Stop looking at me like that."

"I'm just eating my lunch."

"You're playing with fire is what you're doing."

"My apologies. Let's get back to what we were discussing."

Priest shifted on his seat again, and Julien's warm chuckle filled the room.

"Keep it up, *mon cœur...*" Priest said.

"I think I already am."

Priest gritted his teeth and reached for the baguette. As he ripped a piece off and tried to satisfy at least *one* of his hungers, Julien said, "Okay. Tell me some of the things you were thinking."

Priest finished his mouthful and looked at the notepad on his desk. *A get-together with family, a private dinner, a big announcement somewhere public.* But none of that seemed right now, and they both wanted this perfect for Robbie.

"I don't like any of these," Priest admitted, and then both of their phones chimed.

Robbie: Since I have to work this weekend, how about we make date night tomorrow night?

With the three of them having such busy schedules, they'd decided early in their relationship that one night a week, the three of them would go out somewhere on a date. If it fell on Robbie's weekend, they generally picked a night he was free during the week. They could go anywhere, do anything—all that was required was that all *three* of them be there.

Priest and Julien reached for their phones at the same time.

Priest: Sounds good, sweetheart. Julien? Are you free?

Julien eyed him over the desk. "You're bad."

Priest smirked and took another bite of his food as Julien typed.

Julien: I can shuffle some things around. Did you have something in mind you wanted to do?

"He would kick our asses if he knew we were eating your food without him," Priest said, finishing off his lunch.

"It's for a good reason," Julien said. "But I also saved him a dish, so act surprised when I give it to him tonight."

Priest chuckled as another message came through.

Robbie: Welll, I thought it might be fun if we all went out dancing. You know, since Priest owes me.

Priest's laughter came to an abrupt halt as he read that, and Julien grinned.

"You didn't think you'd get out of that, did you?" Julien asked.

"I was hoping," Priest mumbled.

"No such luck. Once he saw you with Valerie, it was all over for you. Our *princesse* won't be satisfied until he's rubbed her off your body...and mind."

When neither of them answered right away, another message came through.

Robbie: Aww, come on. You know you want to, Priest...

As a kissy-face emoji followed, Priest shook his head. "We're never going to be able to say no to him again now that he knows what buttons to push."

"You've got a point," Julien said as he texted back, and when Julien's message came through, Priest said, "Traitor."

Julien: I'd love to spend the night bumping and grinding with you and Priest.

Robbie: Mmm...think about it, Priest. You, me, and Julien, all rubbing up against each other.

Priest: I can do that every morning in the shower.

Robbie: Not to hot, sexed-up music. And *not* in public. That makes it even hotter.

"Fucking hell," Priest said as he aimed his eyes at Julien. "I'm not going to win this, am I?"

Julien didn't have to say it; Priest already knew the answer—no.

Priest: Okay. Pick a place. But can you and Julien please stop talking about grinding all over me, I'm trying to work.

"Liar," Julien said, as he got to his feet and started to pack away the dirty containers.

Robbie: Fine. I was just going to go and get ready for work anyway. I'll think about what moves I want to put on you in there. You know, when I'm all naked, and wet, and—

Priest: Goodbye, Robert.

Robbie: LOL...

Troublemaker.

Julien: Au revoir, princesse.

As they put their phones down, Priest said, "His parents were right: that man is a handful."

Julien stilled, his hands in the bag. "Do you have a little more time right now?"

"Yes, why?"

"I think I just had an idea on what we could do."

"Really?"

Julien sat back down in his chair and grinned. "*Vraiment,*" he said, and as he began to talk, Priest agreed.

Julien's idea was perfect, and not an hour later, the two of them had put together the perfect plan to make Robert Bianchi theirs.

CHAPTER FOURTEEN

I just love his feisty mouth.
Fuck yes, I do ~ Priest

IS THERE ANYTHING sexier than the throbbing beat of a song designed to make your body vibrate, your blood pump, and your inhibitions take the night off?

Well, okay, maybe there's two sexier things—

"Hand, please." The burly man stationed at the front door of CRUSH interrupted Robbie's thoughts as the couple in front of him, Julien, and Priest, disappeared inside.

Robbie offered his hand as a queen might a commoner, and when the big guy took it and pressed the stamp to the back of his palm, he winked at Robbie and said, "You're good to go, pretty boy."

A throat clearing behind Robbie had the man looking over his shoulder. And while Robbie had never really seen the appeal of having a possessive partner in the past, knowing that Julien and Priest were likely giving this guy a look that screamed, *Back the fuck off,* made not only his heart happy, but also something a little further south.

Robbie moved to the side so Julien could step forward, and as he held his hand out, it was all Robbie could do not to reach down and adjust his misbehaving cock.

Julien looked positively yummy tonight. His black pants sat low on his hips, and he'd matched them with a tight white V-neck. It molded to every lean muscle of his body, and around his tanned throat Julien had added a leather strap that made Robbie's mouth water.

As the guy stamped Julien's hand, Julien looked at Robbie and said, "*Une princesse pimpante et un prêtre possessif. Que Dieu me vienne en aide ce soir.*"

Seriously, could he get any hotter?

After months spent with his Frenchman, and taking some online courses, Robbie caught most of what he'd said—or, at least, he thought he did: *A pretty princess and a possessive priest. God help me tonight.*

But Robbie was more inclined to phrase it like: *A sexy Frenchman and a sinful-looking Priest. God, please turn a blind eye tonight.*

Because he was *not* about to behave himself once he got them inside.

As the bouncer said, "You're good," Robbie grinned at Julien and held his hand out. When Julien took it, he tugged Robbie forward and said against his ear, "You're going to drive us crazy in there, aren't you?"

Robbie leaned back slightly and put his fingers to his chest. "Who, *moi?*"

Julien chuckled as he let him go. "*Oui, toi.*"

Robbie couldn't help his mischievous grin as his eyes shifted to Priest, who was now standing in front of the bouncer with his hand being stamped, *and damn*, Priest looked...awesome. Like that first night Robbie had seen them at CRUSH. Broody, command-ing, and powerful, and boy did it work for him.

In jeans and a black button-up shirt, Priest wasn't wearing

anything special. But his thick forearms were bare, and Robbie couldn't help but imagine them wrapped around him. And make no mistake, he planned to have them wound *tight* around him, as one of those hands moved up under his top, and the other down inside his skinny black—

"Robert?"

Priest's voice snapped Robbie back to the present.

"Are you ready?"

In more ways than one, Robbie thought. But since he actually wanted to experience dancing with these two tonight, he decided to keep that to himself a little longer.

"Yes," Robbie said, and batted his lashes, and when Priest kissed his temple, a shiver of anticipation raced down Robbie's spine.

"Then get your ass inside, before I have to fight everyone off it."

Loving the territorial light in Priest's eyes, Robbie touched the tip of his tongue to his top lip, and Julien muttered, "*Merde.*"

"Get inside, Robert," Priest said. "*Now.*" And when Robbie turned to do just that with an extra swing to his hips, Priest swatted him on the ass and said, "Flirt."

FUCKING HELL. PRIEST had known tonight was going to be a test of his self-restraint, especially after Robbie had walked out of their bathroom dressed in skinny black jeans and a black mesh top. But an hour or so in of having that tight body grinding all over him, and his cock was so damn hard he was surprised it hadn't punched through the zipper of his jeans.

Ever since they'd stepped back into the club where they'd first pursued Robbie, to right now, as he stood at the bar taking a self-imposed timeout, Priest had been having a difficult time not giving in to his need to drag Robbie and Julien away somewhere private. But they'd promised Robbie a night out—a night out dancing, to be specific—and Priest wasn't about to shortchange him. Especially since it was abundantly clear how much Robbie had missed it.

This was his element. It was as though the music energized Robbie, and Priest had made a mental note to make sure he and Julien brought their boyfriend out dancing more often.

The bartender slid his drink across the counter, and Priest downed it in one gulp and told his dick to calm the hell down. It would get its reward *after* it made it through the night, that he was sure of. But right now, he wanted to get back to his men.

Priest made his way through the sweaty sea of gyrating bodies, and as he got closer to the spot where he'd left Julien and Robbie, he spotted them when the bright lights flicked their way.

Robbie had his mesh-covered arms wound around Julien's neck, and Julien's hands were molded to Robbie's ass. Their mouths were fused in a tongue-thrusting kiss, and as Priest got closer, his eyes trailed down to where their bodies met below the waist.

The pulse of the music made Priest's cock pound even harder as he watched Robbie bump and grind against the erection Priest knew Julien was sporting, and when Julien raised his head and began to bite along Robbie's jaw to his neck, Robbie tipped his head back and Julien's fingers tightened on his ass.

They were unbelievably sexy together, and the only way Priest could imagine it any better was if they were stripped of their clothes.

As Priest moved closer, he detoured around behind Robbie until he was in Julien's line of sight, and when Julien's eyes caught on him, Priest groaned.

Jesus, Julien looked about two seconds away from dragging Robbie to the floor, and while Julien was less worried these days about keeping his relationship a national secret, fucking their boyfriend in public might still be a little too much.

Priest stopped several feet away from them and made sure to keep a distance, much like he had that first night—and just like then, Julien knew exactly what Priest was thinking.

Julien moved his mouth up to Robbie's ear and whispered in it, and Robbie turned around and fit his tight little ass against Julien's front. As the music switched to a song that slowed to a steady, hip-grinding beat, Julien reached for Robbie's wrists and brought them up behind his neck, displaying their princess for Priest in the best way imaginable.

Robbie's eyes were shut as the music coursed through him, and Julien smoothed his hands down Robbie's sides and covered Robbie's erection. Robbie's sweet lips parted on a needy gasp, and Julien's eyes searched Priest out as he spoke again in Robbie's ear.

Robbie's eyes fluttered open, and Priest knew the second he spotted him. One of the arms he had stretched back around Julien's neck flexed, and then he reached down with his other hand to press Julien's harder against his cock.

That's right, sweetheart, dance for me, Priest thought, as Robbie and Julien picked up the rhythm of the song, and Robbie began to get off to the beat of it.

Priest clenched his jaw tight. He wanted to be pressed up against Robbie's tempting body, to kiss the lips that were parted in pleasure, and with that thought in mind, Priest began to stalk his men through the handful of strangers in his way.

Julien smirked like he knew they'd likely pushed him to his limits, while Robbie dragged his and Julien's hands up under his top until they were stroking his naked skin.

As Priest got closer, he began to imagine all the ways he was going to teach them the lesson of what happened when they teased him, but that was rudely interrupted when someone else got in his way.

"*ROBBIE?*"

THE SOUND of Robbie's name being shouted over the music penetrated Julien's lust-hazed brain. He'd been well into his fantasy of Priest reaching them, sandwiching Robbie nice and tight between them, so they could get their *princesse* so needy and desperate that he demanded they take him somewhere private to finish him off.

But now that was being interrupted by a good-looking guy with dark hair and brown eyes, who had moved to stand opposite them. But more *importantly,* he'd moved to stand between *them* and Priest.

As Robbie's view of Priest was blocked, and the man now in front of him seemed to register, Robbie froze, and his arms fell away.

"Nathan?" Robbie said over the music.

Nathan? The Nathan? As in Robbie's ex? Putain, this was not going to end well. And even though Julien now knew who he was, his first impression of him hadn't changed. Nathan *was* a good-looking guy. *Connard.*

"Yeah, hi," Nathan said, not even sparing Julien a glance, as he flashed a smile that, unfortunately, made his face even more attractive. "Wow. You look great, babe. Gorgeous."

Julien could almost feel Robbie's hackles rise at the shock in Nathan's voice, and just as he was about to reach out and offer a comforting hand, Robbie angled his head up and said, "Of course I do. I went back to being *me.* You know, the kind of gorgeous you don't like."

Nathan took a step closer. "That's not what I meant—"

"No?" Robbie said. "Then what did you mean? You didn't think I'd hide away and mourn *you* forever, did you? Oh, honey, please. My shine came back as soon as the dark cloud I'd been smothered by left. Or, I'm sorry, threw me out and *fired* me."

Nathan half grinned. "Ah, I've missed that. You always were feisty. I've actually been wanting to call you."

Is this guy serious? After the way he'd treated Robbie, Julien was shocked Nathan had the audacity to come anywhere near him. But then again, he didn't seem too bright. He hadn't even noticed that Priest had just come to a stop behind him.

"*Call* me?" Robbie said, and then laughed. "Why would you

want to call me when you were too embarrassed to even talk to me in public?"

"Robbie..." Nathan paused, and when it looked as though he were going to reach out and touch Robbie, Julien decided it was time to make his presence known.

He stepped up behind Robbie and placed a hand on his waist, and Robbie startled as though he'd forgotten Julien was there.

"*Ça va, princesse?*" Julien asked, knowing Robbie would pick up on the question, but at the same time sparing him the indignity of asking it out loud.

"*Oui,*" Robbie said, as he turned his head to look at Julien.

Robbie's eyes were still dilated from the arousal that had been riding him before they'd been so rudely interrupted, and when he licked his glossy lips, Julien knew Robbie saw the same desire in his.

"Hey?" Nathan said, inserting himself again into a moment where he was not welcome. "Aren't you that...that chef guy?"

Robbie's spine stiffened at Nathan's words, but Julien looked around Robbie's shoulder at the man who had once tried to dull their *princesse* and said, "*Oui,* I am. And you're that Nathan guy."

Nathan frowned, obviously confused. But when his eyes lowered to the hand Julien had on Robbie's waist, Julien tightened his fingers and stepped in even closer to Robbie. *That's right, monsieur—Il est à moi.*

"Yeah. Uh, that's right," Nathan said as he looked to Robbie. "I'm Robbie's—"

"Nothing." Priest's voice was firm when it finally cut in. "But I'm Priest, and they are mine."

Nathan's head whipped around, and Julien heard Robbie suck in a breath—no doubt as turned on by Priest in that moment as Julien was.

Arrogant, possessive, and clearly annoyed, Priest was eyeing Nathan as though he were a bug he wanted to crush. But before Priest could say another word, Robbie reminded them all that he was quite capable of crushing that bug himself.

"Was there something else you wanted, Nathan?" Robbie asked.

Nathan's eyes ping-ponged between the three of them, and Julien made sure to wrap an arm around Robbie's waist and kiss the side of his neck, making it clear who Robbie was there with tonight.

"If not, do you mind moving?" Robbie said, as he leaned back into Julien and rolled his hips. "I was really looking forward to having *both* my men's hands all over me tonight, and you're in Priest's way."

At Robbie's declaration, Priest's eyes had a dangerous look. The kind of danger Julien and Robbie loved getting into when it came to Priest.

Nathan stepped out of the way, proving that he did have a brain, and eyed Priest the way a man did when he knew he had no hope. And Priest? It was as though he'd forgotten Nathan was even there.

Priest was all about the men he considered his, and when he ran his finger along Robbie's lips and said, "Have I mentioned how much I love this *feisty* mouth of yours?" Julien knew Robbie had no cause to worry. He was about to get both of their hands all over him right now, judging by the look on Priest's face.

CHAPTER FIFTEEN

Tu es si beau, princesse
- Julien

"WE'RE LEAVING."

PRIEST'S voice was rough, and his grip tight, as he guided Robbie off the dance floor and toward the closest exit. Julien wasn't far behind them, as Priest pushed his way through the crowd and out the doors into the steamy night air.

Robbie couldn't believe what had just happened, and was totally annoyed that Nathan had tried to ruin their date night out. *Nothing like an ex to cock-block a situation*—and the situation had been Julien grinding all over him and Priest eye-fucking them from across the dance floor.

Things had been hot, and about to get a whole lot hotter, until good old Nathan had to go and ruin everything.

Ugh. If it hadn't been for the moment when Julien had all but marked him, and Priest had incinerated Nathan with a death glare,

Robbie might've had to write the whole evening off and ask for a do-over.

As it was, he would file this memory away for whenever he wanted to privately gloat to himself about the night he finally got to tell Nathan to shove it where *his* sun would no longer shine.

"Priest? Priest, would you slow down a second?" Robbie asked, as Priest marched down the side street. But when Priest didn't respond, Robbie shook his head. "Okay, so is this like your version of a caveman? Where you drag me away and remind me who I belong to?"

When Priest still said nothing, Robbie continued, "I mean, it's super hot, don't get me wrong. But didn't we park in the other direction? Out on the main road?"

Priest glanced over his shoulder and said in a clipped voice, "Julien? Here."

Here? Robbie looked at the dark, narrow alcove to Priest's right that had a boarded-up door and empty bottles on the ground, and was about to ask what the hell Priest was talking about, when —*oomph*—Robbie found himself pulled off from the street and pushed up against the brick wall.

Priest was on Robbie's right, closest to the door, and Julien was on his left with his back to the street. The two of them crowded in on either side of Robbie, and his breath left him in a rush.

"Do you know what I hate more than annoying ex-boyfriends getting in my way?" Priest said.

Robbie swallowed as Priest's scorching gaze zeroed in on his lips. "No…"

"I *hate* being interrupted when I'm about to taste you."

Oh, sweet Jesus, I want that, Robbie thought, and he was willing to get down on the filthy ground in his two-hundred-dollar pair of jeans and beg for it. But luckily for him, begging wasn't required.

Priest reached for his chin, angled his face, and then, without another word, took Robbie's mouth in a savage kiss. He bit and sucked at Robbie's lips, and when Robbie opened for him, Priest speared his tongue inside.

Robbie could taste a hint of whiskey on Priest's tongue, and as Priest tangled with him, he smoothed his hand down to Robbie's shoulder and tugged him forward until Priest's back hit the boarded-up door, and Robbie was plastered up against his front.

Robbie put his hands on Priest's chest and moaned, as he licked into Priest's mouth and writhed up against his muscled body. Priest's hand found his ass, and as he hauled Robbie closer, he bucked his hips forward and grunted.

"God, you're fucking pretty," Priest said. "It's probably good I didn't get my hands on you after watching you grind all over Julien."

Robbie shuddered and his chest heaved against Priest's, and before he could find his voice, Julien moved in behind him and pressed a kiss to the back of Robbie's neck.

Robbie's eyes fell shut and he clenched his teeth.

Are they crazy? Any more of this and they're going to make me—

"Come for us," Priest whispered against Robbie's lips. "I want to watch you. Close your eyes, lean back into Julien, and come for us."

Robbie sucked in a gasp of air, as Julien's hands moved to his hips and he pulled him away from Priest to fit his cock against the crack of Robbie's ass.

"He...here?" Robbie said, as Priest pushed off the door.

"Yes," Priest said, and kissed the corner of Robbie's lips as he flicked open the button on his skinny jeans. "Right here, Robert. In my mouth."

THE LOOK ON Robbie's face as Priest lowered to his knees made Priest's already hard cock impossibly harder. He would've given anything for the three of them to be home right then. But since they weren't, this would have to do—because he couldn't wait.

Watching Robbie stand up for himself back there in the club

had taken Priest's annoyance at being cock-blocked and turned it to fuel for his already out-of-control desire.

Fierce and sassy had never been so fucking sexy, as Robbie had turned on Nathan and finally owned who he was. The fact that Robbie had added in that he belonged to *them* was just icing on the cake as far as Priest was concerned, and when his knees hit the ground, Priest was determined to eat that cake. Right here. Right now.

Priest looked up at the two hovering above him, and as the sound of a car horn blasted in the distance, he felt his lips curve. *Hotter in public,* their princess had said. *Okay then, let's do this.*

"Julien," Priest said, and when Julien's eyes found his, Priest pressed the heel of his hand to his cock. That look was nearly enough to get him off. Julien looked close to ripping Robbie's jeans off and fucking him to orgasm. But Priest didn't want them to get arrested, he just wanted to get Robbie off—and so, apparently, did his husband. "Unzip his jeans."

Robbie cursed, and Julien smirked as he reached for Robbie's zipper and drew it down. Priest's eyes immediately fell to the open denim, and he didn't wait around after that.

He pulled the stiff material apart, and when Robbie's flushed cock sprang free, Priest looked up and then leaned forward to lick a path up the underside to the plump head.

"*God,*" Robbie said, and reached for Priest's hair.

As his fingers twisted in the thick strands, Priest glanced at Julien and said, "Feed him to me."

"Oh fuck. Fuck me," Robbie said as Julien wrapped his fingers around Robbie's dick and directed it toward Priest's mouth.

When the salty evidence of Robbie's arousal coated Priest's lips, he growled and then shifted to rub his beard up along the side of Robbie's sensitive flesh, and Robbie's hands tightened.

"That's it, sweetheart," Priest said. "Hold on." Then Priest opened his mouth and swallowed Robbie to the back of his throat.

The shout that filled the darkened street was quickly muffled, and when Priest looked up and saw Julien's hand over Robbie's mouth and Robbie's teeth biting into it to keep quiet, Priest had to practically strangle his own dick to keep from coming.

Fuck they were sexy, and when Robbie punched forward, shoving back between Priest's lips, Priest closed his eyes and let Robbie go at him. He reveled at the painful pulls to his hair and the desperate, almost frantic way Robbie was pumping in and out of his mouth.

It was dirty, rough, and one of the most erotic things Priest had ever seen or heard, and the muffled moans from Robbie made Priest want to give Julien something before Robbie came.

Since they couldn't get inside Robbie right now, Priest had another idea in mind, and as he drew his mouth off Robbie's cock, he dragged his teeth over his swollen lip and said, "Julien?"

Julien's fevered stare found his. *"Oui, mon amour?"*

Priest smiled at the ragged edge to Julien's voice, and he decided to test Robbie's French a little. *"Doigte notre princesse, pendant que je suce sa queue."*

Julien planted a kiss beneath Robbie's ear and asked, "Would you like that, *princesse?*"

Robbie nodded, his comprehension of the language now good enough that he'd worked out most of what Priest had said.

Now all Priest had to do was wait for Julien's next move.

JULIEN COULD FEEL Robbie's entire body vibrating against him, as he kissed his way up Robbie's ear and whispered, "Would you like my finger in you while you fuck Priest's mouth?"

Robbie nodded again, and Julien ground his aching dick against Robbie's ass before he sucked a finger into his mouth and slipped his hand down the back of Robbie's skinny jeans.

As he trailed his finger between Robbie's tight ass cheeks, they flexed, and Robbie whimpered, and when Julien massaged the pad of his index finger over Robbie's pucker, he said to Priest, *"Suce-le."*

Priest parted his lips, and this time Robbie slid inside his mouth without needing any instruction. Julien wound an arm around Robbie's waist, and as his finger penetrated the tight ring of muscle, Robbie slapped a palm on the brick wall beside them and bucked back, and Julien burrowed his finger in deeper.

"*Ah*, damn, Jules... Yeah, right there. Right fucking there."

Julien could see Priest's head moving up and down as Robbie's fingers twisted in his auburn hair, and when Julien sucked on Robbie's ear, he began to talk to him in French, knowing just how hot that got the both of them.

"*Tu es si beau, princesse. Étroit, chaud, comme l'enfer et le paradis à la fois.*"

Robbie's fingers tensed on the bricks, and as he thrust his hips forward, Julien massaged his prostate, and Robbie's head strained back until their cheeks were touching.

"*Encore. Encore,*" Robbie said, and Julien took his lips in a crushing kiss as he slid his finger free and then pushed it back in, rubbing up against the sensitive bundle of nerves. Robbie finally ripped his mouth away and dropped his arm from the brick to grab at Priest's hair.

A long groan left Robbie's lips as he stiffened and his ass clenched, and Julien wished like hell it was his cock inside of him as Robbie came hard down Priest's throat.

Robbie's breathing left him in ragged bursts as he leaned back in search of Julien's mouth. Julien took his lips, and as their tongues rubbed up against each other, Julien freed his hand and pulled Robbie back against him.

When he finally freed Robbie's mouth, they saw that Priest was standing as he reached for Julien, leaned in, and crushed their mouths together, sharing the delicious taste of Robbie.

Julien grunted as Priest growled against his lips, and he knew it would be a race as to *who* got in their *princesse* first tonight.

"Let's go," Priest said, and when they both turned to Robbie, he was re-buttoning his jeans. "Don't get too zipped up. You'll be lucky if you make it out of the garage with how hard the two of us are."

Robbie's eyes fell down to the erections straining behind Julien's and Priest's zippers. "Promise?"

Julien took Robbie's hand, tugged him forward, and kissed that sassy mouth of his. "*Promis.*"

"Shit, okay, let's go," Robbie said, and when they all stepped back out into the street and headed toward the car, he added, "So were you thinking against the wall? Or, *oooh*, over the hood of the car?"

"I swear to God, if you keep talking, it's going to be in the back seat of the car as soon as we get in it," Priest said, his control clearly being tested as much as Julien's.

"Promise?" Robbie said, and then laughed like the teasing, *satisfied* minx he was as they climbed in the car, their final destination and intention having erased all other things but the three of them from this night.

CHAPTER SIXTEEN

Uh, what the what?
- Robbie

"OKAY, I'M OUT unless you need anything else," Robbie said, as he walked out of the back room of The Popped Cherry with his messenger bag slung over his shoulder.

"I think I've got it under control," Tate said as he wiped down the bar. "You have a good break."

"Will do," Robbie said, and looked at his watch. "I shouldn't be too long. It's just down the street, and—"

"I'm sure I can manage." Tate chuckled and flashed that pearly-white grin of his. "Just remember, every minute you're late, your boss will dock your pay. He's mean like that."

Robbie rolled his eyes, Tate had never once docked his pay. He was the best boss Robbie had ever had. "You know, he *is* kind of a hard-ass."

As Robbie walked by, he made a show of lingering behind Tate

and dropping his eyes to emphasize exactly which *ass* he was refer-
ring to.

"I thought you were on your dinner break," Tate said, and
looked over his shoulder.

"I'm going. I'm just appreciating the view as I leave."

"Uh huh."

Robbie laughed and headed toward the back door, and as he
turned the handle and shoved it open, he called out over his shoulder, "Try not to miss me too much."

Tate shook his head and grinned. "I'll try my very hardest."

"See you in a bit." Robbie waved and stepped out into the
humid night air, and as it slapped him in the face, he tried to
remind himself to enjoy it while he could. Soon enough, the cooler
temperatures would come, and then the snow, and then the—*oooh,
the cuddling.*

Yeah, this winter was looking up for him. Even if he had to
hibernate, he didn't think it sounded all that bad if he got to be
locked in his house with Julien and Priest. In fact, he might just
pray a little for that exact scenario.

With that thought in mind, Robbie popped the locks of his car
and climbed inside. As he cranked the AC on high, he tossed his
bag on the passenger seat and sent off a quick text to Elliot to
make sure he was on his way.

Once he was all buckled in and his phone was in the mount,
Robbie flicked on his lights, put his car in reverse, and headed
down the narrow street behind the bar to the main road. As he sat
there waiting for a break in the traffic, his phone started to ring,
and when he saw who it was, he grinned.

It'd been nearly two weeks since the three of them had gone to
Oshkosh, and with his weekend off approaching once again, they'd
been debating on whether to go out and visit one of the local
wineries before it got too cold to go anywhere at all.

Robbie thought it was a fabulous idea. *Julien, Priest, and copious
amounts of wine? Count me in.* Plus, it was also a do-over from that
one time they all were there, but not really. He liked the idea of

revisiting the hotel where Julien and Priest had decided to make him theirs, and let them, well...make him theirs.

"Good evening, Mr. Priestley," Robbie said. "How are you doing tonight?"

Priest's chuckle made Robbie smile, and as he caught a break in traffic, he merged onto the main road.

"I'm doing well, sweetheart. How are you?"

Great now, Robbie thought. *I love it when he calls me that.* "I'm doing good. You caught me, though. I'm heading out to meet another man for dinner."

"Is that right?"

"It is..."

"Hmm, well, if I were an insecure man—"

Robbie snorted, but Priest kept talking despite the interruption.

"—I might be inclined to ask who. But since you woke up this morning with me inside you, I'm feeling pretty—"

"Arrogant?" Robbie said, even as he squirmed a little in his seat at the memory.

"I was going to say...confident."

Robbie made a turn at the light and was glad he was on his own with the ridiculous grin that curved his lips. "Whatever. Arrogant. Confident. *Priest.* The three words all mean the same thing and fit."

"How about lucky? That word fits too. Since we *all* got lucky this morning."

Yes, we did, Robbie thought, as his mind wandered back to the way Julien had stretched out in front of him and watched as Priest had taken Robbie nice and—

"You're going to meet Elliot tonight, aren't you?"

—slow. "Huh?"

"Robert, are you driving?"

"Uh, yes, sorry."

"How about you pay attention, then. I'd hate you to—"

"Oh *shit*," Robbie said, as red and blue lights caught his eye in the rearview mirror. "A cop is pulling me over. *Ugh*. I must've been speeding without even realizing it. Great."

Robbie's heart began to hammer and his palms started to sweat, which was ridiculous, because all he likely did was break the speed limit. He flicked on his indicator and pulled his car over to the side of the road.

"Just stay calm and don't talk too much," Priest said.

Um, hello, did Priest forget who he was talking to?

"Yes or no answers only. Or silence. Silence works too," Priest continued. "That way, if you need to fight a fine—"

"A *fine?*"

"A speeding ticket," Priest said. "There's nothing incriminating to hold against you."

"Shit. This is not making me feel very *confident* right now," Robbie said, and turned off the engine.

"You're going to be fine. You didn't do anything wrong. Call me as soon as he's gone. Okay?"

Robbie let out a sigh. "Okay. Oh, Priest?"

"Yes?"

"Can you call Elliot and tell him I'm going to be late?"

"Yes. Now hang up and remember, don't try and explain yourself and *don't* talk too much."

Robbie rolled his eyes and ended the call, then he wound down the window and placed his hands on the steering wheel. With his eyes glued to the rearview mirror, he told himself to stay calm as the police officer got out of his car and started toward him.

I did nothing wrong, except maybe speed a little. I have nothing to worry about. Stay calm.

"Good evening, officer," Robbie said as a flashlight found him and he tried for his best smile.

"Good evening. I'm Officer Bailey. Do you know why I pulled you over tonight?"

Robbie thought about what Priest had said to him—*yes or no answers*—and since he wasn't one hundred percent *sure* he'd been speeding, Robbie shook his head. "No, sir."

"You were speeding. I clocked you doing fifty-five. Could I see your license and registration, please?"

Shit. Damn Priest for distracting me. "Uh, my license is in my bag."

"Okay. You can proceed."

Robbie reached into his messenger bag, grabbed his wallet, and then pulled his registration from the glove box. He handed Officer Bailey both items, and as he shined the flashlight over them, Robbie put his hands back on the wheel where they could be seen.

Robbie stared up at the officer and thought it probably wasn't a good time to notice how good that uniform looked. But he made a mental note for later when he got out of this, because he was totally going to get Julien and Priest to dress up like that and arrest him.

"Mr. Bianchi, do you know what the speed limit is here in town?"

Robbie was about to automatically answer when he heard Priest's voice again—*silence works too*—and decided in this case to keep his mouth shut.

"It's forty-five," Officer Bailey said. "That means you were doing ten over the legal speed limit."

Robbie wanted to kick himself in the ass. Really? This was the last thing he needed. God only knew how much the fine for this was going to cost him.

Officer Bailey tapped Robbie's paperwork on his palm and then said, "I'm going to go and check this out, and then I'll be back. Don't move from your vehicle. Do you understand?"

"Yes, sir," Robbie said, and as the officer went to walk away, he flashed his light inside the back window, and then stopped and bent over to look inside.

Robbie's eyes shifted to the side mirror, and when Officer Bailey straightened and came back to him, instead of walking away, Robbie gripped the steering wheel a little tighter. This did not seem good.

"Mr. Bianchi, I need you to get out of the car for me, please."

Uh, what the what? Robbie frowned, and when he didn't move or respond, Officer Bailey said again, "I need you to get out of the car."

Finally, Robbie found his voice and decided to hell with not saying anything. "Why?"

"I have reason to believe there are drugs in your car, Mr. Bianchi. Can you please step out?"

Wait... What? Drugs? Robbie stared blankly at the officer as though he didn't quite understand, and if he hadn't been so blindsided, he might've thought it strange that Officer Bailey's lips twitched.

"Mr. Bianchi? Please step out of the vehicle."

You've got to be shitting me. Robbie didn't have any drugs in his car. He'd never touched a drug in his life—well, except for back in the day, like, once. This was absurd.

Robbie pushed open the car door and got out, knowing the sooner this guy looked in his car and realized there was nothing in there, the sooner he'd let him go. Then Robbie could ask Priest if he had any recourse against delusional police officers.

As Robbie shut the door behind him, Officer Bailey said, "Stand right there, please." Robbie chewed on his bottom lip as the officer once again peered in his passenger window. "There's a small packet on the floor of your vehicle that I'd like to take a closer look at."

Robbie turned around to look, and Officer Bailey held a hand up and said, "Don't move, sir."

"Sorry," Robbie said automatically, but was racking his brain trying to think of what the hell this guy was looking at.

"Do you mind if I take a look?"

What could he say, *no?* Then what would happen? Robbie's nerves were a wreck, but at the same time, he knew he had nothing to hide. "Go ahead."

As the officer opened the car door, Robbie wished like hell that Priest was there with him. He'd know exactly what to do.

"Okay, Mr. Bianchi," Officer Bailey said as he got out of the car. "Do you want to explain to me what this is?"

Robbie's eyes almost bugged out of his head as he stared at the small rectangular baggie the police officer was holding up in front of him. What the fuck was that? It sure as shit wasn't his.

"Mr. Bianchi?"

Robbie's breathing was coming a little faster now, and when Officer Bailey took a step closer, Robbie thought he might pass out.

"You got nothing to say?"

As disbelief started to cloud Robbie's mind, he thought of his cousin Vanessa and how one mistake had almost cost her her life, and Robbie knew his best course of action here was to shut his mouth and wait until he could get to Priest, or call Priest, or—

"Right. If you've got nothing to say for yourself, then go ahead and give me your hands. You're going to be detained right now and taken to the station for further questioning."

Oh my God, Robbie thought, as the police officer put the cuffs on him. *I'm going to be calling Priest, all right. I'm going to be calling him from jail.*

CHAPTER SEVENTEEN

What the shit is going on?
-Robbie

AS ROBBIE SAT in the back of the police cruiser on the way to the station, he stared at the partition between him and Officer Bailey and tried to work out how in the world he'd ended up there.

Ever since the handcuffs had been clicked into place and he'd been escorted to the back seat of the car, Robbie had been freaking the fuck out.

How was he ever going to explain this to his family? To Priest? To *Julien?* Especially after he'd given Julien such a hard time for needing Priest to bail him out back in the day, gloating that he'd never gotten a speeding ticket in his life.

Yeah, well, look where that karma got you, Bianchi. Handcuffed in the back of a cop car, and taken in for questioning about drugs. Drugs!

This was insanity. He couldn't even think of a logical answer as to why that bag was in there. Or *how* it got in there. It was just *there*. Which he was sure the cop was going to love as an explana-tion—not to mention Priest.

Robbie shut his eyes, his leg doing a nervous jig as he thought about the phone call he was going to have to make when he got to the station: *I'm sorry, Priest, I just happened to get arrested for having drugs in my car. I swear they aren't mine.*

Yeah, okay. Priest was going to think his family had some serious drug problems for sure, and just when he'd finally managed to convince him they were all somewhat normal.

Robbie shook his head and then glanced out the window, and it wasn't until the cruiser began to slow down that he realized he hadn't *really* been paying attention to where they were going.

Officer Bailey had told Robbie that he was taking him to the station. But Robbie had been so preoccupied with how to go about saving his ass that it was only now registering that they'd been driving *much* longer than they probably should've been to get to the closest precinct.

When the car came to a stop, Robbie peered outside, and when all he saw was, well, nothing, his heart just about up and stopped.

Where the hell are we?

Robbie looked around, and all he could see for miles were trees. Lots and lots of trees, and then Officer Bailey got out of the cruiser and shut the door behind him, making Robbie jump.

When Officer Bailey opened the door and reached inside to take hold of his arm, Robbie started to shake his head.

"I, um— Sorry. *Where* are we?" Robbie asked, as he again scanned his surroundings, but all he saw was a dark forest and a sketchy-looking dirt road lit up by the cruiser's headlights.

Shit, maybe Officer Bailey isn't really a cop, Robbie thought. That possibility hadn't even crossed his mind. But it did now, and as panic started to take over common sense, Robbie tugged his arm back.

Officer Bailey's grip didn't loosen in the slightest, and Robbie seriously thought about kicking him in the shins and making a run for it. But that was when a figure stepped out into the path of the cruiser's headlights, and Robbie's plans all came to a grinding halt —right along with his brain.

Priest? No. His mind had to be playing tricks on him, because there was no way that Priest was standing out here in the middle of nowhere. This was him hallucinating, right?

Officer Bailey glanced over his shoulder, and when he smirked, Robbie saw it. *What the shit is going on?*

Robbie's eyes flew back to the spot where he'd imagined—*no, seen*—Priest, and as Office Bailey began walking, towing Robbie along with him, relief flooded Robbie's body.

As they came to a stop, Robbie took in the pressed suit Priest was wearing and noted it was different to the one he'd left for work in that morning. Priest eyed the man in uniform with a stern expression that Robbie was still trying to understand.

"And what have we got here, Officer Bailey?" Priest asked, as though he knew the man who was the star of Robbie's worst night ever.

"Nothing too bad," Officer Bailey said, as he reached into his pocket, pulled out a key, and handed it over to Priest. "He was actually pretty good until the end. Got a little mouthy then."

Robbie's eyes widened like saucers as he looked between the two, incredulity now shoving aside his confusion, as he finally realized that whatever this was, it had all been orchestrated by—

"Did he now?"

—*Priest.*

Officer Bailey chuckled. "He did. And I'm going to let you uncuff him. If he kills you out here, I just might take his side. See you around, Priest. Mr. Bianchi."

Robbie turned to watch him head back to the cruiser, and then he rounded on Priest, his mouth hanging open, his brain still working overtime as it tried to catch up.

Priest hooked a finger over the chain of the handcuffs, and as he tugged Robbie forward, he said, "It was only a matter of time before a troublemaker like you ended up on the wrong side of the law. Wouldn't you agree, Mr. Bianchi?"

CHAPTER EIGHTEEN

We want him to feel as though he's walking into a dream.
One where he wants to stay forever
- Julien

HE WANTS TO kill me, Priest thought, as Robbie's eyes narrowed and his dainty jaw clenched. Those usually pouty lips of his had gone from twisted confusion, to parted in shock, and were now pulled into a seriously pissed-off line.

Oh yes, Robbie was about to rain holy hellfire down on him, and Priest couldn't wait. It reminded him of how far they'd come, and where they'd both begun, and that was exactly where Priest wanted Robbie's mind to go to tonight. A little trip down memory lane.

Keeping his expression serious, Priest said, "I asked you a question, Mr. Bianchi," and that finally made his little spitfire explode.

"You're asking," Robbie said. "You're asking *me* a question?"

Knowing exactly what buttons to push with Robbie, Priest nodded. "Yes. And you still haven't answered."

"I...I don't even know what to say to you right now. Did you *seriously* just have me arrested?"

"No," Priest said, because technically, Robbie hadn't been arrested. Not really. "Although it is rather handy that Craig cuffed you. I didn't ask him to do that."

A look of utter disbelief crossed Robbie's face, and then he began to laugh hysterically, almost delirious in his incredulity, as though he thought Priest had lost his mind, and maybe he had. But if that were the case, so had Julien, who was waiting for them to arrive not far from there.

As Robbie glared at him, clearly trying to work out the finer details as to why he was standing in the middle of the woods at night, Priest tugged on the chain again, drawing Robbie closer.

When Robbie staggered forward, and seemed to realize what Priest was doing, he raised his bound hands and flattened his palms on Priest's chest.

"Uh, what do you think you're doing?" Robbie said with so much attitude, it was all Priest could do to keep his lips in a firm line. "You're not getting anything from me until you start explaining."

Priest let his gaze roam over the perfectly sculpted eyebrow now winging up, the lined eyes shooting daggers his way, and the pointy chin, angled so high up that Priest couldn't help himself from reaching out and taking hold of it.

"Well, that's unfortunate," Priest said. "Because we want everything, Robert Bianchi."

Robbie opened his mouth, about to tell him to *back up* or *go to hell*, no doubt. But as Priest's words sank in, he seemed to realize what he'd just said, and the furious light that had been lit a second ago turned into a...curious one.

That's right, sweetheart. Remember the first time I said that? Remember where we all began.

Robbie licked at his lips. "What do you mean you want *everything?*"

And it was that moment that Priest knew he had him. Robbie

had finally gotten past his annoyance and realized that something else was happening.

Priest smirked and began to walk backward, and this time when he pulled on the chain, Robbie followed.

"Priest?" Robbie said, as he looked around again. "Where are we?"

"Why?" Priest asked. "Are you scared?"

"Well," Robbie said, "I was arrested, handcuffed, and brought out to the middle of the woods and handed over to a crazy man. So..."

Priest stopped walking and pulled Robbie in until he could wrap an arm around him. "So?"

"I'm not scared at all. Does that make me crazy too?"

Priest took in all of the elegant lines of Robbie's face. "Crazy in love, maybe."

Robbie blinked, and before he could say anything else, Priest said, "Let's go. Julien's waiting for us."

JULIEN LOOKED OUT at the peaceful forest that stretched for miles in front of him, and enjoyed the relaxing sounds that came with nightfall once you left the city behind.

He was standing on the wraparound porch of the little cottage Sofia and Antonio had told them about back in Oshkosh, wondering how their son's story was going to play out in comparison to theirs.

Julien smiled, thinking about the tongue-lashing Priest was likely enduring after their elaborate ploy to get Robbie out there alone and unsuspecting. But when he had suggested his plan, Priest had thought it absolutely perfect. Insane, but perfect for them.

Nothing had ever been normal when it came to the three of them, and it only seemed fitting that Robbie would have a tale like that of a thief, stealing a car, to tell for many years to come.

Julien gave the porch a final look before the other two arrived.

This was where the magic tonight would begin, where the new chapter in their journey would start, and he had been particular on how he wanted to set the stage. He wanted Robbie to feel as though he was walking into a dream. One where he wanted to stay forever with Julien and Priest.

The sound of leaves crunching had Julien tugging at his collar, and he found he was a little bit nervous. This was a first for him.

Oui, he'd been married for many years. But Priest had been the one who'd proposed, and it had been so special. Every element of that night had been carefully thought out and designed to sweep Julien off his feet, and tonight they were hoping to do the same for Robbie.

Priest stepped through the trees first in a suit that looked totally out of place, but added to the overall ambience they were going for this evening. They'd been trying to decide how to play this whole scenario out, and had finally agreed in the end to put forward the version of themselves that Robbie had first fallen for —the prick and the priest.

As Priest walked toward him, Julien took in the powerful frame under his tailored jacket, the tie knotted at the base of his throat, and his long legs as they ate up the distance between them like he was in a hurry to get closer.

Priest's eyes were zeroed in on him, and as he drew near, Julien caught sight of Robbie walking beside him.

His eyes were wide as he took in the scene all around him, and as they walked up the stairs, Julien finally had a chance to drink in the sight of Robbie.

Still dressed from work, Robbie wore his black tailored pants, burgundy shirt, and black vest, and when he finally spotted Julien and saw what he was wearing, Robbie's mouth fell open. He looked to Priest and said, "Am I dreaming?"

When Priest said nothing, Robbie turned back to Julien and said, "If I am, please don't wake me up."

SOMEWHERE AROUND PRIEST telling him that they wanted *everything*, to now, as Robbie stood in front of Julien, who was decked out in his *Chef Master* uniform, with *Julien "the Prick" Thornton* stitched above the pocket—Robbie's emotions had been in a tailspin.

At first, he'd been furious at Priest for freaking him out. But when his nerves had finally calmed and his brain had decided to show up to the party, Robbie's heart had begun to race for a very different reason.

He recognized this place. He wasn't sure how, because he'd never been there before. But from the moment Priest had led him off the path, and they'd come out of the forest into this clearing, Robbie had had an immediate flash of recognition.

There was a little cottage with a dozen or so lanterns illuminating a path up to the stairs, where there was a wraparound porch covered in ivy and twinkle lights that gave the place a magical feel.

It had a charming quality that was otherworldly in the dark seclusion of the night—and as the three of them now stood on the porch with one another, Robbie realized that they really *were* secluded. There was nothing on either side of them but trees, and off in the distance, you could hear the sound of...water, maybe?

"*Bonsoir, princesse,*" Julien said, in that smooth, sensual cadence that wrapped around every fiber of Robbie's being and pulled him back to the present. "You seem to have gotten yourself into a little bind."

Julien took Robbie's cuffed hands and leaned down to press a kiss to the back of them, and when he raised his eyes, a shiver raced up Robbie's spine.

The expression in Julien's eyes was the same one he'd seen in Priest's a second ago. The one that had made Robbie's heart skip a few beats, and then begin to thump extraordinarily fast.

Something was going on here tonight. Something big.

"I wasn't sure you'd make it back alive, *mon amour*," Julien said, as he glanced at Priest. "But now it makes more sense."

Priest slipped a hand into his pocket and pulled out the key Officer Bailey had given him.

"I was lucky," Priest said, as he handed it to Julien. "But I thought I'd leave him shackled until we made it back to you for safety reasons. Plus, you were my accomplice. If he's going to strangle us, it should be together."

As Julien reached for the key, Priest's words registered with Robbie, and he tried to work out what exactly *Julien* was guilty of.

"The flour in the back of your car, *princesse*." Julien winked as he pulled Robbie in. "I told you I was a thief that night at CRUSH. And tonight, we wanted to steal you away from the rest of the world."

Robbie took in a shaky breath as the cuffs around his wrists loosened, and Priest said in his ear, "But your heart? Your heart, we want to steal forever."

Priest then moved to stand alongside his husband, and as Robbie took in the handsome picture they made, he worried that his legs might give out from under him.

His lawyer and his chef. Robbie couldn't have imagined a more perfect fit for him than these two men, and when they both moved down to one knee and looked up at him, Robbie's hands flew to his mouth.

"Robert Antonio Bianchi," Priest said, and though Robbie tried to focus, he was finding it difficult with the tears now blurring his eyes.

"You are the brightest part of our lives," Julien said. "And from the moment you walked into it, we knew you were meant to be ours."

Julien took Priest's hand and entwined their fingers, forming that bond, that connection, that Robbie loved the most about them.

"We've been planning to ask you for some time now," Priest said, and Robbie bit down on his lip to stop his chin from quivering. "But we wanted your parents' blessing first."

"And when they gave it," Julien said, "they told us about this place, and everything, as it always does with you, and us, fell into place."

Oh my God, Robbie thought, as he finally realized why this all felt so familiar. This was where his parents had gotten engaged. Where the greatest love story he knew began. In the little cottage with the lights, where there was nothing in the world but you and love, and Robbie remembered his ma telling him one time, *That's all that matters in the end, Robert, not who. Out there, love is* all *that exists.*

"Robert?" Priest said, gently smiling.

Then Julien's dimple appeared. "*Princesse?*"

Then they both held their free hands out to him and proved his ma right. "Will you marry us?"

CHAPTER NINETEEN

This is the beginning of forever.
And if you come with us, we'll show you the rest of the way
- Julien & Priest

"*YES*," ROBBIE SAID, and fell down to his knees. "A thousand times over, yes."

As the lights flickered over Robbie's face, Priest took in the beautiful picture he made. The shimmering blue eyes, the pretty flushed cheeks, and the trembling in his body as what was happening—what *had* happened—began to wash over him.

Julien brought Robbie's hand up and pressed his lips to the center of it.

"*Je t'aime*, Robbie," Julien whispered.

"*Je t'aime aussi*," Robbie replied, making Julien grin as he entwined their fingers. "Oh my God. I can't believe you want to marry me. That both of you do."

Julien looked to Priest, and Robbie did also, and when Priest pressed a kiss to Robbie's palm, his emotions threatened to overwhelm him.

"We do," Priest said. "We love you. *I* love you, sweetheart. But that's not all we want. There's something else we'd like to ask of you tonight."

Robbie swallowed, and just as Priest was about to continue, Robbie put a finger to his lips and said, "Wait..."

Priest paused, thinking that maybe Robbie was feeling rushed. But then a lovely smile crossed his lips and he said, "You didn't let me say it back."

Priest blinked. It wasn't often that he lost his words, but when Robbie moved his hand to cradle Priest's bearded cheek and said, "I love you too," Priest had a hard time remembering what he'd been going to say.

As he sat there staring at the young man who'd walked into his and Julien's lives not too long ago, Priest wondered what he'd ever done to deserve not only one great love in his life, but two.

"You wanted to ask me something else?" Robbie said, and a soft laugh escaped him. "I'm not sure my heart can take anything else."

"Yes. This is important," Priest said. "*You* are important. And we want you to understand and feel that."

Julien nodded. "We want the world to understand that you are loved by both Priest and myself, *princesse*. Regardless of a piece of paper."

Robbie let go of Julien's hand for a second to brush away a tear. But as soon as it was gone, he reached for him again.

"I do understand that," Robbie said. "I know this can't be legally recognized, but—"

This time Priest put a finger to Robbie's lips. "But taking our names can be."

Robbie's mouth opened and shut several times. "Wh...what?"

"Our names," Priest said. "We both kept our own when we married."

"But with you," Julien said, "we would be honored if you would take them, and legally make them yours. We think Thornton-Priestley has a nice ring to it."

Robbie let go of both their hands to cover his mouth. His eyes were round as saucers, and all the love and happiness he was experiencing was shining right out of them.

"Are you serious?" Robbie said, trying to blink back his tears and failing.

"*Oui*, very serious," Julien said. "But only if you want—"

"I want to," Robbie said, and launched himself at Julien, who wrapped his arms around Robbie's waist and kissed him until he shook, and when he pulled back and reached for Priest to do the same, Julien chuckled at his exuberance.

When Robbie finally let them go, he sat back on his heels and said, "This *is* a dream. The most beautiful, wonderful dream I've ever had."

"*Non, mon cher petit*. This is the beginning of forever," Julien said, and as they all got to their feet, he reached for Robbie's hand. "And if you come with us, we'll show you the rest of the way."

———

ROBBIE FELT AS though he were in a daze as he slipped his hand into Julien's. His heart was so full it was close to bursting, and as he looked out at the twinkling lights all around them, he wondered if it was physically possible to be as happy as he was without passing out from the rush of it.

"Show me," Robbie whispered, and then looked to the two men who had just made every wish of his a reality.

Julien's smile was dazzling as he tugged Robbie forward, and as they followed the wraparound porch to the back of the house instead of going inside, Robbie's curiosity was piqued. This evening was not going anything like he'd expected, and he was starting to suspect he had no hope of guessing what these two had in store for him.

As they made a turn to walk toward the back of the cottage, Robbie looked over his shoulder to see Priest following. His hands were in his pockets, his attention fastened on the two of them, and when he caught Robbie's eyes, the smile that crossed his mouth made Robbie's entire body respond. That smile was like gold, and Robbie swore to himself he would spend the rest of his life making sure Priest continued to look at him that way.

Robbie grinned, and Priest indicated with a nod that he should turn around, and what Robbie saw when he did, took his breath away.

Julien let go of his hand and stepped aside, and Robbie slowly walked forward to where the back porch opened up to a set of stairs leading to the ground below. There, lighting up the forest floor like stars, were dozens of lanterns, as far as the eye could see.

Robbie looked over his shoulder to see Julien and Priest standing side by side. "I've never seen anything more beautiful...ever."

Robbie reached for the rail to hang on, knowing there was a very real possibility his legs were about to give out.

How it was possible to feel so much and still be standing, he had no idea. But when Julien reached him and said, "I have," and kissed him before heading down the stairs, Robbie gripped the rail a little tighter and watched as Julien disappeared into the trees.

"May I?" Priest said as he came up beside Robbie and crooked his arm.

Robbie slid his hand through Priest's offered elbow and said, "Thank you. I feel a little..."

"Off-balance?"

Robbie chuckled. "Off-balance. Breathless. So happy my entire body might float away from the high of it?"

"Well don't do that," Priest said as he guided Robbie down the stairs. "Not when there's so much down here waiting for you."

As they reached the bottom, Robbie looked out ahead of them and whispered, "This place is like a fairy tale."

"Fit for a princess, then?"

Robbie nodded, and as Priest guided them forward, Robbie became aware of something he'd heard earlier. He'd been so distracted by what he was feeling and seeing that he hadn't realized the sound of rushing water—the sound of a waterfall—was much louder now.

As Priest weaved them through the golden glow of the lights, Robbie took in the beauty of the untouched slice of paradise they had somehow been granted access to tonight. Then Priest drew them around a corner, and Robbie gasped.

"Oh my God." Robbie could barely believe what he was seeing. He stared at Julien, who stood on a deck in front of a table that was draped in white, with the moonlight shining down over him, and the backdrop of the most gorgeous waterfall Robbie had ever seen in his life.

"I can't... I don't... I don't know what to say," Robbie managed, as he tried to look at everything all at once. There were candles on the table, three chairs around it, and lanterns *all* over the place, and nothing in his wildest dreams could've ever come close to a night like this.

"I believe our chef is waiting on you, sweetheart."

As Priest's words floated around him, Robbie tore his eyes away from the most romantic setting he'd ever seen. "Then let's not make him wait any longer."

JULIEN STOOD IN awe of the two men walking his way, and allowed the heady feeling of love to envelop him. Over the past several months they'd been navigating their way through this relationship one day at a time.

They'd experienced incredible highs and some devastating lows. But when Robbie said *yes* to them back there on the porch, Julien knew that from here on out, whatever they were dealing with, the three of them would always be able to get through it together, as one.

As Priest stood aside to let Robbie climb the steps, he looked up to Julien and winked, and Julien thought his heart might just stop. He knew tonight was Robbie's night. But as Julien waited for his *princesse* to reach him, he couldn't help but feel this was a renewal for him and Priest also. An affirmation that their love was just as strong now as it had been eight years ago.

"Welcome to your dining room for the evening, *princesse*," Julien said.

"It doesn't seem real."

"I know," Julien said, and glanced over his shoulder at the waterfall in the distance. "I didn't believe your mother when she said it was here."

"Neither did I," Robbie whispered as he tilted his head back to take in the scene in its entirety. "This whole place, it's exactly the way she described it."

"*Oui*, it is. The original owners passed it down to their children, who updated a few things, like this deck," Julien said as he placed a hand on Robbie's lower back. "I promised her you'd take lots of photos."

The candlelight reflected off Robbie's shimmering eyes. "That's the one thing she always regretted."

"I know," Julien said, and then drew his fingers down Robbie's jaw line. "Will you take a seat? Let me dazzle your taste buds?"

Robbie looked at three silver-domed place settings. "Did you do all this?"

"With some help," Julien said as Priest came to them.

"He's being modest." Priest pulled a seat out for Robbie. "He did nearly *all* of this."

Priest's compliment made Julien's heart warm as he walked around the table and pulled the cork from the bottle of Pinot he'd paired with tonight's meal. Once Robbie and Priest were seated, Julien poured them both a glass, and then he went about removing the covers.

"Oh, wow, Jules. This looks incredible," Robbie said as he peered down at the meal in front of him. "Is it duck?"

Julien nodded as he took a seat on the other side of the table, next to Priest. "*Oui.* It's *Magret de canard aux cerises avec une sauce au Porto.* Seared duck breast with cherries and port sauce."

"You two are totally spoiling me. This sounds delicious," Robbie said as he took his napkin and draped it over his lap.

"It is," Priest said. "It's a meal that reminds us of a very special moment in our lives."

"What's that?"

"I was testing this meal on Priest for the restaurant the night you first called us from CRUSH," Julien said, and Robbie frowned.

"When I— *Ohhh.*"

Robbie's cheeks flushed, and Julien looked at Priest, who had a mystified look on his face, as though he couldn't believe where they'd all ended up from that one night.

"Mhmm," Julien said as they all picked up their knives and forks. "I decided right then that this meal would be one that I kept specifically for us, and now that includes you."

Robbie shook his head and looked around again. "I still can't believe I'm here. Sitting in a place I only ever imagined in my head, with the both of you."

"I can," Priest said. "We'd been looking for you. Once we found you, this was only a matter of time."

Robbie sighed. "It feels too good to be true."

"That's how you know for sure it is," Julien said. "Nothing this powerful could ever be anything but real."

Robbie nodded, his eyes twinkling, and before he took his first bite of food, he said, "Do we get to stay here for the whole night? Please say yes."

Priest eyed him, his lips twitching a little. "You mean, out here with two crazy men in the middle of the woods with nothing but the clothes on your back?"

Robbie playfully smiled, his joy over the evening bubbling right up out of him. "Or off my back. I'm not picky."

"Then yes. I believe you get to stay here for *two* whole nights with those crazy men," Priest said, which seemed to please Robbie immensely.

"And *then?*" Robbie said, looking to Julien.

"Then," Julien said, and winked, "they're going to take you home and marry you."

CHAPTER TWENTY

Sometimes dreams really do come true.
If you wish hard enough
- Robbie

"DID YOU HAVE enough?" Julien asked, as Robbie finished the final bite of his chocolate soufflé and sat back.

Had he? Robbie didn't think he'd ever been more satisfied by a meal in his life. Not that that was a surprise, considering a world-class chef had cooked it. *My world-class chef. Wait, no—my* fiancé.

"*Oui*," Robbie said with a grin. He was so damn happy right now, he was surprised his mouth wasn't stuck in a permanent smile. "That was amazing."

"*Bien.* I'm pleased."

"And I have to say, being served by the winner of *Chef Master* in his sexy *uniform* far surpasses my earlier idea of having you both dress up and play good cop/bad cop."

Priest reached for his glass of wine and chuckled. "Oh, I don't know. That idea certainly has its merit."

"Yes, well, we all know which cop *you* would be," Robbie said to his *other* fiancé—*yeah, okay, that's never going to get old.*

He still couldn't believe where he was and what had happened here tonight. He was now engaged to Julien and Priest, and no matter how much time passed, his brain kept coming back to that over and over again.

"What are you thinking about, *princesse?*" Julien said. "You have a *very* dreamy smile on your face."

Robbie didn't doubt it. "Um, yeah, how could I have anything but? Look at this place."

"While the place is lovely," Priest said, and lowered his glass back to the table, "I find myself distracted by something else entirely."

Under the intense scrutiny of Priest's stare, Robbie felt almost...shy. "You do?"

"I do," Priest said. "Now there's two words you should start practicing. We're looking forward to hearing you say them very soon."

Robbie couldn't explain why, but he suddenly felt as nervous with the two of them as he had on their first date. It might've had something to do with the way they looked with the candlelight flickering over their handsome faces, and a waterfall streaming down behind them. They looked like two gods who had come to whisk him away and keep him for all eternity.

At least, that was how Robbie saw their story going, and he wanted to memorize this exact moment for the rest of his life.

"If you're done," Julien said, "would you like to take a look inside the cottage?"

I'd like nothing more. "Yes, please."

As Julien and Priest got to their feet, Robbie's gaze travelled up their tall frames, and then he closed his eyes for a second and made a wish.

When they reopened, Priest said, "Are you okay?"

Robbie pushed his chair back so he could stand. "Yes. I was just making a wish."

Julien smiled. "A wish?"

"Mhmm," Robbie said, and when Priest reached for the plates and started stacking them up, Robbie gathered up the napkins.

"Do you do that often?" Priest said, as he placed the plates into the basket he'd pulled from under the table.

"Sometimes," Robbie said, handing over the linens. "And has there ever been a place worthier of a wish than this? This place is... It's magical. And you know what? Sometimes the wishes even come true."

"Do they?" Julien asked, as he handed Priest the wine glasses.

"Oh yes," Robbie said. "I wished *hard* all the time for the both of you, and look what happened."

The two of them chuckled as Priest shut the lid on the basket, and Julien leaned down to blow out the candles.

"Okay, cheeky boy," Julien said as he came around and held out his hand. "I hope you wished to go inside, because that's where you're headed."

That was more than fine with Robbie. He couldn't wait to get inside, strip down to nothing, and then crawl between the sheets with these two. He wanted to both thank and worship them for the best night of his life, and while they *were* out in the middle of nowhere, Robbie thought it best that they go inside for that. He wasn't a huge fan of the idea of rolling around in nature bare-assed, just in case something other than his men decided to, you know, take a bite.

The three of them headed back through the lit garden, and when they reached the door of the cottage and Julien held it open, Robbie stopped and said, "Is there somewhere I could maybe go and, um, freshen up?"

"*Oui*," Julien said, and then pointed down a narrow hall. "Down there to your left."

"You'll find your toiletry bag already in there," Priest said.

"Just so you know," Robbie said, "I don't normally approve of the scheming you two have been up to behind my back. But since it worked out so well for me, I'm going to overlook it this one time."

"How very magnanimous of you," Priest said, as Robbie walked inside and headed straight for the hall. He would check the cottage out in the morning when the sun was up, because right now, there were other things he wanted to do—*two* other things, to be precise.

"I thought so," Robbie called over his shoulder, and just before he stepped into the bathroom, he looked back to see both men watching him. "I'll be out soon. Be sure to miss me a *whooole* lot while I'm gone."

Robbie disappeared into the tiny room and had the fleeting thought that if they were stuck in the middle of nowhere for the rest of their days, he sure wouldn't mind.

Not one little bit.

⸻

"HE SAID YES," Priest said, as the bathroom door clicked shut and he and Julien walked into the kitchen.

"*Oui*, he did," Julien said. "Quite emphatically. Several times."

Priest put the basket up on the counter, and as he opened the door for the dishwasher, Julien reached out to help.

Priest brushed his hand away. "You cooked. I'll take care of this."

Julien leaned back against the sink and crossed his arms, a smile playing on his generous lips. "So was he very angry about the police escort?"

Priest turned the tap on and rinsed off the plates as he stacked them one by one into the washer. "He was very...Robert-like."

Julien laughed. "So he was furious."

"Ah, yes. Until he realized something else was going on. Then... then he was, as always, curious." Priest washed off the utensils next, and once they were in the holder, he added the soap and set it to start. "This place, this dinner... Julien, you made it so special for him. He's never going to forget this."

Julien put his hands on Priest's chest. "*We* made it special for him. The place was all Sofia. But I have a feeling we could've asked him down at a jail and he still would've said yes."

Priest wrapped his arms around Julien's waist and kissed him softly, slowly, until Julien's hands slid over his shoulders and his fingers found Priest's hair.

"*Je t'aime*, Joel," he said against Priest's lips. "So much."

Priest ran his hands up Julien's back as he kissed his way to his ear. "I love you. You make everything in my world make sense. You make all of *us* make sense."

Julien caught Priest's lips again in a kiss full of love, full of forever, a kiss that only got better with time, and when they pulled apart, he brought his hand down along Priest's cheek and traced a thumb across his lips.

"Let me go and get out of this uniform and wash up a little," Julien said. "There's that small en suite at the front, and after cooking this afternoon, I'm—"

"Perfect?" Priest said, as Julien stepped back, their hands still linked.

"You're biased."

"I'm right. I bet Robert would agree."

As Julien let go of one of his hands and was about to free the other, Priest pulled him back in and kissed him again, more in love with his Frenchman than he ever had been.

Julien started to laugh and pushed him away. "Quit it."

"I don't want to."

"Give me ten minutes and you can kiss me all you like. Not all of us could shower and change before we got here tonight."

Priest let him go. "Fine, leave me."

"Never." Julien backed out of the kitchen, and as he reached the door, he said, "Not ever."

Priest rinsed and washed the wine glasses, then cleaned up the rest of the kitchen and flicked off the light. As he made his way through to the bedroom, he checked the doors were locked, and the lights outside were turned off. He could hear the shower still running down the hall, and knew he wouldn't have much longer until Robbie appeared. So Priest switched on the bedside lamps, pulled the covers back, and went about getting undressed.

Tonight couldn't have gone better. When Sofia had told them about the place and Julien suggested they see if it was still around, Priest could never have imagined what they'd found.

The new owners had renovated the cottage to what it was today—a secluded, romantic oasis for honeymooners or special getaways, and tonight, an engagement fit for a princess. It'd been perfect, in every single way.

Priest folded his pants and shirt over the chaise longue in the room, and once he was stripped down to his boxer briefs, he put a bottle of lube under the pillow and got into bed. He and Julien had left Robbie a little gift with his toiletries tonight, and Priest wanted to gauge his mood once he arrived before deciding which direction to lead them all in—and he didn't have to wait long.

Minutes after Priest settled in with his back against the head-board and the sheet across his lap, Robbie walked into the bedroom. With his hair slicked back, Robbie's high cheekbones made Priest want to kiss his way along them to his ear so he could tell him how beautiful he was—because truly, he was exquisite.

He had a towel wrapped around his trim waist, and as he walked to the end of the bed, Robbie's blue eyes never strayed from Priest.

"Did you have a nice shower?" Priest asked, when Robbie came to the foot of the bed.

"I did," Robbie said as he fingered the knot at the edge of his towel.

"And did you find everything okay?"

Robbie's lips curved, giving away the fact he had indeed found what they'd included for him tonight. "I did."

"And do you plan to share?"

"Only for the rest of my life," the flirt said, and then he pulled the knot free. As Robbie tossed the towel over the end of the bed, Priest's eyes lowered to the barely there hot-pink briefs they'd picked out and packed for their princess to wear tonight.

"Turn around. Show me the back," Priest said, his voice gravelly.

As Robbie slowly pivoted to face the door, Priest stroked over the sheet between his legs, because *Christ*, Robbie looked fucking unreal. The briefs were tight, low-cut, and cupped his spectacular ass, and across the curves Priest wanted to get between was the word *PRINCESS* with a glittery little crown over the *I*, much like the one Julien always drew.

The smooth, creamy skin of Robbie's back made Priest's mouth water, and when he glanced over his shoulder and saw Priest palming himself, Robbie grinned.

"You like?"

"So damn much," Priest said, as Robbie turned back to face him. "Get up here."

Robbie climbed onto the end of the bed, and as he got closer, Priest kicked the sheet off and Robbie pulled it away. When it was gone, Robbie licked his lips and continued up the mattress until he was straddling Priest's lap, and as soon as he was close enough, Robbie connected their mouths.

Priest opened for him in an instant, and when Robbie slid his tongue inside, Priest smoothed his hands around to the ass he'd just been admiring. Robbie moaned and took Priest's face in his hands, angling it just the way he wanted to get a deeper taste, and as he rubbed his swelling dick up against Priest's, a groan tore from Priest's throat.

"Jesus," Priest said as Robbie raised his head and stared down at him. "You're so fucking beautiful. You feel incredible."

"So do you. So damn good." Robbie threaded his fingers through Priest's hair as he shifted up to his knees to roll his hips forward, and Priest squeezed his ass, bringing him even closer.

Priest flicked his tongue over the nipple near his mouth, and when Robbie's fingers flexed in his hair, Priest bit down on it, making Robbie thrust into him.

"You want it hard, like that?" Priest said as he looked up at Robbie's flushed face and tongued his nipple.

"Mhmm," Robbie said. "Do it again."

Priest smirked. "Bossy." He slipped his hands into the elastic of Robbie's briefs to cup his bare ass, as he lowered his head and bit and sucked at Robbie's nipple.

Priest kneaded the firm cheeks until Robbie was rocking against him and all but panting, and he could feel Robbie's pre-cum soaking through his briefs.

"Shit, you need to..." Robbie rolled his hips forward again. "You need to stop or I'm going to—"

"Come?" Priest said as he sat back against the headboard.

"Yes," Robbie said as he ground his hips down and arched into Priest's touch. "*God*. Yes..."

"Well, you're not going to want to do that just yet," Priest said, as his eyes shifted over Robbie's shoulder to where Julien was now standing, naked as the day he was born. "Julien just got here, and we have plans to—what did you say?—spoil you."

THE SCENE THAT greeted Julien when he walked into the bedroom had his cock stiffening and his feet moving faster.

After he'd finished washing up, he'd debated putting anything back on. But in the end had decided it was just going to get in his way and opted for his preferred state of dress—which was to be *undressed*. It was a decision he was now glad of, as he took in the way Robbie was grinding all over Priest's lap in those cheeky pink briefs, and Julien made a promise to himself.

He would watch Robbie do exactly what he was doing right now *minus* the briefs, by the end of this night.

Robbie looked over his shoulder, ran his fevered eyes down to Julien's cock, and licked his lips. *Putain*. Robbie and Priest were so intoxicating to watch together that Julien reached for his dick and began to stroke.

"Damn," Robbie said, and went to move off Priest's lap to his side, but Julien shook his head.

"*Non,*" Julien said. "You stay right there. Joel? *Écarte tes jambes.*"

Priest reached for something under his pillow and tossed it toward Julien, then opened his legs, which widened Robbie's straddle and emphasized what a fantastic ass he had.

Julien eyed the bottle of lube as he moved up the bed to kneel behind Robbie. "*Dieu.* Pink is always my favorite color on you. Pink cheeks, pink lips..." He trailed his fingers along Robbie's spine until he reached the edge of his briefs, then dipped them inside and down Robbie's crack, making him moan. "Your pretty pink hole. You look lovely in any shade, and tonight's no exception, *princesse.*"

"*Ah...* More, Jules," Robbie said, turning his head so his breath ghosted on Julien's lips. "I want more."

Julien stroked his finger over Robbie's hole, and when Robbie sucked in a breath, Julien said, "I'm going to give you a whole lot more, *je te le promets.* But first—*embrasse-moi.*"

Julien crushed their lips together, and as he did, he massaged the pad of his finger over Robbie's eager entrance. Robbie's ass flexed, and then he gasped and pulled his mouth free to curse, and Julien saw that Priest's hand was now working Robbie's cock.

Julien eyed his husband, saw a glimpse of the black briefs he still wore, and knew that Priest had to be as hard as both him and Robbie. So Julien removed his hand from Robbie's briefs and said, "Let's get these off you."

Robbie nodded and hurried off Priest's lap to shimmy out of his briefs, and Julien was right: Priest's enormous cock was practically busting through the black material.

When Robbie kicked his briefs aside and looked back to Priest, who'd shifted down the bed and put a second pillow behind his head, his hand found his dick, and Julien did the same. It wasn't often they got Priest stretched out like this for them to visually feast on, and both of them were taking a second to enjoy the moment.

His auburn scruff and thick, messed-up hair on the white pillows only added to Priest's rugged appeal, and once you added in the muscles, the treasure trail, and those snug boxer briefs outlining his heavy erection, it was a miracle both Julien and Robbie didn't come right then and there.

Priest spread his legs a little wider and reached down to rub his covered cock and balls, and Robbie was back on the bed in a heartbeat after that. As his knees hit the mattress, Robbie looked at where Julien was still situated between Priest's calves, and Julien nodded to Priest's working hand.

"Why don't you get between us tonight, *princesse*? Give Priest a helping hand."

Robbie grinned and then moved to settle between Priest's thighs, on his knees. With his naked back now facing Julien, Robbie gave a final glance over his shoulder as he bent down over Priest, and when he gave his ass a little shake, Julien smirked.

Oh, oui, Robbie understood without any more words that the *more* Julien had promised him minutes ago was about to be delivered in full.

CHAPTER TWENTY-ONE

If this is what our marital bed is going to be like,
sign me up for life - Robbie

PRIEST LOOKED DOWN to where Robbie was now naked, bent over, and running his teasing mouth all over his covered dick, and clenched his teeth together in an effort not to tell him to take the damn boxers off.

He was trying to remember why he'd kept them on in the first place, but as Robbie's breath dampened the material molding them to his throbbing cock, Priest was starting to believe it had been a really stupid idea. Julien was naked and hard, kneeling behind Robbie's bent-over frame, and the hungry way he was watching Robbie mouth Priest's dick wasn't helping matters in the slightest.

Priest wanted out of his confines. He wanted Robbie's mouth on his flesh, and when he raised his eyes to Julien's, Priest bucked up. Those jade eyes looked as though they were glowing, as Julien ran them all over him and licked along his lower lip, and Priest changed his mind.

He wanted out of his confines, and wanted Robbie's *and* Julien's mouths on him. Fuck, he might even beg for it.

Robbie's fingers crept into the sides of Priest's boxer briefs, and as he began to pull them down and his cock sprang free, Priest looked down in time to see Robbie's tongue come out and swipe a long, wet path from root to tip.

Robbie moaned as he reached out to angle him upward, and then swirled his tongue around the wide head, where he dipped his tongue into the slit, making Priest curse. Robbie removed his lips and aimed his flirty eyes up at Priest, then he did it again, and that was it. Priest reached out to take a handful of Robbie's hair and direct him, and as Robbie sucked him, deep between those sweet lips of his, Priest looked up to find Julien zeroed in on the two of them.

Usually on the other end of this scenario, Priest reveled in the switch tonight, and opened himself up to the two men watching and working him over, and when Robbie raised his head and looked over his shoulder at Julien, whatever passed between them was exactly what Priest had been hoping for.

Robbie shifted a little to the side until Julien was bent down beside him, a hand now planted firmly on the mattress by Priest's hip, as Robbie held Priest's cock up for him like a fucking gift.

Priest's body was as taut as a tripwire, as their mouths hovered on either side of his aching erection. He wanted this more than his next goddamn breath, and when Julien and Robbie ran a tongue up either side of his shaft, and then took turns sucking him into their mouths, Priest groaned and slammed his head back into the pillow.

Fucking hell. The two of them licked, sucked, and then kissed one another around the head of his dick, until they were both moaning between Priest's thighs, and finally he said, "*Shit.* No more."

They both looked up, and Julien grinned. "What do you think, *princesse?* Do *you* want more?"

Robbie grinned like the devil—*a really fucking pretty one*—and then nodded as Julien moved back to his position behind Robbie, and Robbie climbed up over Priest's body, straddled his waist, and then leaned down to say against Priest's lips, "I want a whole lot more."

Priest growled and ran his hands around Robbie's hips to his ass, and then thrust up, rubbing his hard cock under Robbie's balls. Priest then spread Robbie's cheeks for Julien, who picked up the lube and poured a liberal amount down his crack, and when Julien tossed it aside and slid his finger along the slippery path and into Robbie's hole, Robbie cried out and Priest sucked his lip.

"That kind of more?"

"Yes, *ah*..." Robbie moaned again when Julien added a second finger, making Robbie writhe on top of Priest, leaving a sticky path in his wake.

Priest ran his hands up and down Robbie's sides, and Robbie planted his hands on either side of Priest's head to get more momentum, and as he began to rock back on Julien's fingers, Priest reached down to stroke Robbie's cock.

"Oh God," Robbie said as he stared down into Priest's face. His eyelids heavy with arousal. "I... Jules... Fuck—"

Julien looked around Robbie to Priest, and his hungry expression was exactly the same as their princess's, as Priest slid his hands back down to join Julien's and added a third finger in Robbie's stretched little entrance. They moved in and out of him, making Robbie whimper, and then Priest said, "Hands and knees, sweetheart. Get up over me. Let Julien watch us together like this."

Priest and Julien removed their fingers, and Robbie moved into position, placing his palms by Priest's head, and his knees by his sides, and when Priest nudged the wide head of his shaft against Robbie's entry, he shoved back onto him.

Priest thrust up off the bed, and as Robbie's body enveloped him, Priest shut his eyes and clamped his hands on Robbie's thighs. It felt so fucking good that Priest's toes curled and his balls threatened to explode. But when he finally managed to get some of his damn control together, Priest opened his eyes to see Robbie looking down at him with an expression of lust wrapped up in a whole lot of love.

As Robbie began to move over him in a sensual body roll, Priest ran a hand up to his neck and pulled his head down to kiss him, and Robbie went wild. He ran his hands through Priest's hair and moaned as he held on. Then he found the right pace for himself, and began to ride Priest until he was tearing his mouth free and panting.

"Ah, ah, *ah*..." Robbie said as he moved on top of him. "Damn. Priest."

"Mmm," Priest said, his hands molding to Robbie's ass as it flexed, and when he buried his head in Priest's neck, Julien came into view. His eyes were fastened to where Priest was penetrating their princess, and his cock was hard as a steel rod. "You ready for Julien, princess?"

"*Yes*," Robbie said, his voice reedy and thin.

"Good, because he's looking at you like you are the best thing he's ever seen." Priest pulled out but kept his hands in place to hold Robbie open for Julien, then he kissed Robbie's cheek and said, "And you know what? He's not fucking wrong."

JULIEN MOVED FROM his knees to his feet, and as he positioned himself behind Robbie, he ran the tip of his cock over his stretched hole. Robbie moaned and then pushed up until he was hovering over Priest again on his hands and knees, and as he looked over his shoulder, his eyes found Julien's as he slowly sank his cock into Robbie's glorious body.

Robbie tipped his head back and moaned Julien's name, and Julien put his hands on Robbie's waist and began a steady pace in and out. As Robbie's body grew accustomed to the fit of Julien's, he began to move to the same rhythm, and Julien leaned down and pressed a kiss between Robbie's shoulder blades.

"*Très bien, princesse.* I love the way your body fits mine."

Robbie trembled and reached back to grab at Julien's leg. He dug his fingers in as Julien began to move again, and when Julien saw Priest crane up and bite and suck at Robbie's chest, he pulled out and then tunneled back inside.

"Ah... *Fuck*," Robbie said as his arms faltered and he fell down over Priest, who chuckled and reached up to stroke Robbie's cock and balls, then behind to Julien's tight sac as he powered back inside their princess.

"He making you feel good, sweetheart?" Priest said by Robbie's ear.

Robbie panted. "So fucking good."

Julien leaned forward and wrapped his arms around Robbie's waist until his front was flush with Robbie's back, and when he caught Priest's eyes on him, Julien began to roll his hips, nice and slow, until Robbie was whimpering and searching out Priest's mouth.

As the two kissed, Julien continued to move inside Robbie's body until his control threatened to give out on him, and then he pulled free, and Priest was right there to take his place.

As his huge cock sought out its target, Robbie's hole acted like a beacon, and Julien helped guide Priest the rest of the way inside. Priest was long enough that he was able to get right up inside Robbie and then some, and as Robbie took him in with no problem at all, Julien was close to coming.

Beautiful, sexy, and totally uninhibited, Robbie was theirs, from the tip of his gorgeous head down to the soles of his pretty feet, and when Priest pulled out several minutes later and Julien replaced him, that had never been more apparent.

Robbie shoved back onto him, and this time Julien took his shoulder and pulled him up against his body so he was now on his spread knees, straddled over Priest. Julien reached down to work his cock for him, and Robbie wrapped an arm up around his neck.

They were in the same position they had been in that night at CRUSH. But this time there were no clothes between them and nobody else in the way, and Priest was watching them with an untamed look that had Julien's hand pumping Robbie a little faster.

"I'm going to watch you come all over him tonight," Julien said in Robbie's ear. "And then, *princesse*, we're going to come in you."

Robbie's breathing accelerated, as did the movement of his hips, when Julien began to drive in and out. Robbie tipped his head back, and Julien kissed along his neck until Robbie moaned and his ass clenched. Then his entire body stiffened, and Robbie shouted out Julien's name, as he came all over Priest's hard dick and the hand working it.

Julien let go of Robbie's spent cock to take hold of his chin so he could kiss him, and when he groaned into Julien's mouth, Julien's balls tightened, and he came in a rush.

"Mmm," Robbie said, as Julien's chest heaved behind him. "Kiss me again, Jules... Fuck."

Julien obliged as his dick slid free, then they both looked down at Priest, who said, "You better *both* get over here—now."

ROBBIE FELT ABOUT as amazing as Priest looked. Sprawled out under Robbie's spread legs, he was on his back, his hard cock in his hand, with Robbie's cum all over him.

Julien had made damn good on his promise, and as he moved up alongside Priest to kiss him, Robbie shifted back down to his knees and—

"Oh fucking *hell*, Robert."

—sank down on Priest with his slick, hot hole—courtesy of their Frenchman.

"He feels good, *oui?*" Julien whispered against Priest's ear as they both looked up at Robbie. "Our fiancé."

"He feels amazing and well used...in the best way ever." As Priest grabbed a handful of each ass cheek, he pulled Robbie down until all three of their faces were close. "One of you better fucking kiss me in the next three seconds or—"

Robbie didn't let Priest finish. He crushed their mouths together as Priest began to move in him, and when Robbie raised his head to let out a moan of toe-curling ecstasy, Julien took his place.

Damn. The two of them were so incredibly hot, and seeing them side by side like this, their mouths melded, Julien's hand on Priest's face, made Robbie's hips move a little faster. As his dick stirred back to life, Robbie put his hands on Priest's chest and pushed up until he was seated, and began to ride him until Priest was hitting Robbie's prostate.

Priest pulled his mouth free to let out a groan, and his hands found Robbie's hips as he began to tunnel up in to him. Robbie swiped his fingers through his cum and used it to slick his dick, and as Julien whispered something in Priest's ear and then kissed him, that was it for Priest. He clenched his teeth, arched his head back into the pillows, and then came inside Robbie in a hot flood of release.

It was the perfect end to a perfect night, and as the three of them caught their breaths, Robbie reached for the towel he'd tossed at the end of the bed, cleaned himself off, and then looked down at the two staring up at him. "Well, if that's what our marital bed is going to be like, sign me up for life."

Priest grabbed Robbie and tumbled him down between him and Julien. "It was too late anyway. You already said yes."

"Mhmm," Julien said in his ear, and then kissed Robbie under it. "You're stuck with us for life now."

"Sounds like heaven to me," Robbie said, as he turned his head to kiss Julien.

"It does, doesn't it?" Julien whispered, and then smiled against Robbie's lips.

Robbie looked to Priest to see his eyes were shut and his mouth was relaxed, as he lay there silently, his breathing even.

It was amazing. After all this time of *not* sleeping, Priest seemed to be making up for it. He could now fall asleep in the blink of an eye and stay that way for hours, and while some might be a little miffed at that after what had just happened there tonight, Robbie merely turned to his side and cuddled into Julien to watch over him, both of them happy that Priest could now find peace so quickly when he lay down beside them.

"Sweet dreams, *princesse*," Julien said as he switched off the lamps.

Robbie smiled into the pillow and knew nothing would compare to the dream he'd walked into tonight, and whispered back, "Sweet dreams to you, Jules." Not a second later, he drifted off into a blissful sleep.

CHAPTER TWENTY-TWO

Dumbstruck.
Apparently, that's what Logan Mitchell makes my men.
I just might have to kill him
- Priest

"STOP FIDGETING," PRIEST said in Robbie's ear, as he stood behind him with Julien on Logan and Tate's front stoop.

It was Sunday night, and when they'd gotten back from the cottage, Logan had called and invited them over for drinks if they weren't busy. Since their new house was only three blocks from the Mitchells', Robbie had jumped at the chance to be able to tell someone other than his family his big news, until they'd walked up the pathway to the front door. Now he seemed a little...apprehensive.

Robbie tilted his chin up and then said haughtily, "I'm *not* fidgeting."

Priest's lips quirked, and he thought, *Nice try.* "Yes, you are. Nervous about something?"

"Nervous?" Robbie gave a little laugh. "Why would I be nervous? I've known Logan and Tate for years."

"*Oui*," Julien said, as he trailed a finger under Robbie's chin. "But I believe Priest was asking if you were nervous about telling them we got engaged this weekend."

Robbie scraped his teeth over his lower lip. "Why would I be nervous about that?"

Priest leaned in until their lips were barely a whisper apart. "I don't know. Why would you be?"

Robbie's cheeks flushed pink, and just as he was about to reply, the front door was pulled open, and he whirled around to face Tate.

"Hey, guys," Tate said as he ran a hand through his disheveled hair. "Come in, come in. Logan's in the, ah"—Tate cleared his throat and stepped to the side—"he's in the kitchen."

"Thanks for having us over tonight," Robbie said as he walked inside.

"Of course," Tate said, and Priest noticed the slightly rumpled shirt he was wearing. "You can head straight through. You remember the way, Robbie."

Robbie nodded and disappeared toward the kitchen with Julien following.

As Priest passed by Tate, he pointed to his shirt. "You missed a button."

Tate glanced down, and sure enough, two of the center buttons were off. He'd either been running late and rushing or—

"At least it's only one," Tate said with a wry grin. "If you'd been five minutes later, who knows how I'd be greeting the door."

Exactly what Priest had suspected. No wonder Logan wasn't the one to greet them; he was probably in the kitchen trying to get himself under control...or having a stiff drink.

"We can always do this some other time," Priest said, making Tate laugh.

"Nah, it builds character for him to have to wait for it occasionally."

Priest barked out a laugh, as Tate shut the door behind him. "That or drives them to drink."

"Either way, Logan will survive," Tate said. "Come on in."

Priest headed through the beautifully decorated home, and while the style wasn't really his, Priest had to admit, the Mitchells' place was cozy and inviting.

Over to his left, there was a fireplace that had a TV mounted above it and a sitting area facing it. The front bay window let in the moonlight tonight, and as he followed Tate through that space and past an elegant dining area, Priest heard the chatter of the other three men in the kitchen.

As he and Tate stepped inside, Priest spotted Julien standing on one side of a long kitchen island and Robbie beside him with an arm tucked through the crook of Julien's elbow, head resting on his shoulder.

Logan was standing on the opposite side of the counter with a cutting board, lemons—one of which had been cut into segments —and a knife. There was a tequila bottle on the marble, and two flipped-over shot glasses beside it.

Ahh, Priest thought, as he wandered down toward his men. So the licking, sipping, and sucking had most certainly started before they'd arrived.

"Okay, old man," Logan said to Robbie. "What can I start you with tonight?"

Robbie pinned Logan with a withering stare. "Who are you calling old man? You're the one who turned—"

"Say it, and you'll regret it," Logan said, pointing the knife at Robbie.

Robbie rolled his eyes. "Oh, whatever," he said, and then he looked at Priest, and the grin on his face was pure mischief.

"You going to tell me what you want?" Logan said.

"I'm *thinking*," Robbie said, and pursed his lips. "Do these two first." When Logan raised an eyebrow, Robbie seemed to realize what he'd said and laughed. "I mean get them a *drink*. Geez, Logan, get your mind out of my men's pants."

Priest kissed Robbie's temple and said, "Don't be too hard on him, sweetheart. Tate's already doing that."

"Oh really?" Robbie said, as the rascal looked between Logan and Tate. "In that case, how about a Cock Tease? Do you know how to make one of those?"

Logan turned toward Tate and drawled, "I'm positive one of us does. Right, Tate?"

Tate flashed Logan a grin. "Ah huh. I'm fairly familiar with that one."

"Aren't we all," Julien said, and looked over Robbie's head to Priest, making it clear to everyone in the room exactly who the holdout was in their particular threesome.

Logan scoffed and began to slice the other lemons on the board. Then he looked at Priest and said with a curl to his lips, "Now why doesn't it surprise me that *you're* the control freak in this relationship?"

Priest eyed Logan. "Because despite your tendency to be a pain in the ass, you're one of the smartest people I know."

Logan stopped slicing and looked at Robbie and Julien. "Did he just give me a compliment?" Julien smirked as Robbie nodded, and Logan continued, "Can someone please note that down somewhere? And for the record, Priest, I'm never a pain in the ass to the people I love. I'm careful to make it an enjoyable experience. Right, Tate?"

"Oh my God," Robbie said. "How many drinks have you had?"

"One shot of tequila," Logan said. "And a nice, long suck of Tate's—"

"Lemons," Tate said, and then shoved a bottle of raspberry and vanilla rum Logan's way. "Here, two ounces of each of those, and I'll grab the cranberry and pineapple juice. What can I get for you, Julien?"

"He'll have a Tom Collins, and Priest will have an Old Fashioned," Robbie said.

Priest smiled and slipped his hand down over Robbie's ass, as

Julien winked at him and said, "*Merci de prendre soin de nous, princesse.*"

Robbie's face flushed, and Priest's eyes shifted to Logan, who was laughing at him.

"You all right there, Robbie?" Logan said. "Or do you need a seat in case your knees give out on you?"

Robbie turned back to face Logan. "Shut it, Logan, or...I don't know, go suck on Tate's...lemon."

"Is that what we're calling it now? Good to know." Tate laughed as he mixed Julien's and Priest's drinks and then slid them across the counter. "Why don't you three come with me? We can get the fire pit going and settle in while Logan gets some food ready for us."

"Would you like some help?" Julien asked Logan.

"You know what?" Logan said. "I think I might. It's not every day one gets the opportunity to cook with one of the greats."

"And let's be real, any help you can get will improve the meal," Tate joked.

Robbie followed Tate's lead and headed outside, and Priest stopped to look back at Julien, who was walking around the counter to where Logan was holding out an apron to him. Deciding to give Logan a little bit of his own medicine, Priest crossed his arms and looked at the pair.

"Hey, Mitchell?" Priest called out from the back door, and once Julien had his apron on, Logan turned to face Priest. "Don't even think about flirting with my husband while I'm not here."

Logan smirked. "Worried we're about to heat up the kitchen?"

Priest didn't crack a smile as he eyed Logan's smug face, then he looked at Julien. "And you, try to be a little less attractive or something, would you?"

Julien laughed at Priest's stern expression.

"I'm serious," Priest said. "The whole country knows that when you cook, you only get hotter. So, Mitchell, behave yourself."

"Oh relax, Priest," Logan said. "I'm a happily married man."

"So are we, and look what happened to us."

"Priest, you wound me," Logan said. "You really think I'm going to hit on your husband? And here I thought we'd come so far."

Priest shrugged, and when Logan finally started to bristle a little, he laughed. "I'm just fucking with you, Mitchell. Enjoy your cooking lesson. You're learning from the best."

Logan hurled a lemon in his direction, and when it missed, he muttered, "Fucker," and shot the finger at Priest as he walked out the back door.

A COUPLE OF hours later, as Robbie finished off his latest Cock Tease, he felt the buzzed sense of relaxation wash over him.

He shifted back between the men flanking either side of him, and he knew that Julien and Priest were wondering when he was going to tell Logan and Tate their news. He was building to it, really, he was. But there just hadn't been the right moment, or, you know, the right amount of alcohol.

It wasn't that he was afraid to tell them. It was just that, after the way Logan had reacted to the three of them when they'd first gotten together, Robbie had started to second-guess the response he might get now.

Robbie had known Logan and Tate for a long time, and considered them family—and if he said this out loud and saw anything but the joy he felt about it all, he wasn't quite sure how he'd deal with that.

Robbie's eyes shifted to the man he'd once fancied himself in love with, and he let his gaze trail over Logan's coal-colored hair, those laughing blue eyes, and the pressed polo shirt and shorts.

Logan would always be one of the most attractive men Robbie had ever seen. But he'd come to realize that the love he felt for Julien and Priest was so much more than the infatuation he'd had for Logan. These two men beside him owned him body and soul. Exactly the same way, Robbie supposed, that Tate owned Logan, and that was what it all came down to: that feeling of belonging.

It all makes sense now...

"Earth to Robbie," Logan said, but it wasn't until Julien said in Robbie's ear, "*Ça va, princesse?*" that Robbie snapped out of his daze.

He turned his head until his lips were only inches from Julien's. "Mhmm. I was just thinking."

"I don't even want to know about what," Logan said.

Robbie licked his lips and then decided, what the hell. Now was as good a time as any. "My fiancés, actually."

All conversation ceased at that little announcement, and when the words Robbie had said registered, Logan looked between all three of them and said, "Fiancés?"

Robbie bit into his lip and waited, and when no one said anything, he was about two seconds away from demanding someone speak.

Then, finally, Logan did. "Okay, I don't know if you two are brave or just crazy to take him on for life."

Robbie's mouth fell open at the same time Logan and Tate got to their feet. And as they walked around the fire pit, Robbie realized Logan was messing with him.

"Excuse me," Robbie said as he stood and faced off with Logan. "As if people didn't say the same thing to Tate about you."

"I believe you were probably one of them." Logan smirked as he reached for Robbie and pulled him into a hug. "But we proved you all wrong. It's nice to see you doing the same thing."

Robbie wound his arms around Logan's waist and grinned into the side of his neck.

"I'm happy for you," Logan whispered, and kissed his cheek. "I'm happy for you all."

Robbie wasn't sure why he felt so emotional, but when he pulled back, he found himself wiping a tear from the corner of his eye.

Tate was busy shaking Julien's and Priest's hands, and when all three looked at Robbie and Logan, Tate nodded and said, "I want to thank you two for finally giving Robbie someone to dream about besides my husband."

Robbie eyed Logan and made a show of rolling his eyes. "Oh please, his charm hasn't worked on me for a long time."

Tate scoffed. "And here I thought that day would never come."

"Neither did I," Priest said, making Robbie look in his direction. "What? You must admit, when we first met, you were rather besotted by him."

Robbie's face heated with embarrassment under Priest's steady gaze and crooked grin.

"You didn't exactly keep it a secret," Tate pointed out.

"It's not *my* fault," Robbie said. "Everyone who meets Logan is dumbstruck. It's like a rite of passage. His face is too perfect or something. But then he opens his mouth and—"

"Excuse me," Logan said. "You are in my house, you do remember that, right? Buzzed on *my* liquor."

Robbie adopted a fake pout and batted his lashes. "Mhmm. It's really good, too."

"Plus," Logan said, crossing his arms, "no one I know has ever complained when I've opened my mouth."

Robbie started laughing, delighted by the familiar volleying with Logan. It had always been that way with them, and he knew it always would be. Then Julien managed to snag everyone's attention.

"I have to agree with Robbie on this one," he said to Logan. "I remember the first time I met you. The night Priest sent me to The Popped Cherry. I have to admit, I was rather... What did you call it, *princesse?* Dumbstruck?"

Robbie's mouth fell open as he remembered the exact moment he'd seen Julien sitting at Tate's bar. He'd told Logan that he couldn't go and serve him because it was, well, Jules, and just like the cocky bastard Logan was, he'd sauntered right up to Julien, not having a clue who he was, and taken his order.

Julien chuckled at Robbie's expression, and when Robbie's brain kicked back in, he said, "Wait, you thought Logan was *hot?*"

"Again, I'm right here," Logan said.

Julien's eyes twinkled as he stared at Robbie. "Is. He *is* hot. So is Tate. How many times have you told me this?"

"Yeah, but you and Priest are—"

"Married? *Oui.* And you are engaged. That doesn't mean we're blind, *mon cher petit.*" Julien winked. "But don't fret; I was merely biding my time with him until someone prettier got the courage to come and talk to me."

"I wasn't nervous that night," Robbie lied.

"You were *so* nervous that night," Logan said.

Tate laughed. "It's true. He went on and on about how he'd watched every episode of your show. Then he refused to go and serve you—"

"So you got me instead," Logan said.

Priest's and Julien's rumbling laughter had Robbie death-glaring at Logan and Tate. "*Ugh*, you two suck."

"Just a little payback," Tate said.

"Plus," Logan said, "I got you to go over and talk to him, and look at you now? You're engaged to the man. So I'd say you owe me."

"Actually, that's not true," Priest said, and Robbie could've kissed him for that. "Julien would've found a way to talk to him one way or another. I sent him there for that very reason. There-fore, I would say that Robert owes *me*—for the rest of his life."

Priest's voice had dipped a register, to that sexy place it went whenever he was naked and inside Robbie or Julien, and when Robbie met his wicked gaze, he saw the heated desire and love swirling in Priest's grey eyes.

"I'm, uh, suddenly getting a little...tired," Robbie said, and patted his mouth in a fake yawn that no one bought.

Julien held his hand out, and when Robbie took it and snuggled into his side, Tate stood back with Logan.

"We're thinking about a ceremony in early October," Priest

said, as they all walked back toward the house. "We'd like it if you two could be there."

"We wouldn't miss it for the world," Tate said.

"Good," Robbie said, as they stopped in the kitchen. "I mean, you'll get an invitation, of course. It's going to be at my parents' lake house where we used to spend our summers. My sisters are organizing everything, which basically means Bianchi madness will follow."

Logan chuckled. "Well, count us in. We have to come and see the blushing bride on his wedding day."

As they made their way through the house, Robbie grinned. "Just make sure you bring your tissues."

Logan opened the front door, and when Priest and Julien stepped outside, he said to Robbie, "My tissues?"

"Yes," Robbie said, as he looked into Logan's handsome face. "Because I'm going to be so beautiful you're going to cry your eyes out for having let me go."

Logan's eyes softened, and he leaned forward and kissed Robbie's cheek. "In that case, I'll be sure to bring three boxes."

As Robbie straightened, Tate winked at him and said, "See you at work."

"See you then, Mr. Mitchell," Robbie said, and then jogged down the stairs to join Julien and Priest.

Logan called out, "And what will we be calling *you* next month?"

The three of them took one another's hands, and as they walked down the path, Robbie called out over his shoulder, "Come to the wedding and you'll find out."

CHAPTER TWENTY-THREE

Robbie has taught us how fun life can be
when you travel a little lighter—figuratively speaking, of course
-Julien & Priest

October...

IT'S A GOOD weekend for a wedding. It's a good weekend for a wedding. It's a good weekend for my *wedding.* At least, that was what Robbie was telling himself, but the ominous cloud rolling in over the lake wasn't boding too well for him. "Val? You gave the right address for the flowers, didn't you?"

"Uh huh," Val said from the couch in their ma and pa's great room.

"And the caterer? He knows where he's going. Right, Felicity?"

"Yes, Roberta. Unruffle thy feathers—"

"I mean, I can see chairs down there," Robbie said, ignoring her, as he walked closer to the French doors that led out to the deck of the Bianchis' summer lake house. "But I don't see flowers.

I don't see flowers, I don't see programs, and...where are the bows? I don't see the organza bows on the chairs like I asked for."

As a fat drop of rain hit the glass pane of the door, Robbie jerked back as though he'd been hit in the face with a pie.

"Is that *rain?*" he said, his eyes widening as another drop hit, then another, and then another. "Oh my God." Robbie whirled around to face his sisters, who were all sitting on the couch sharing a bucket of popcorn. "*Why* is it raining?"

Felicity handed the bucket to Val, got to her feet, and walked to Robbie.

"Because today is *Fri*day, and you are getting married tomorrow," she said as she put her hands on his shoulders. "It's allowed to rain today."

"No. No, it's not," Robbie said. "If it rains today, the ground gets muddy, the chairs are white, and then *ugh*." He spun back to see that the raindrops were falling a little faster now. "What a disaster."

Felicity wrapped her arm around Robbie's waist and laid her head on his shoulder. "It's not going to be a disaster," she said. "Well, unless Penny's water breaks."

Robbie's head whipped around to pin his oldest sister with a glare that spoke of his feelings on that. Penny was six days late with no baby in sight, and he'd like to keep it that way—for at least forty more hours. "I swear, you better keep your legs shut—"

"If only you'd had that talk with her nine months ago, brother," Val said, and Penny picked up a piece of popcorn and threw it.

"Don't worry," Penny said, and smoothed her hands over her *very* swollen belly. "This kid seems comfortable where she is for now."

"As am I," Robbie said. "For now. She can arrive any time after midnight tomorrow."

"Why then?" Val laughed. "Is that when you turn back into a pumpkin?"

"No, it's when he turns back into our loving brother, Robbie," Felicity said. "Instead of this high-strung bridezilla version."

"Oh, whatever," Robbie said. "I just want this to be perfect. It's only going to happen once."

Felicity bumped shoulders with him. "Or twice if you're Julien and Priest."

Robbie grinned at the mention of their names and knew he was incredibly lucky to have a family who not only understood him, but was willing to embrace the unique and wonderful men he'd fallen in love with.

"Yes, well, *once* for me," Robbie said. "But since they've done this before, I want it perfect. I want to make it different this time."

"Umm, pretty sure you've got that covered," Felicity said. "Your sisters are organizing it—and hello, us Bianchi bitches know how to throw a party—your father is walking you down the aisle, and your nonna is going to be sitting with your ma in the front row with a box of tissues. From what you've told us, they don't have a whole lot of family—"

"Try none. Well, none worth mentioning," Robbie said, and thought about how extraordinary Julien and Priest were despite that fact.

"And now you're about to give them an enormous one. From what I've seen, they're loving that as much as they love you. So see? It's already different and perfect."

Felicity was right: he needed to stop worrying and enjoy this. Julien and Priest would be back with groceries for dinner any minute now, and Robbie didn't want them to see him losing his cool.

"You're right," Robbie said, then turned back to look out the doors.

"Of course I am."

Robbie smirked at his sister and hugged her in close, and that was when he noticed that the rain had stopped, and as the sun began to shine, a smile curved his lips.

There, now *it's perfect. No one's going to rain on my damn parade.*

"HOW MUCH DO you think Robbie is panicking right now?" Julien said, as he peered out the windshield of the Range Rover.

They'd barely made it into the car with the groceries before the rain had started to fall, and as Priest pulled to a stop at the lights leading out of the parking lot, he chuckled. "I think it's a pretty safe bet to say a whole damn lot."

Julien laughed as he looked at the lone black cloud that seemed to have rolled in. But it didn't look like it would hang around too long. "*Oui*. At least his sisters are with him and he's not sitting there alone watching this."

"Right," Priest said. "I'm sure they know how to deal with a Robbie meltdown better than we do."

"Or know how to provoke one," Julien said with a grin. "Sisters are really good at that kind of thing."

Priest reached for Julien's hand and laced their fingers together. "I love seeing you like this."

"Like what?"

"Happy," Priest said. "Free to be able to talk about Jacquelyn with a smile on your face. It's been a long time coming. There's many things I love about Robert, but giving you that freedom is high on the list."

Julien stroked his thumb over Priest's where their hands were joined.

"You both gave me that," Julien said softly. "You kept me functioning. Kept me safe and alive, to make it to this point."

As Priest watched the road, Julien took in the strength of his arms and hands, and knew as long as Priest was by his side, he'd *always* feel safe.

"You know what I love?" Julien said.

"What's that?" Priest asked, his eyes on the road.

"The exact same thing as you."

Priest frowned and looked at Julien.

"I love the way Robbie makes you smile and laugh. It's relaxed, easy, and a little…goofy."

"Goofy? Do you want to walk the rest of the way back to the lake?" Priest asked.

Julien chuckled. "*Non*. I'd rather sit here and watch you scowl." He ran his hand down Priest's arm. "I just mean that he brings out a more carefree side to you, that's all. It's wonderful, and is high up there on *my* list of things that I love about our *princesse*."

When Priest pulled up at a red light and looked at him, Julien said in all seriousness, "You deserve to be happy, *mon amour*. You know that, right?"

"I've always been happy with you."

Julien's smile softened. "I know that. But I mean in *all* aspects of your life. We tend to hang on to our baggage a little too tightly, you and me. I think Robbie's been great at teaching us just how fun life can be when you travel a little lighter."

"Figuratively speaking." Priest chuckled. "But I agree. We'd always hoped for that, for someone who could balance us out. But I never knew how *complete* he'd make us feel. Does that make sense?"

"It does," Julien said, because he'd been feeling the same thing. "I can't wait to see where we go from here. From this weekend on."

Priest gave a half smile that was so charming it made Julien's pulse spike. "I can't even begin to imagine."

"It won't be boring," Julien said. "That's for sure."

"No, it certainly won't be," Priest said, and winked. "In fact, I think it's going to be pretty damn spectacular. With you two in it, how could it be anything but?"

"*Espèce de flatteur, va.*"

"That's a step up from goofy," Priest said. "I'll take it."

"Mhmm. A big step," Julien said, and then noticed that the rain had stopped. "Look. The crisis has been averted."

"For now," Priest said, and Julien shoved at his arm.

"Don't jinx us."

"You're right. We have enough to get through before tomorrow. The rain doesn't need to add to it."

Priest wasn't wrong. They had dinner with Robbie and his sisters tonight, then *he* was finally going to meet Robbie's nonna, Cheryl Bianchi.

"I think we'll be just fine, *mon amour*. I have a good feeling about this, but we better get home soon. If Robbie's sisters are anything like him, I really don't want to deal with four hangry Bianchis."

Priest chuckled, but didn't argue. Instead, he pressed his foot a little harder on the gas and got them back to the lake house in record time.

AFTER DINNER WITH his sisters wrapped up, Robbie led Penny into the living room along with Julien and Priest, while Val and Felicity took care of the dishes. It was closing in on eight o'clock, and their parents were due to arrive any minute now.

His nonna had spent the week at his ma and pa's house, and they'd been waiting for his father to get home before heading to the lake house. Tomorrow was all set to be a full-on Bianchi affair —*God help them all*—but Robbie wouldn't have wanted it any other way.

As he and Priest helped lower Penny down into the seat, Julien handed her a couple of cushions.

"I feel like a shipping container with you two helping me up, moving me along to the next spot, and then lowering me down." She shook her head. "I'm probably as heavy as one, too."

As she settled into the seat, Priest straightened and said, "Not at all," at the same time Robbie said, "I'd say you're at *least* a few tons shy of a shipping container."

Priest's eyes widened, and he looked truly worried, as though he might have to step in and save Robbie from a pregnant woman. But when Penny started to laugh uproariously, he visibly relaxed.

"You're lucky I can't get up right now," Penny said when she calmed. "Or I'd kick your scrawny ass for that."

"Excuse me," Robbie said, and turned his head to look at the ass in question. "It's not scrawny." Then he looked to where Priest had just sat with Julien and decided to tease them a little. "You two don't think I have a scrawny ass, do you? I'm positive I've never heard *either* of you describe it that way..."

Julien snorted, and Priest's eyebrow winged up, and just as they looked about to answer, the front door opened and they all turned toward the hallway. Robbie walked in the direction he knew his parents would be coming down, but before he disappeared around the corner, he threw a wink over his shoulder at his men and said, "I'll leave you to discuss that with Penny. I'll be right back."

Robbie headed down the hall, where he saw his nonna handing her coat to his father, and when she turned around to see him, Robbie noticed she was a little frailer than she had been the last time he'd visited, but that didn't stop the smile that lit her face.

"Robert, come and give your nonna a hug," she said, holding her arms out, and Robbie wrapped his arms around her and kissed her on the cheek.

"How are you doing, *vecchietta?*"

"*Psh*. Who are you calling old? I'm doing quite well, thank you very much," she said, reaching for her new walking cane, as Robbie straightened and let her go. "And from what I'm hearing, so are you?"

Robbie looked over his nonna's head to his ma, and when she nodded and offered a reassuring smile, he knew that his *unusual* situation had already been explained—somehow.

God bless his ma.

"I *am*...yes," Robbie said, and held his arm out. As Nonna slipped her hand through the crook of his elbow, Robbie led her toward the living room.

"If you come with me, I'd like to introduce you to—" Robbie drew up short on the word *fiancés*, suddenly feeling a little unsure of himself. It was one thing for her to know about them, but to actually say it out loud to his seventy-six-year-old nonna? Well, that was something else entirely.

She apparently did *not* feel the same way. "Your handsome men, I hope?"

Robbie's eyes widened, and when she grinned at him, she said, "I might be old, Robert, but I haven't lost my memory. It's that lovely fellow from the TV who cooks, am I right? And the handsome lawyer who helped Vanessa? They used to pick you up in the same car."

Well, then. It seemed no explaining was necessary. "That's right."

"Of course it is. I'm not blind."

Clearly. Robbie laughed. "Okay then, come with me and I'll introduce you."

As Robbie directed her through to the living room, Julien and Priest got to their feet and smiled. Then they made their way over to Nonna so she wouldn't have to go too far.

"Nonna," Robbie said. "I'd like to introduce you to Julien, and Pri—Joel, you already know. We all call him Priest because his name is—"

"Mr. Priestley, I remember." As Nonna sized them up, Julien greeted her the way Julien always did: a dreamy kiss to the back of the palm designed to make hearts melt, and Nonna's was no exception.

"*Bonsoir, mademoiselle,*" Julien said. "Robbie has told me so much about you. It's a pleasure to finally meet you."

"The pleasure is mine, Mr. Thornton," she said, squeezing his fingers. "I own one of your cookbooks."

"*Vraiment?*"

"That means *really*," Robbie said, making his nonna smile wider.

"Look at my grandson learning French."

"He's very good at it," Julien said, and Robbie preened at the compliment.

"I'm not surprised. He's always known how to talk, in any

language available to him. And yes, really. It's your French pastry cookbook."

"Oh, *oui, très bien*. We'll have to exchange recipes one day. Robbie's been trying to teach me your pasta sauce. But I'd love the opportunity to cook with you some time."

"My word," Nonna said, and then turned to Robbie. "Did you hear that? He wants to cook with me."

Robbie chuckled and kissed her temple. "Of course he does. You're the best."

She turned to Priest, and Robbie had to admit, he'd been curious about how this meeting would go from the moment he'd started dating Priest. These two knew each other, and Robbie wasn't so sure how his nonna would react to him dating Vanessa's ex...uh, lawyer? Especially considering how much he used to argue with said lawyer at the time.

But as it always seemed to happen when it came to Joel Priestley, no one ever quite reacted to him the way Robbie expected.

"I had a feeling I'd be seeing you again."

Priest looked at Robbie and smiled. "You're a smart lady, then."

"Almost as smart as you, for finally snatching this one up," she said, and Robbie grinned.

"I agree," Priest said, as he took her hand. "How are you, Cheryl?"

"I'm very good, and *very* excited to finally be able to attend one of my grandchildren's weddings." Nonna looked around Priest to Penny, who rolled her eyes.

"We all are," Ma said, as Robbie's parents joined them in the living room.

"We're excited too," Priest said. "We can't thank you enough for agreeing to host it here."

"Oh, don't be silly," Ma said. "We wouldn't have it any other way. But...since it *is* the night before the wedding, and we have a lot to do tomorrow, I think it's time that Robert comes with me."

"Wait? *What?* I have to sleep somewhere else?" Robbie said.

"Yes," his ma said, as she took Robbie's hand. Then she looked at Penny and said, "How are you?"

"Still pregnant," Penny groused, as their father helped her to her feet.

"You poor thing. Go with your pa. He's going to help you upstairs. And Julien, Joel? Did Robbie show you the room you are staying in tonight?"

"Hang on," Robbie said, as Penny disappeared with their father. "They're getting married tomorrow too. Why do I have to sleep somewhere else?"

"Because *they're* already married, dear," his mother said as though it were the most normal thing. Then she patted his arm. "There, there, don't pout. That's your own fault, remember."

Priest and Julien tried to cover a laugh, and Robbie rolled his eyes. "That's not fair."

"Would it help if we told you we'd miss you?" Priest asked, and Robbie poked his tongue out.

"I'll keep your men company until they head off to bed," Robbie's nonna said, as Julien took her hand and escorted her to the couch.

"That would make us very happy," Julien said, and then came over to kiss Robbie on the cheek. "*Bonne nuit, princesse.* I can't wait to see you tomorrow."

When Robbie frowned, Priest started to laugh.

"*Ugh*, fine. Let's go," Robbie said to his ma. "I need my beauty sleep anyway."

"No, you don't," Priest said, and kissed his other cheek. "But you do need to rest. Good night, sweetheart. We'll see *you* tomorrow."

Robbie and his ma headed upstairs and toward the bedrooms he and his sisters used to stay in whenever they came here for the summer. They were on the opposite side to the two guest rooms, which he figured was his mother's intention, and when they finally got to Robbie's room, she sat down on his bed and indicated the spot beside her.

"Felicity told me you asked her to do the ceremony tomorrow."

Robbie nodded as he sat, and when he took her hand in his, Robbie heard her sniff. "Ma? Are you all right?"

"Oh, yes. Don't worry about me. I'm just..." She cupped Robbie's cheek. "I'm just feeling a little bit emotional. That's all."

Robbie placed his hand over hers and then kissed it. "Good emotions?" he asked, wondering if she was at all second-guessing the unusual union her son was about to enter into. "I know this might be a little awkward for you and Pa, but—"

"Robert? Shh...baby. Stop worrying. They're good ones. I'm happy and a little bit sad that my baby boy is all grown up. But mostly I'm so proud of the man you have become."

Robbie's eyes welled, and when she let go of his hand to cradle both his cheeks, she said, "You have always been my sweet boy. The one who had a smile for everyone and wanted nothing more than to be loved. And for that reason, I always worried about you the most. That you would give your love to the wrong person —until now."

Robbie didn't realize until she'd wiped away a tear that he was crying. But when she leaned in and rested her forehead to his like she used to when he was a boy, there was nothing he could do to stop it.

"A person would have to be blind not to see how much those two men love you. This might not be conventional, and it might not come with a legal document attached. But from the moment they asked your father and me for your hand in marriage, they became part of this family, and our family does not embarrass us, Robert. So tomorrow, you go out there and be proud of who you are, because that's the man I raised, and that's the man they love."

Robbie wrapped his arms around his mother's waist, and as she kissed the side of his head, he shut his eyes and held on tight until, finally, he felt together enough to let go. He had the best family in the world. He'd known that a long time ago, but as he sat there with his mother, now going over tomorrow's plans, Robbie realized that not only was he excited about marrying Julien and Priest, he was also excited to give them this.

A family who would love and accept them—and occasionally drive them up the wall—and no amount of money could ever buy that kind of love or happiness.

CHAPTER TWENTY-FOUR

Damn, the two of them make me feel like...wow
~ Robbie

"*BONJOUR, MON CŒUR.*" Priest's voice wrapped around Julien like a caress, as the sun crept between the sheer curtains of the lake house guest room and roused him from his sleep. "The sun is rising, the rain is gone, and you and I are marrying a princess today."

Julien smiled before he even opened his eyes, and when he finally did and turned his head, Priest rolled him to his back.

"*Bonjour*," Julien said as Priest stretched out alongside him, his head propped up on his palm. "You're awake early. Couldn't sleep?"

"I could..." Priest said, as he lowered his head and pressed a soft kiss to Julien's lips. "I just found that I liked what was here better than anything in my dreams."

Julien grinned against Priest's mouth, a sleepy chuckle rumbling from his chest. "Aren't you charming this morning."

Priest kissed his way over to Julien's ear and nuzzled in under it. "I'm charming every morning."

"*Non*, you are not." Julien laughed as he rolled to his side and Priest slid his leg between his, and then slipped his hands into the back of Julien's white briefs. "You are usually broody and silent until you are showered and caffeinated."

Priest eyed him for a minute, and then shrugged. "Fair point. But I'm never like that on my wedding days."

Julien put his hands against Priest's chest and tested the muscle there. "True. You always seem to wake up very *energized* on those particular days."

"You should know; you've been there for both of them."

Julien kissed along Priest's jaw, and when he hummed in the back of his throat, Julien pushed him to his back. As he placed a palm on either side of Priest's head, Priest stared up at him, his grey eyes taking in every feature of Julien's face, as though he were memorizing it for all eternity.

"I love the way you look at me," Julien said, as he ran his fingers through the thick auburn strands, and Priest widened his legs so Julien could settle between them.

"I love looking *at* you. Honestly, I don't know how I got so lucky that I get to do that for the rest of my life." Priest ran his hands up Julien's back and then traced his fingers down one side of his face. "You have such a beautiful soul, Julien. I always knew that. It's right there in everything you do and say. But every day I spend with you, that I see you with Robert? I swear, I fall more in love with you. How is that possible? When I already love you so much?"

Julien's eyes blurred as he kissed Priest's fingertips, then he shifted down the bed until he could lay his head on Priest's chest.

As Priest's heart steadily thudded in his ear, Priest wrapped his arms around him, and Julien said, "I don't know. But I understand how you feel." Julien looked up at Priest. "He's shown us new ways to love each other. Kind of incredible, isn't it?"

"Yes. It really is."

Julien smiled, thinking of their *princesse* sleeping somewhere else in the house, and knew that Priest was missing him just as much as he was.

"Did you text him yet?" Julien asked.

"No," Priest said, and then smiled. "But he texted us about fifteen minutes ago."

Julien chuckled and looked over to their phones on the nightstand. "Of course he did."

"Ah huh," Priest said, and then reached over to grab his. "I thought I'd wait for you to wake up so we could give him a call."

Julien kissed the center of Priest's chest as he shifted up the bed so his head was propped up on the pillow against the headboard. As he unlocked the phone, Priest turned it around and showed Julien the message.

Robbie: Good morning! Happy wedding day! I hope you both slept well. I tossed and turned ALL night. This bed is too big for just me. ~sigh~ I can't wait to see you both today. Or text you. Or call you...

Julien grinned, and could see the pout behind those words as clearly as if Robbie was standing in front of them. When neither of them had responded, a second message had come through, then a third, and then a fourth.

Robbie: Or you know, you could call me maybe?

Robbie: Great, now I have that song in my head.

Robbie: Where are you two? The sun is up. Don't tell me you're actually sleeping in, Jules. Really? Today?

Julien shook his head. "You could've texted him back. Put him out of his misery."

"I could have," Priest said, as Julien got off him and moved to sit up. "But I find that I'm a little weak this morning. One suggestion from him that he come over here, I would've caved like a house of cards."

Julien held his hand out for the phone, and when Priest gave it to him, Julien leaned down and kissed him on the lips. "I don't blame you at all, *mon amour*. I would've done the same thing. But I think the two of us can handle him."

"That's what everyone keeps telling us," Priest said.

"Then let's see if they're right." Julien hit Robbie's number, and not halfway through the first ring, their *princesse* answered.

***

ROBBIE STARED AT the second hand of the clock as it *tick-tick-ticked* its way around too damn slowly for his liking. It was creeping up to seven thirty now, and he'd been staring at it since five.

Ugh, so much for beauty sleep. He'd tossed and turned all night in the bed he used to sleep in just fine whenever they'd come to the lake house. But not last night. No. He'd lain there most of the night thinking how big it felt, how...empty, and had come to the decision that he never wanted to sleep anywhere alone ever again.

Figuring Julien would be up by now doing his yoga—*or if he's lucky, Priest*—Robbie sent them a quick message to let them know that he was up too. Just in case they wanted to, you know, call him on their wedding day.

Robbie stared at the phone, waiting for a reply, and when nothing came through, he sent off another text, and then another, and when he *still* got no response, Robbie let out a deep sigh and texted: **Where are you two? The sun is up. Don't tell me you're actually sleeping in, Jules. Really? Today?**

Feeling slightly desperate, and a little pathetic for how much he missed them, Robbie tossed back the covers and walked over to the large windows that overlooked the lake, and just like that, he forgot all about his restless night.

The morning sunlight was shimmering across the calm water and filtering through the property's tree line to electrify the vibrant colors of the fall leaves. The rich shades of red, orange, and yellow made the morning appear as though it were bathed in gold, and the arbor that had been delivered yesterday evening sat still and silent, beautiful in its solitude, as it overlooked the sparkling water.

Robbie could see his mother down there already, slipping the bouquets of orange roses, burgundy chrysanthemums, and yellow daisies into the organza bows, and Felicity was behind her putting the programs on the chairs with little gold pumpkins on top to hold them in place.

Robbie brought a hand to his heart to try and calm its erratic thudding. But he knew it was no use. *This* was his wedding day. This moment? He'd never have again, and as he stared out at the morning greeting him, he knew it was going to be perfect.

The sound of his phone buzzing had Robbie turning away from the window to see Priest's name and number, and he quickly snatched it and hit answer, before turning back to once again soak in the magnificent view.

"*Bonjour, princesse,*" Julien said, and Priest added, "Good morning, sweetheart."

"Good morning," Robbie said, and bit his lower lip as he imagined them across the house in the guest room, lounging in bed together.

"How are you this morning?" Priest asked, and if he'd called five minutes earlier, Robbie's answer would've been much different.

"I'm wonderful."

"*Oui*, you are that," Julien said, making Robbie want to swoon. "But how are you *feeling*? You said you couldn't sleep in your text?"

Robbie leaned against the wall and watched his mother and Val begin to decorate the arbor with the same beautiful flowers as the bouquets. "Yeah, last night was *long*."

"We're sorry to hear that," Priest said. "Why don't you try and get another hour or so in now?"

"Are you kidding? I couldn't sleep now if I tried," Robbie said. "Plus, I just looked outside and realized..." Robbie trailed off, wondering if they'd think him silly.

"What, *princesse*?" Julien said. "What did you realize?"

Robbie felt his cheeks heat even though he was standing on his own. "Just that I don't want to miss any part of today. Not one second of it. This is our wedding day."

"Yes, it is." Priest's confirmation sent a shiver racing up Robbie's spine.

"It's beautiful out there this morning," Robbie said. "Have you seen? It's the perfect day."

"Of course it is, sweetheart. We wouldn't let it be anything other than perfect for you."

Robbie chuckled as he fiddled with the hem of his pajama top. "I miss you both," he confessed, and then shook his head. "That sounds dumb, I know, but—"

"It doesn't sound dumb at all," Julien said. "We miss you too, and can't wait to see you today."

"Oh yeah?"

"*Oui.*"

"So you haven't forgotten what I look like?" Robbie said. "You don't need me to come and *remind* you, maybe?"

"I told you he'd do this to me, didn't I?" Priest said, and Robbie could hear the smile in his voice.

"Do what?" Robbie asked.

"Test his control," Julien said. "Priest is feeling a little bit *weak* this morning when it comes to you, *princesse*. Better stay out of his path until he can claim you."

Robbie *loved* the sound of that, like, a whole lot.

"But to answer your question," Julien said, "*non*, we have not forgotten what you look like. *You* are quite unforgettable, *mon cher petit.*"

Robbie lost his ability to form a coherent sentence, because damn, the two of them were making him feel like...wow.

When Robbie didn't answer, Julien said, "Robbie? Are you there?"

"Yes, I'm just—" Robbie paused as his eyes shifted to the clock he'd been cursing earlier, and he realized that, *oh shit*, he only had four hours to get everything ready and look the best he'd ever looked in his life, and that suddenly didn't seem like long enough. "I have to go. It's nearly eight o'clock. Why didn't you tell me it was nearly eight?"

Julien chuckled. "*Désolé*."

Robbie ran a hand through his hair as he walked to the mirror in the bedroom, and when he saw his reflection, his eyes widened in horror. "Yes, well, now that I know, I need to stop talking to you two and go and get pretty."

Priest hummed. "You're already pretty."

Robbie shook his head. "Trust me, if you saw me right now—"

"I'd feel exactly the same way," Priest said. "But go, before I try and convince you to come over here."

Robbie grinned to himself. "I love you. Both of you."

"*On t'aime aussi*," Julien said.

Reluctant to end the call, even though he knew he needed to get moving, Robbie lingered. "I'll see you soon."

"We'll be the ones waiting for you at the end of the aisle," Priest said, and Robbie's breath caught as he conjured up that image.

"I can't wait."

"*Au revoir, princesse*," Julien said, and then ended the call, and Robbie kicked his ass into high gear and went off in search of his sisters. It was time to get this day officially underway, because the sooner it began, the sooner it would end, and then he would belong to those two amazing men for the rest of his life.

CHAPTER TWENTY-FIVE

We are meant to be with one another,
and if that means we want an awful lot—then so be it
- Robbie, Julien, & Priest

"WELL, WHAT DO you think?"

Priest's voice had Julien turning away from the French doors, where he'd been watching the guests below locate their seats. As Priest walked out of the bathroom dressed in a classic tuxedo, Julien ran his eyes over the polished shoes, up the long, tailored legs, to the fitted black waistcoat, and the black buttons on the crisp white shirt. Then, knotted at the base of his throat, was an elegant black bow tie. His beard had been trimmed close, his hair swept back, and his grey eyes were watching Julien closely.

Julien walked over, smoothed his fingers down Priest's lapel, and said, "*J'en ai les jambes qui tremblent.*"

"*Merci,*" Priest said, as he took Julien's hand and stepped back to look him over. "*You* look devastating. Robert is going to want to run down the aisle when he sees you."

"Then we better get down there, *non?*"

"Yes, I suppose we should," Priest said, looking at the clock. It had just turned twelve forty-five, and the ceremony was set to begin at one. "I imagine most of the guests are already here."

"*Oui*, that was what I was just looking at," Julien said, and he tugged on Priest's hand, leading him to the doors. "Did you ever think in a million years that we would marry into a family who not only accepts us, but has invited their friends and family to celebrate their son marrying two men?"

As Priest shook his head, they watched Felicity lead Elliot to his seat, and Valerie help Penny down the aisle to a padded one off to the side—poor, *still pregnant* Penny.

"No," Priest said, and brought Julien's hand up to kiss it. "But I can't say I'm that surprised, considering the kind of man Robert is."

"*Oui.* It all makes sense now, doesn't it? How caring he is. How open with his heart."

"It does, and it shows. There's a lot of love down there for him right now."

"And even more up here in this room," Julien said, as he looked back to the scene below. Robbie's sisters and Sofia had created a fall fantasy wedding for the man they all adored, and the only things now missing from it were his grooms. "It's time we go down there now and join them, don't you think?"

Priest nodded, and Julien knew that he understood what he meant. For so long, the two of them had been on their own due to circumstances beyond their control. But today they not only joined their lives with Robbie's, but also with his sisters, his parents, his nonna, and soon a niece.

The man who had burst into their life with his radiant smile and sunny disposition was about to hand over those who made him that way, for them to love as well. That was a gift neither Julien nor Priest would ever be able to repay. But it was one they would deeply cherish and respect for the rest of their lives.

"YOU KNOW, YOU don't clean up so bad."

Logan Mitchell's voice broke through Priest's thoughts, as he stood to the side of the bustling lawn of the lake house. He'd just finished making his way through all the *hellos* with Julien to the Bianchis—and the extended Bianchis—and had excused himself to take a moment or three to think about what he was going to say today to Robert.

Priest wasn't exactly the best when it came to endearing himself to others; having grown up in a situation so far removed from this one, he found that conversing with this crowd was like learning a whole other language. The Bianchis were fun, vibrant, and loved one another fiercely, and Priest wanted to make sure they understood just how much Robert meant to him.

All caught up in his head, Priest hadn't even seen Logan and Tate arrive, but as Logan held his hand out, Priest shook it, and noted how sharp Logan looked in his grey suit with a tie that matched his blue eyes.

"Thanks," Priest said, brushing a fallen leaf from his lapel. "You don't look so bad yourself. Then again, you never do."

Logan's lips curved into a smile that rendered most mortals stupid. "I'll take that, thank you. Your *Robert* has a nice family here. I just finished talking to his sister, Felicity? I have to admit, I always wondered where he sprang from."

"They're extremely nice," Priest said, and then looked at everyone starting to take their seats. "Very welcoming, too, considering our unusual circumstances."

"I still can't believe it myself, to be honest," Logan said, serious as ever. "The three of you...married? But before you go ahead and do this today, there's something I really need to talk to you about."

Priest eyed Logan cautiously, hoping he wasn't about to start any shit over the three of them again. Priest already had enough on his mind, and that was the last thing he wanted to think about. "What's that?"

Logan frowned and put a hand on Priest's shoulder. "Why in the *world* did you two let Robbie pick out the music for your wedding ceremony today? Felicity just told me. Have you lost your minds?"

Logan's words were so unexpected that Priest let out a loud laugh, causing several people to look their way.

Logan grinned and clapped him on the shoulder. "I mean, come on," he said. "This is Robbie. Who knows what he's going to be skipping down the aisle to?"

Needing that laugh more than he realized, Priest said, "As long as it's not Starship, I'll consider it a win."

"I think you and Julien have lost your minds, but...personally, I can't wait." Logan looked over his shoulder to Tate and Julien, now gesturing he and Priest to join them. "Looks like I won't have to either. I better go take my seat. I believe the show's about to start."

Priest shook his head as he said his goodbyes to Logan, and then made his way to Julien. Priest took his hand, and they headed toward the front, where Felicity was waiting for them.

"Is everything okay?" Julien asked.

Priest nodded and said, "Everything is perfect. Let's get this started. I'm ready to see our fiancé."

"It's time," Felicity said, and as the soft strains of a violin began, Julien smiled, and the two of them walked past the front row of chairs, where Robbie's mother and nonna sat.

Priest and Julien stopped to kiss their cheeks, and when the women blushed and shooed them along, Priest thought it absolutely charming. It was wonderful to see a little bit of Robbie in them, as he and Julien walked to the arbor, and then turned to face the French doors of the deck, where Robbie and his father had just stepped into view.

The sound of a door opening caught everyone's attention, and when they turned in their chairs, a collective gasp filled the silence.

Robbie looked simply stunning as he stopped on the deck with his father, and the sunlight caught in the caramel highlights of his hair. He'd styled it in a very demure part to the left, which allowed his gorgeous face to be the main attraction of the day—and what a face it was.

With his delicate nose, those high cheekbones, and his sweet, shining lips curving into a shy smile, Robbie had rendered the two men waiting on him mute as they continued to take in every single detail.

Robbie had paired his elegant black tuxedo with a cream shirt and a lilac vest, cravat, and handkerchief, and as his father led him across the deck to the stairs, all Priest and Julien could do was watch in awe.

"*Mon Dieu, il est magnifique,*" Julien whispered as Antonio led his son down the stairs to the head of the aisle, and Priest thought, *"My God" is right*, because surely only God could've created someone as incredible as Robert Antonio Bianchi.

ROBBIE STOOD AT the window of the front living room, trying to think of anything other than the sudden attack of nerves that had hit him around ten minutes ago. But ever since Felicity had told him that Julien and Priest were outside waiting, Robbie's palms had begun to sweat.

All morning he'd been kept away from them, been told he had to stay on the opposite side of the house and not to look out any of the windows, and while he'd usually sneak a peek, this time he'd actually done as he was told, wanting the first time he saw them to be a surprise.

Now it was here. *The* moment. It was about to happen as soon as—

"Robbie?"

—his father came and got him.

"Yeah, Pa? I'm over here," Robbie said as his father shut the door and walked into the living room.

When Robbie turned around, his father stopped and said, "Wow."

Robbie looked down at his tuxedo, and then back to his father. "Yeah?"

"Oh yes," Pa said as he stopped in front of Robbie and straightened his cravat. "You're going to make those two men cry when they see you. *Sei bellissimo.*" Robbie blushed as his father kissed his cheek. "Are you ready?"

"I think so," Robbie said, and then took in a deep breath and let it out.

His father dropped his hands away, held his arm up, and said, "Okay?"

Robbie nodded and took the offered arm. "Okay."

As they walked toward the door, Robbie concentrated on how to breathe and let his father lead him through the house toward the back deck. As they got closer to the French doors, Robbie could see all his family and friends seated in the chairs facing the lake, and as he passed by Val, who stood off to the side at the sound system, she did a silent squeal and mouthed, *You look gorgeous.*

Robbie ordered himself not to cry—for God's sake, he wasn't even outside yet—but when the door was pulled open and everyone turned around to look at him, Robbie thought he just might faint. As if sensing how he was feeling, his father paused for a moment, and Robbie dug his fingers into Pa's sleeve as he got his bearings.

He scanned the familiar faces staring up at him. From Penny, to Elliot, to Logan and Tate, Robbie's eyes roved over cousins and friends, to his ma and nonna, and then, finally, he found the two men standing at the end of the aisle waiting for him—and Robbie tightened his grip on his father's arm.

Priest and Julien were standing side by side, and as always, whenever they came into view, the rest of the world faded away.

Priest looked exactly the way Julien often described him. Like chaos wrapped in classic sophistication. That shock of flame-colored hair was brushed away from his attractive face, and made the polished black tuxedo he wore look as though it was trying to tame all the fire burning within. But when Priest's steely gaze connected and locked on his, there was nothing Robbie wanted more than to catch on fire and burn up the rest of his nights with him.

Unable to keep his eyes from shifting to the man on Priest's left, Robbie braced himself for the full impact of Julien—but that still didn't help when it hit.

In a black morning suit, with a white vest and a printed dove-grey tie, Julien looked exceptionally handsome. Timeless in a way that made your breath catch and your heart beat a little faster, Julien looked like a prince who'd stepped out of Robbie's very own fairy tale and had come to sweep him off his feet, and he was in real danger of swooning in front of his entire family.

"You good?" Pa said under his breath, reminding Robbie that there were people waiting for him.

Robbie somehow managed a yes, and as his father led him down the stairs and over to the aisle, Robbie kept his eyes trained on Julien and Priest. When they stopped for a moment, Robbie knew what they were waiting for, and not a second later, it began.

The swelling violins of "All the Way" by Frank Sinatra flooded out of his father's outdoor speakers and into the open air, and as soon as the tune made its way up the aisle to Priest and Julien, the smiles that crossed their mouths had Robbie's feet moving.

The words seemed to carry him up the aisle as though he were floating, and Robbie knew there had never been a more perfect song for them than this. When he finally reached them, and they both held a hand out, Robbie slipped his fingers free of his father's arm.

"Thank you," Robbie whispered.

Pa nodded, and then looked to Julien and Priest. "Same rule applies with this one as it does with my wife, gentlemen. You make my son sad, you answer to me, *capito?*"

As Priest and Julien nodded, Robbie took each of their hands, and they guided him beneath the arbor between them. Robbie swallowed and wondered if he should say something, but before he could locate his tongue, Felicity cleared her throat.

She looked lovely in her burgundy dress, with yellow daisies in her wavy hair, and when she smiled at him, Robbie couldn't help but grin back.

"Now that we're *all* here," she said, "would you three like to begin?"

Julien and Priest each squeezed Robbie's hand, and as if that somehow reawakened him from his dreamlike state, Robbie found his voice and was finally able to answer with them, "Yes."

"Very good," she said, and then looked out at the people behind them. The people Robbie had completely forgotten were even there.

"Welcome, everyone, to this wonderful and...unique day we're here to celebrate," Felicity started. "And really, would we expect anything other than that from Robbie? No, we wouldn't, and while he asked me to stand up and perform this ceremony for the three of them this afternoon, I am not actually needed..."

Robbie's mouth fell open, as Felicity stepped forward and kissed his cheek, then she walked around them all and said to the guests, "Julien and Joel have asked to take it from here, and I think they will do a much better job than I would anyway." Then she went and took a seat.

Robbie had turned to watch her go, and when Priest and Julien moved around to stand in front of him, facing one another, Robbie realized that they were now all center stage—or center arbor, as it were—and his pulse began to race.

"*Princesse*," Julien said, and as he smiled, that dimple Robbie loved appeared on Julien's right cheek, and Robbie was mesmerized. "*Je t'aime et je t'adore*. I love and adore you. I have from the moment I sat down at a bar and you batted your pretty lashes at me. That was the night I fell under your spell, and I've been captivated ever since."

Robbie's chin began to quiver, and when Julien took a step

forward and placed Robbie's palm on his chest, Robbie sank his teeth into his lower lip to try and hold back the emotions threatening to overwhelm him.

"You, *mon cher petit*, radiate light and laughter and make me smile whenever you are near. Your joy for living is contagious, and has taught me to celebrate that which is gone and not mourn it, giving me back my sister when for so long she was lost to me. You love with every fiber of your being, and when I see you look at Priest with the same expression in your eyes that I feel in my heart, I can't explain why, but that makes me love you even more."

Julien paused and then ran his fingers down the side of Robbie's face. "You look at me, and my soul rejoices. You make it happy, every single part of it. *Je veux être avec toi pour toujours.* I want to be with you forever, and I would love nothing more than if you would take my name and be my husband."

A tear slipped free and ran down Robbie's cheek, and when he nodded and was about to try and speak, Julien kissed the tear away and whispered, "Not yet..."

"Robert," Priest said, and as Julien took a step back, Robbie's attention focused on Priest, whose eyes had darkened to that stormy grey Robbie loved. "You and I, we had a rather...interesting beginning."

As unbelievable as it was, Robbie's lips twitched, just as he suspected Priest had intended. Then Priest rubbed his thumb over the back of Robbie's hand and kept talking.

"Most of the people sitting behind me right now know this about us. Or so I've recently found out. But here's the thing about interesting beginnings: they are what hooks us and make us want to come back for a second look. Interesting beginnings are what makes us stop and take notice, like a bright yellow tie in an elevator or a car thief in an alley. They're what made me stop. They're what made me look twice. And what I saw staring back at me both times was a man I knew I wanted to look at for the rest of my life."

Robbie's entire body trembled under the power and weight of

Priest's words, and when he raised Robbie's hand and pressed a reverent kiss to the inside of his palm, Priest closed his eyes for a moment, and Robbie sucked in a seriously shaky breath.

"You once told us that you make wishes," Priest said, and opened his eyes. "Today, you have made mine come true. I love you. *We* love you. And I want today to be the last time we ever wake up *without* you. Your father told me and Julien the night we asked him if we could marry you that we wanted an awful lot."

Robbie's eyes widened slightly, that piece of information a new one, and Priest chuckled.

"And he's right. We do want an awful lot. We want you, we want us, and we want forever. You are an exceptional man, Robert Antonio Bianchi. I can't wait to see where each day after this will take us when we've already come so far, and I, too, would be honored if you would take my name with Julien's and agree to be our husband."

Robbie wasn't sure how he was still standing, but as he stared into the two most arresting faces he'd ever seen, he said, "Yes. I want that. With every single part of me, I do. To both of you."

Robbie brought both of their joined hands to his lips and kissed them, shutting his eyes for a moment as he tried to gather himself. When it was clear that wasn't going to happen anytime soon, he opened them back up and let the tears fall free.

"Last year," Robbie said, as he looked between Julien and Priest, "around this time, there was a moment where I thought there was something wrong with me. That there was something I needed to change about myself because no one I ever dated stayed with me; they always moved on. But it turns out I was wrong." Robbie smiled. "They didn't move on because there was something *wrong* with me. They moved on because they weren't either of you. The two of you are where I'm supposed to be, I have never been surer of anything in my life than I am of that."

Robbie blinked away his tears and swallowed. "Most people don't understand us. But they don't need to. We love one another. We are meant to *be* with one another, and if that means you want an awful lot, then I do too. Because nothing, and I mean *nothing*, would make me happier in this entire world than becoming Robert Antonio Thornton-Priestley."

Applause rang out behind Julien and Priest, and Robbie had been so caught up in their moment that it almost shocked him to hear it. But when Julien tugged him forward and kissed his lips, Robbie melted into his arms before turning to Priest, who mirrored the embrace but then pulled a ring box from his pocket and opened it up.

Sitting on the black velvet cushion inside were three matching silver bands that each held a ruby, a sapphire, and an emerald embedded side by side. Robbie gasped, and his hands flew to his mouth, as Julien picked up the first band and said, "May I?"

Robbie held his left hand out faster than he could blink, and didn't care in the slightest when everyone chuckled at his exuberance. He wanted that ring on his finger. Not only because it was exquisite, but because of what it represented.

After Julien slid it into place, Priest handed Robbie the box with the other two. "All of these bands have a part of our original wedding bands melted into them. We not only wanted the stones to represent us—you the sapphire, Julien the emerald—"

"And you," Robbie said, "the ruby."

"Yes," Priest said. "We also wanted them to represent our marriage merging with this marriage."

Robbie touched one of the bands as though they had magical powers, and in a way, they did. They held all the love between the two men in front of him, plus all the love he had to give, which made these rings the most powerful symbols in the world to him.

As he picked one up, Robbie slipped it onto Priest's ring finger and then turned to do the same to Julien, and once they were all in place, Robbie stared at the pair of them in a daydream and said, "My husbands."

Julien's lips curved into a pleased smile and Priest's twitched in amusement, and then Felicity called out, "I'm pretty sure that makes you all husband, husband, and husband. You may kiss, um, each other?"

That was good enough for Robbie, and as Priest and Julien wound their arms around his waist, Robbie kissed the both of them and thought that while life as Robert Antonio Bianchi had been pretty damn good, life as Robert Antonio Thornton-Priestley would be *twice* as extraordinary.

EPILOGUE

Five Years Later

JULIEN EXECUTED THE perfect dive into the deep end of their pool, and as the cool water sluiced over him, he swam the length of it underwater until he popped up through the surface and heard the sound of a high-pitched giggle and clapping hands.

Julien pivoted toward the stairs at the shallow end, where Robbie sat with his back to the tiled wall. His hair was slicked back and he had a pair of sunglasses on, and standing between his legs, jumping up and down with glee was a grinning toddler dressed in a hot-pink, frilly swimsuit with matching pink floaties on her chubby little arms.

Her grey eyes were smiling as they focused on Julien, and as he swam closer, she said, "Catch, *Papounet*! Catch."

Julien stood and held his arms out. She walked to the edge of the step and took a flying leap of faith toward him, and Julien swooped her up in his arms. Water droplets splashed up into her laughing face, and as they clung to the russet-colored curls that had escaped, she swiped them away and said, *"Merde."*

Julien's eyes widened, but before he could react, Robbie said, "Chloé Thornton-Priestley. You do not use that word, young lady. How many times do I have to tell you that?"

Robbie had certainly perfected *that* little speech over the past few months, their daughter, Chloé, having become quite the mimic of her fathers' less-than-perfect language choices at times. And it didn't matter *which* language they used; the impressionable little three-year-old was developing a rather well-tuned ear for it.

Chloé adopted a pout that rivaled Robbie's, and then she turned her big bright eyes on Julien. "Oh, *non.*" Julien chuckled. "Your daddy is right. Don't even try that look on me, *bichette.* It won't work."

"What are you talking about? It always works," Priest said as he walked through the door to the deck and headed toward the loungers.

It was Friday afternoon, and Priest was still in his suit, shirt, and tie, but had removed his jacket. He had a bottle of sunscreen in one hand, a little white hat with pink polka dots in the other, and three towels under one of his arms.

As he reached the sun chairs, Chloé beamed at him, and Julien waded over to the edge, already knowing the routine. Priest dropped two of the towels onto the chair, and when he turned toward the pool, he smiled at the little girl, who called out, "Papa. Come in the pool, Papa."

Priest crooked a finger at her, and when Julien hoisted her up over the edge, Chloé's little feet were moving before they landed. She raced over to where Priest stood with a towel, and when she got there, he wrapped her up in it and blew a raspberry kiss on her cheek.

Chloé giggled and tried to squirm away, but Priest bundled her up and lifted her into his arms, rubbing his beard along her smooth cheek. "How's my favorite girl this afternoon?"

"*Bien*," she said with a grin, and then Priest looked at Julien and Robbie.

"And my favorite men?"

"*Bien*," Julien said as he pushed away from the edge of the pool, and watched Robbie walk to where Chloé now had her arms wrapped around Priest's neck.

"We're all good," Robbie said. "But this one is picking up someone else's bad habits. Isn't she, *Jules?*"

Chloé's bottom lip stuck out, and when Robbie raised an eyebrow, she said, "I'm sorry, Daddy."

"Good girl," Robbie said, and kissed her on the cheek. Then he did the same to Priest and scrunched his nose up. "Ohhh, it *tickles*."

Chloé laughed like a loon, and Priest rolled his eyes. "When was the last time you put some sunscreen on, *bichette?*"

"She's due for some more, actually," Robbie said. "But she's getting hangry, so we were just cooling off before we headed inside to fix dinner."

"In that case," Priest said, as Robbie picked up a towel to dry off his hair, "we might head inside, get her bathed and dressed, and we'll meet you two in the kitchen."

"I don't wanna to take a bath, Papa," Chloé said, but Priest was already walking toward the door.

"You know the rule, young lady," Priest told her. "Bath before dinner. Especially after the pool."

"But I don't *wanna*," Chloé said, with plenty of attitude to spare.

Julien couldn't stop the chuckle that left him. He aimed his eyes at Robbie and said, "*Oui*, she's definitely picking up on other people's bad habits, isn't she, *princesse?*"

Priest pulled open the door and then looked back. "Both of you have bad habits," he said, and then winked. "That's why I love you. Twenty minutes work for you?"

"Twenty minutes is *parfait*," Julien replied, as Priest disappeared inside with Chloé.

As the door shut behind them, Robbie took his sunglasses off and tossed them on the lounger before diving into the pool. When he surfaced in front of Julien, he made sure to slide right up against him until Julien's back was against the wall, and Robbie was against his front.

"Mmm," Robbie said, as he kissed his way up Julien's jaw to his ear. "Twenty minutes seems like an eternity without a sassy little three-year-old to watch over."

Julien spread his arms out along the edge of the pool and wrapped his legs around Robbie's waist. "It does, doesn't it? So how are you going to spend it, *princesse?*"

"Well," Robbie said as he flicked his tongue over Julien's earlobe, and then ran his hands down to the erection in Julien's shorts. "I could show you some of those bad habits you seem to think I have."

Julien chuckled and turned his head to nip at Robbie's lower lip, and when Robbie moaned and opened up to him, Julien let go of the pool's edge to take hold of Robbie's face so he could get a much deeper taste of that sweet, tempting mouth.

Stolen moments like this one, and the ones that came at nightfall, were taken whenever they could now that Chloé had entered their lives.

As Robbie pulled back, Julien kissed his way up his jaw and said, "Teasing me is certainly a bad habit, husband."

Robbie shut his eyes and tilted his head to the side. "I'm not *teasing*, just giving you a preview. Tomorrow's date night, and Chloé's spending it with her aunt Penny and cousin Shayla."

Julien raised his head and saw that Robbie's eyes were close to sparkling. Penny had moved into the city around a year after they had gotten married. It had worked out perfectly in the end, since right around the same time, the three of them had started talking all things...baby. "I didn't know that."

"Mhmm," Robbie said. "I thought we might go dancing. It's been a little while, and I'd like to feel you and Priest all over me, and all up...*in* me—*all* night."

"*Putain.*" Julien cupped Robbie's ass and pulled him in close. "Does Priest know yet?"

"No," Robbie said. "I thought I'd tell him tonight when I give him *his* bath."

"*Dieu,*" Julien said, then chuckled and made himself let Robbie go. "You need to leave...*now.*"

Robbie flashed a cheeky grin as Julien swam to the other side of the pool.

"Go, troublemaker," Julien said. "I'm sure Priest could do with a hand downstairs about now."

"I'm sure *you* could do with a hand right now," Robbie said, but moved to the stairs as he'd been told.

As he climbed out of the pool and the water streamed down over his lean frame, firm ass, and long legs, Julien was starting to think telling Robbie to go had been a mistake.

He palmed himself as Robbie strutted up the pool's edge to the lounger, and after he picked up his towel and dried off, Robbie slung it around his neck, keeping that perfect ass on full display as he walked over to the door and called out, "Tomorrow night?"

"*Oui,*" Julien said, as Robbie aimed a final flirty look over his shoulder. "Tomorrow night." Then Robbie disappeared inside.

ROBBIE COULD HEAR the sound of water splashing and laughter as he headed out of the bedroom, now dressed and ready for dinner.

He hadn't bothered with a shower, figuring he'd take one once Chloé was asleep, so he'd just pulled on some shorts and a shirt before heading down the hall to the main bathroom, where he knew he'd find the two who were making such a ruckus.

When he got to the open door, Robbie did his best not to make a sound, so he could take a second to enjoy the sight that greeted him.

Priest was kneeling on the plush bathroom mat beside the

bathtub with his sleeves rolled up, and water soaking through his shirt where Chloé had splashed him. He had a grin on his face and a small container in his hand, and when he scooped up some of the water and said, "Shut your eyes, shut your eyes, shut your eyes," Chloé squeezed her eyes shut and angled her head up toward him.

Priest guarded her closed eyes with his free hand, as he tipped the water over the remaining suds in her hair, and when she opened them back up and swiped at them, she said, "Again, Papa. Again."

Priest chuckled. "The soap is all gone, *bichette*, and we have to get you out and dressed for dinner."

"That's right," Robbie said, and when Priest and Chloé looked at him, Robbie couldn't have stopped his smile if he tried. The likeness between the two looking up at him was so unreal that at moments like this, when they were side by side, it never failed to stop Robbie in his tracks.

When they'd first discussed using a surrogate to have a child, both Robbie and Julien had shocked the hell out of Priest by agreeing they wanted the baby to be biologically his—and Chloé was a dead ringer, except her hair was a couple of shades darker.

"You want to help *Papounet* make pizzas tonight, don't you?" Robbie said, and Chloé's eyes lit up.

"Pizza?"

"All the pizza you can eat," Robbie said as he pushed off the door and handed Priest a bath towel. "So you better get out and get dressed."

When Chloé gripped the edge of the tub and tried to get to her feet, Priest moved up on his knees, scooped her out, and then wrapped the huge towel around her.

As he got to his feet, Priest kissed Robbie's cheek and said, "Thanks, sweetheart."

"You're welcome," Robbie said, as he looked down at Priest's wet shirt. "Why don't I get her dressed for dinner while you get changed? I think you're as soaked as she is."

"I think you might be right," Priest said, as he looked down at the little girl and tapped her on the nose. "For someone who complains about taking a bath, young lady, you sure do have fun in them."

Chloé aimed an *it wasn't me* look at Priest that had him shaking his head. "She gets that from you."

Robbie scoffed as he wrapped his fingers around Chloé's, and they all walked out the bathroom door. "Kind of like she enjoys playing in her bath, like you?"

"Mhmm. Exactly like that." Priest winked, and even after all this time, Robbie's cheeks flamed, and as he walked off toward the bedroom, Robbie heard him chuckle.

"Daddy?"

"Yes, *bichette?*" Robbie said, pulling his eyes away from Priest's retreating back.

"I want to dress up for dinner. Like a princess."

Ah, I'm so proud. "Well, of course you do," Robbie said as Chloé waddled along beside him in her enormous towel. "Let's go and see what you've got, shall we?"

Robbie guided her into her bedroom, plopped her down on one of the little white stools that went with her tea party setup, and then opened her closet with a flourish.

"Right," Robbie said, adopting his most fabulous voice, making her entire face light up with a grin. "Let's see here. No," he said, and tossed a little blue skirt aside, then he went for a pink one and did the same. "No, no, no."

Robbie continued as Chloé laughed, then he paused on the sparkly purple princess dress that his mother had given her for Christmas, looked over his shoulder at her, and nodded.

"This," he said, and pulled the dress out and held it under his chin. "*This* is the one."

Chloé bounced in her seat, and when Robbie held a hand out, she jumped off her chair and raced over to him.

Robbie brushed out her soft curls and dried them, then helped her pick out some silver slippers to match, and once she was dressed and fit for receiving, Robbie heard the distinct sound of a cook in the kitchen, and made a show of sniffing the air.

"Mmm. I smell something yummy," he said.

Chloé tugged on his hand, pulling him toward the door. "It's *Papounet!*"

"Are you sure?"

"*Oui,*" she said, as she picked up her taffeta skirt and headed toward the door like a princess on a mission.

As she hurried off in Julien's direction, Robbie followed. One of her favorite things to do was watch Julien cook. Not that that was a huge shock—she was a smart one, after all. But what was so endearing about it was the pure joy both she and Julien got whenever he let her help out.

Chloé was his number one assistant, both here and at the restaurant, and they all had a feeling that they had a budding young chef in their midst—either that, or a princess in waiting.

"ROBERT'S BEEN GONE awhile," Priest said, as he looked at the clock hanging above the fireplace. He and Julien were watching a movie on TV, as the day finally wound down and Miss Chloé was being read her bedtime story.

This week had been long, and Priest was looking forward to spending some quality time with his family over the next couple of days. Julien snuggled into his side and pressed a kiss to his jaw, and Priest wound his arm around his shoulders and tugged him close.

"This is nice," Julien said, and Priest kissed the top of his head.

"It is. I swear, sometimes I forget what it's like to sit in silence."

Julien laughed, his chest vibrating against Priest's side, making him smile. "Well, snatch up the minutes while you can. I don't think silence is going to be a common thing in this house for many years to come now. Chloé is talking more and more these days. Her speech is incredible. Both English and French."

"Of course it is," Priest said. "She's learning from the best."

"Arrogant much?" Julien said.

"Am I right?"

"*Oui.* But you're also arrogant."

"I believe when it's in reference to our child, it's called pride."

Julien grinned at him and nodded. "I believe you would be right. It's not like that's a huge surprise, though. She has your genes, *mon amour.* She was bound to be intelligent."

"My genes, Robbie's attitude, and your...persuasive ways. I almost feel sorry for the world. It hasn't seen the likes of someone like our Chloé." Priest craned his head to look over his shoulder again. "Speaking of persuasive ways, where is Robert? He goes in for one book and I swear we don't see him for two hours."

"Aw, don't fret. You'll get your turn with the *princesse* soon enough. In fact, he has something special planned for us tomorrow night, I'm told."

"Does he?"

"Mhmm," Julien said, and stroked his fingers down Priest's chest. "He's going to tell you tonight while he washes your back."

Curious, and liking that idea, Priest flicked off the TV and said, "Let's go find him."

Julien pushed to his feet, and when Priest stood, he couldn't help but take Julien's lips in a long, sweet kiss. "Hmm, thank you for dinner, *mon cœur.* You and Chloé did an excellent job."

"We did, didn't we?"

"Yes. Maybe we'll see a father and daughter restaurant one day," Priest said as he took Julien's hand and walked with him down the hall toward Chloé's room.

"That's up to her to decide. But should she want to, I would love nothing more."

When they got to the bedroom door, they found Robbie, all right. He was stretched out on top of Chloé's pink duvet with his arm wrapped around her shoulders and a picture book open on his chest. She was snuggled into his side, still wearing her princess dress, and the purple taffeta was sprawled all over Robbie's legs, making Priest and Julien smile.

"Our two *princesses*," Julien whispered. "Sleeping beauties."

Priest wrapped an arm around Julien's shoulders as he drank in the sight. "They make quite a picture, don't they?"

"*Oui*. They do," Julien said, then kissed Priest's cheek. "This family, you, them. You own my heart. All of you."

Priest pulled Julien in close to his side and kissed his temple, and as he looked over at the two sleeping soundly on the bed, he couldn't have said it better himself.

This family they had created was unlike any other, and yet perfect for them. It was built with love and acceptance, and if that was what one got from wanting an awful lot, then so be it. Because when the day finally arrived for him to take his last breath, Priest would be fully content knowing, *we did it our way*.

THANK YOU

Thank you for reading
CONFESSIONS: THE PRINCESS, THE PRICK, & THE
PRIEST

I hope you enjoyed the final chapter of Robbie, Julien & Priest's
journey. If you did, please consider leaving a review on the site you
purchased the book from. The men would be MOST grateful.

If you would like to talk with other readers who love this series,
you can find them **HERE** at
Ella Frank's Temptation Series Facebook Group.

COMING SOON

Phantom Desires
MM Standalone
Coming 2019

SPECIAL THANKS

I would like to thank everybody who picked up *Confessions: Robbie* and took a chance on a love story that made its *own* rules.

As we all know, Robbie Bianchi—sorry, Robbie Antonio Thornton-Priestley—has never walked to anyone's beat but his own, and Julien and Priest were the perfect couple to take each of his hands and walk with him.

I have loved writing every single word of this book (even the harder ones) and yes, there were definitely difficult moments to get out. But now that this story has been told, I couldn't be more pleased with how it turned out.

So on with the thank yous!

Brooke Blaine. Thank you so much for putting up with my crazy breakdowns this year. I feel like I had more than usual, and you were right there as always to talk me through it and say, "Pull yourself together, woman." You make my writing better, you help me see things in ways I might not have even thought of, and without you, my books wouldn't be half of what they are.

But seriously, can we write together again soon...please?

Miss Zaza. You have been an absolute godsend throughout this series. From book one to book four, you have been there lending both the English and French sides of your brain to me, and I can't tell you how impressive that is. Also, how grateful I am to you. I can't wait to finally meet you in December and give you a big hug!

Thank you, Arran, for always taking my work, chopping it up, and making it that much better for it. I know I always joke around here with you but seriously, you make my story so much better just by showing me what I DON'T need.

Judy...LOL! This book had me emailing you several times over, but as always, you had my back! Thank you, woman. You know how much I love you! Thank you so much for being the final eyes on my books.

Sarah & Jenn at Social Butterfly PR —ladies, you are a helpful hand when needed, a positive spin on a gloomy day, and I'm not sure how you do all you do with such a small amount of time in a day, but you do. Thank you for always being there, even when you have so much going on.

Thank you, as always, to my readers! A special shout-out to Chloé, who Brooke and I will be meeting in December—thank you for the use of your name! I think it fits their little miss so well.

Until next time,
  MUAH!
  Xx Ella

ABOUT THE AUTHOR

If you'd like to get to know Ella better, you can find her getting up to all kinds of shenanigans at:

The Naughty Umbrella

And if you would like to talk with other readers who love Robbie, Julien & Priest, you can find them at
Ella Frank's Temptation Series Facebook Group.

Ella Frank is the *USA Today* Bestselling author of the Temptation series, including Try, Take, and Trust and is the co-author of the fan-favorite contemporary romance, Sex Addict. Her Exquisite series has been praised as "scorching hot!" and "enticingly sexy!"

Some of her favorite authors include Tiffany Reisz, Kresley Cole, Riley Hart, J.R. Ward, Erika Wilde, Gena Showalter, and Carly Philips.

Want to stay up to date with all things Ella?
You can sign up here to join her newsletter

For more information
www.ellafrank.com

58192774R00157

Made in the USA
Columbia, SC
17 May 2019